THE SECRET EMPIRE

A Steam Punk Adventure Romance
Book One of the Atlantea Discovered Series

By A J Burton & C Leov-Lealand

Quintessence Publications
New Zealand

The Secret Empire

A J Burton & C Leov-Lealand /Quintessence Publications Ltd
29 Russell St
Waihi, 3610 New Zealand
http://longshippublications.blogspot.co.nz/

Publisher's Note: This is a work of fiction. Names, characters, places, and incidents are a product of the author's imagination. Locales and public names are sometimes used for atmospheric purposes. Any resemblance to actual people, living or dead, or to businesses, companies, events, institutions, or locales is completely coincidental.

Book Layout ©2013 BookDesignTemplates.com

Ordering Information:
Quantity sales. Special discounts are available on quantity purchases by corporations, associations, and others. For details, contact the "Special Sales Department" at the address above.

The Secret Empire/ A J Burton & C Leov-Lealand -- 1st ed.
ISBN 978-0-9876624-1-5

Dedication

**To Ruth and Charlotte
with love.**

**To JayJay
thanks for all her support
and her frequent useful critiques.**

Acknowledgements

With grateful thanks to Meryl Nicholas, Lisha Young,
John Mallett, Lynne Roberts, Jeanette Currie, John
Crossley, Helene Karkeek, Jillyanne Puata, Colleen
Pearson, Kathy Ross, Julie Russell, Lynley Carpenter &
Karen Thriscutt.

Cover design by Nils Dannemann
http://www.fireflycovers.com

Cover Model – Thanks to M J Burton.

Plato's account of Atlantis as translated by Benjamin Jowett. This is the original mention of the existence of this aggressive nation state.

"Many great and wonderful deeds are recorded of your state in our histories. But one of them exceeds all the rest in greatness and valor. For these histories tell of a mighty power which unprovoked made an expedition against the whole of Europe and Asia, and to which your city put an end.

This power came forth out of the Atlantic Ocean, for in those days the Atlantic was navigable; and there was an island situated in front of the straits which are by you called the Pillars of Heracles; the island was larger than Libya and Asia put together, and was the way to other islands, and from these you might pass to the whole of the opposite continent which surrounded the true ocean; for this sea which is within the Straits of Heracles is only a harbour, having a narrow entrance, but that other is a real sea, and the surrounding land may be most truly called a boundless continent.

Now in this island of Atlantis there was a great and wonderful empire which had rule over the whole island and several others, and over parts of the continent, and, furthermore, the men of Atlantis had subjected the parts of Libya within the columns of Heracles as far as Egypt, and of Europe as far as Tyrrhenia.

This vast power, gathered into one, endeavored to subdue at a blow our country and yours and the whole of the region within the straits; and then, Solon, your country shone forth, in the excellence of her virtue and strength, among all mankind. She was pre-eminent in courage and military skill, and was the leader of the Hellenes. And when the rest fell off from her, being compelled to stand alone, after having undergone the very extremity of danger, she defeated and triumphed over the invaders, and preserved from slavery those who were not *yet subjugated, and generously liberated all the rest of us who dwell within the pillars.*

But afterwards there occurred violent earthquakes and floods; and in a single day and night of misfortune all your warlike men in a body sank into the earth, and the island of Atlantis in like manner disappeared in the depths of the sea. For which reason the sea in those parts is impassable and impenetrable, because there is a shoal of mud in the way; and this was caused by the subsidence of the island."

−QUOTATION SOURCE

http://ancienthistory.about.com/od/lostcontinent/qt/072507Atlantis.htm

1

THE BOW OF THE BRIGHTLY COLORED GREEK MERCHANT SHIP *LILAEA* PLUNGED DEEPLY into the wild seas, right up to her painted eyes. Battered by the elements, she ran before the late summer storm. Her square sail had torn from the boom hours before, the remnants whipped to destruction in the howling wind. The helmsman, together with six strong crewmen held the long wooden tillers steady. They struggled to hold the ship on course. Torrents of stinging salt spray whipped bare arms and exposed faces with unrelenting fury. Sets of green foam topped waves chased the *Lilaea* across the Mediterranean as if the storm's sole purpose was to smash her hull into splinters and drag her crew down into the sea's murky depths.

A huge wave picked her stern up in a watery fist, flinging the ship headlong down a foaming face. To broach, and fall tumbling down through this wave would be the end of them all.

Captain Agapitos looked up; the rope stays were tight and creaked ominously as the wooden mast hummed in the high wind. His crew were exhausted from hours of fighting the storm. He could see them look his way with the eyes of terrified children who had found themselves in a nightmare where death seemed but a heartbeat away.

Agapitos steadied himself by gripping the treacherous deck with his bare toes which were white and bloodless with the effort. He blinked to clear the salt water lashing his face as the wind sliced the tops from the waves and drenched the ship with stinging spray.

Something warm touched his shoulder and he turned his head and found himself face to face with his passenger, Helena, a high ranking priestess at the temple of Delphi. Her woolen cloak flapped wildly in the howling wind, she was gripping it with her arm to stop it being torn from her body while her other hand was braced on his shoulder.

"Get back to your cabin!" Agapitos shouted above the howling wind as the ship once again plunged into another trough sending a surge of green water over her bow.

"I feel helpless in my cabin!" Helena shouted back. "Is there anything I can do to help?" The ship began to rise again as another giant wave lifted her upwards to a crest. Around them the ocean was a vista of breaking waves, the crests blown from them by the hurricane wind.

"This is man's work. If you want to help go back to your cabin and pray for all our souls. I have never seen such a storm. I need to be sailing my ship, not worrying about you," the captain growled. His fear of the sea overpowering the etiquette required when speaking to a Priestess of Apollo.

"I cannot think of a reason for Poseidon to be offended," replied Helena. She grabbed a rail and hung on as the merchant ship made a terrifying slide into another trough, her hull bucking and surging sickeningly.

"I beg you to pray for us. I will offer the sea God a gold coin for your prayers!"

"Very well, I shall pray some more. Do your best. You are one of Corinth's most courageous captains!" Helena made a mad dash for the door of her cabin as the ship rose skyward once more.

"Pray for me!" cried Agapitos, but his words were flung unheard into the roar of the storm. If the young priestess heard his plea she failed to acknowledge it.

As the *Lilaea* rolled violently to port the captain cursed himself for making a direct course to Ortygia in order to get his passenger to the crowning of King Theron. I was a fool to accept the extra gold and promise good speed to the crowning ceremony, he thought. I have sailed my *Lilaea* into unknown waters and placed her in mortal danger and now the Gods will make me pay their price.

As if agreeing with Agapitos' dark thoughts the sky was shredded by a brilliant shaft of jagged lightning which rent the heavens open. The thunder that followed seconds later was deafening and the captain tightened his grip on the rope line beside him, trying to gather his thoughts and fight the fear which knotted his stomach and threatened to overwhelm him.

The men at the tiller looked at him in desperation. Fear written on their faces as they strained with all the muscle they possessed to keep the *Lilaea* running with the wind.

This storm is as fierce and violent as I have ever seen in the Mediterranean, he thought. I have no choice but to run before it. Who knows how far from Ortygia we are now? Who cares? Survival is all that matters. We must uphold our nerve and keep the ship afloat. No storm lasts forever.

Another flash of lightning shredded the sky, for an instant revealing the blinding tumbled fury of the squall. Some of the crew cried out, their strident voices consumed by the fury of the wind and the earsplitting thunder that followed.

Again the ship was lifted upwards on a monster wave; she teetered precariously on the edge of a watery cliff before she was flung like a ponderous wooden spear into the abyss below. As the ship surfed down into the trough she momentarily stalled, then another great swell lifted her skywards. Agapitos looked instinctively to the port side and saw what every sailor fears most in a storm. A foaming monster of a wave on their beam reared up out of the gloom. It was a rogue wave, a ship killer, coming out of nowhere. To Agapitos the wave looked solid, as if made from green jade. White froth tumbled down the slopes high above him in an avalanche of snowy spume.

"Turn to port! Turn to port! Hurry!" screamed Agapitos cupping his hands to his lips, trying to make himself heard above the howling wind. His words had no effect, as the helmsman could not hear him. Thoughts and words failed the captain. All he could do was hold on to the rope and watch, slack jawed in terror, as the green wall of water began to hang over the ship.

The wave caught them beam on and the ship slid sickeningly sideways as the water broke over her. The breaker poured over the decks, sweeping all before it. There were screams as the men holding the tillers were tossed aside as the tiller beams swung violently to starboard, forced by the weight of water on the steering oars. Some of the crew scrambled to give assistance but a second huge wave followed the first and those who were not holding on were swept away. The port sweeps, extended as storm stabilizers, were shattered by the force of the ocean. Cries of distress came from the rowers who were wounded as the oars broke. For a moment the *Lilaea* wallowed sluggishly in the water. Agapitos watched as the second wall of water drained from the deck. Our lives are in the hands of the Gods, he thought, and Poseidon God of the Sea does not appear to be in a forgiving or merciful mood today. He looked up as another wave crested then crashed over the stalled ship. He closed his eyes, held onto the rope line with both hands and cursed the Gods.

2

CAPTAIN KLAUS MEINBACH SAT AT AN ornate military desk in his cabin attending to the ship's log. He dipped a metal tipped quill in a small bottle of ink hung on complex brass gimbals and wrote in a precise elegant script: 'The 3rd day New Spring, 812, 0800 hrs. I am maintaining standard patrol. Easterly course 70 leagues from the coast of Atlantea and abreast of home port Atlantis. No sightings of pirates or Uitlander trading ships. A tempest is approaching from the East. I have ordered the crew to keep a weather eye out, as storms often blow the

Uitlander ships closer to our shores.' He signed it with a flourish Klaus Meinbach, battle cruiser, *Hieglund*. There was a knock at his cabin door.

"Come in," he said, blotting his entry. Navigator Vielung, his second in command entered. He was a small man whose regulation sword seemed too long for him.

"Permission to secure for rough weather captain," Vielung requested.

"Permission granted. Steer North East, we don't want to take this sea beam on. Have the boiler room coal bunkers filled. The crew won't be able to replenish them once it gets rough."

"Yes sir! I'll order all lamps switched on and the gun ports closed." affirmed Vielung.

"Very good Vielung, carry on, I will attend the bridge shortly."

Vielung shut the door leaving the captain to continue his paperwork. Klaus sighed, continuing to fulfill the meticulous administrative requirements set by the Atlantean Navy. Battle cruiser *Hieglund's* bow lifted slightly and Klaus felt the shudder as his ship plowed through a set of larger swells ahead of the storm front. The feel of the ship moving under him, the increasing throb of the engines vibrating through the hull made the captain lift his head. Klaus felt his ship speak to him as a rider feels his mount. Every noise, every creak and groan had a meaning and a reason for being. He could close his eyes and see the helmsman making small corrections then feel the change transmitted through the hull. His eyes returned to his paperwork; his hand picked up his quill again. He continued writing but part of his mind lingered still with his ship. The storm was moving fast, but he had faith in his crew and the speed with which they would make the ship secure for foul weather.

The *Hieglund* was 5000 tons of riveted steel hull and hardwood decks. She was the strongest of the coastal patrol fleet; sleek, elegant and many times larger than the crude wooden Uitlander vessels that strayed into Atlantean waters. With ten rifled cannon arrayed on her gun deck, she could easily defeat any craft which the Uitlanders could bring to bear against them. Indeed, an entire fleet of their oar and sail propelled vessels would be no match for her firepower. The steam dreadnaught was one of the reasons the Atlantean people were protective of their waters and technology. They needed to be.

The primitive races were treacherous and constantly warring with each other. Should they attain Atlantean weaponry they wouldn't hesitate to use the armaments against his people. Klaus knew this; every citizen knew this. By keeping their race pure the archipelago that made up the Atlantean Empire had become prosperous and all powerful.

Klaus put his pen in the holder and placed his correspondence in a wooden tray. It was good to stand and feel the gently rolling deck under his feet. Carefully he put on his charcoal naval uniform jacket trimmed with silver braid and buttons. His captain's rank was marked by additional blue trim and three red pips. He donned his silver braided stiff black cap, buckled on his sword and put a brace of pistols in his holsters. Now the captain of the *Hieglund* was ready for action. As he climbed up to the bridge deck, the sound of ringing bells made marines and sailors scramble to their heavy weather stations. His men saluted as their captain strode past them seeming oblivious to their presence; but they knew their captain missed nothing. Klaus felt proud of his men; they were the best trained, most loyal crew in the Atlantean fleet. He entered the pilothouse, noting that the helmsmen held her great wooden spoked wheels steady on the new course, and all hands were at their stations.

"Ship is battened down and ready for heavy weather, captain," said the first mate, throwing a snappy salute.

"Very good, carry on," said Klaus returning the salute. The Atlantean navy insisted on correct protocol at all times. A ship of the line had never lost or retreated from a naval engagement in Atlantea's eight hundred year history and all ratings from cabin boys to the captain himself knew failure was never tolerated by their masters ashore. In this way the navy kept the secrets of their islands theirs and theirs alone.

Klaus replaced his cap with a metal helmet. Attached to the front was a telescopic device which he pulled down in front of his right eye. He looked ahead at the dark clouds and rain sheets of the approaching storm. Large cresting waves preceded the rough weather; it would be a long day. He watched as a new set of large waves rolled towards the ship. Her high prow and broad shoulders shoved the waves aside effortlessly, sending spray outwards in a huge surge. The *Hieglund* dipped her bow into the next wave as tons of water poured over her decks; she lifted again, her twin screws driving the battle cruiser up the face of the next swell.

"Head straight into the wind." ordered Klaus "This is a major storm. We will take it on the nose day and night if we must. Reduce to three hundred revolutions."

"Aye sir," said the helmsmen in unison as they held the battleship directly into the cresting seas. A huge sheet of green water came foaming up over the foredeck. The water spilled spectacularly down her sides as the water drained through the scuppers.

"Nothing but an Atlantean ship will survive this storm." remarked the first mate. "Those Uitlander Greeks, Persians and Mesopotamians will all be sent to the bottom of the sea this night, mark my words."

Klaus did not respond to the first mate's remark, but felt smug satisfaction at his ship's performance as he braced for the next wave.

3

IT WAS DAWN ON THE SECOND DAY OF THE STORM. There was a brief lull in the weather but rain clouds could be seen approaching from the stern. Helena, priestess of Apollo, stood holding on to a rail in the shelter of the high poop deck. Her ship had been driven far off course. She had made prayers to Poseidon promising a sacrifice of a goat from the sacred temple herd. Her prayers and promises seemed all in vain, but somehow the battered ship had survived the night.

The exhausted, hungry and thirsty crew were repairing the sail and trying to make the ship seaworthy again. The ship was holding her own but could not take much more punishment. Helena heard the captain bellowing orders, trying to attend to several matters at once.

No one noticed a huge grey and brown Leviathan surface under the ship. With a mighty thrust the creature's huge head pounded devastatingly into the hull below the waterline. The ship rolled to the port side; wood splintered. The crew fell and slid across the deck towards the foaming cold sea. Barrels of wine and water broke loose with the blow, rolling across the deck, crushing limbs and creating carnage.

The Leviathan turned away from the stricken vessel and dived. Gradually the ship righted herself. Water poured into the hull around some of the boards which had been sprung by the impact. The crewmen dropped to their knees praying to Poseidon to call off his creature of the deep. Helena raised her arms in supplication, promising chariots of gold to the sea God; her prayers desperate to assuage the rage of Poseidon's minion.

Out of the blue the monster's huge tail thrust high out of the water close to the hull and smashed down on the deck of the ship. The sounds of cracking timbers and cries of agony rent the air.

The *Lilaea* began to list as her hold started to take in much water. They were doomed now. Resigned to their fate some of the crew threw themselves into the sea. Then, as if ordered by some higher power, the huge sea creature turned away from the wreckage it had created. A powerful plume of air blew from the top of the broad head, and then it dived into the deep.

Helena's thoughts turned to Hades, the Lord of the Underworld, and the calm voyage across the river Styx which would soon be their next voyage.

Unexpectedly an incredible apparition appeared on the horizon. It was a ship like no one had ever seen before. Instead of a mast, the vessel seemed to have a tall chimney which, like a kiln, belched a black fume into the wild airs of the storm. Her huge black hull carved through the waves with total disdain, as if the storm waves were nothing.

Was this the vessel that would take them all to the afterlife? Helena wondered. Is this craft Poseidon's personal water chariot powered by magic? Now all she could do was die with dignity. Helena went into her cabin. Perhaps there was time for her to dress in her priestess robes so she could die as befitted her status as an honored Priestess of Apollo and devotee of dolphins.

"Ship off the starboard quarter." yelled a signalman.

Klaus spun his view scope to that portion of the ocean. There lay a brightly colored Greek merchant ship listing badly, the mast smashed across her deck. Her crew stared incredulously at the big steel ship which bore down on them with her smokestack belching black smoke. Klaus smiled grimly. No doubt these Uitlanders are thinking my ship is a work of one of their ridiculous Gods, he thought.

The first mate ordered everyone to action stations on deck.

"Stand by the grappling hooks," he bellowed through a bull horn, "Marines fix bayonets. Show the Uitlanders who rules the sea."

The wreck which had been the *Lilaea* settled further down in the water, wallowing as waves washed over the decks. Men were running on the decks of the black ship. The surviving crew watched in stunned silence as the great ship pulled abreast of them; grapples were thrown and the wreck was hauled roughly alongside. Two wide ramps crashed down onto the shattered deck. Black uniformed men carrying long rods with sharp knives attached ran down the ramps. They moved in tight groups amongst the crew.

"Put your hands on your heads, you Greek scum! Move up the ramp into the ship." commanded one of the uniformed men. The bewildered crew were herded roughly up the ramps into the black ship. One man who resisted was picked up bodily and thrown overboard. A loud boom startled them all. A rod held by one of raiders spat fire at a sailor who had pulled a knife on him. The crewman was lifted into the air by some unknown force, his torso ripped apart. He screamed and fell bloodied and dying onto the deck.

Helena was on her knees praying for a safe passage into the afterlife, when she was disturbed by a pounding on the cabin door. The wooden door was no match for the force applied to it and it splintered, crashing to the floor. Black uniformed men swarmed into the cabin. When they saw Helena standing before them in her glowing white robe they halted their headlong rush. Her eyes blazed defiance. She stood tall, daring them to make the next move. Their leader shouted in a guttural form of Helena's own language.

"You will come with us now!"

Two men forced her out of the cabin. They waded through the rising water, avoiding the flotsam and the remains of the shattered cargo which covered the deck, pushing Helena roughly towards one the ramps. Bruised and bedraggled, Helena was the last to leave the stricken vessel. As she looked up at the black ship she saw the word *Hieglund*, emblazoned in red upon the hull in large bold letters, which invoked thoughts of demons and other minions of Hades. Despite her great fear and terror, Helena walked forward with her head held high; her dignity was all she had left to display.

To captain Meinbach's amazement a blonde woman in white and gold robes appeared from the stern cabin, prodded and shoved without any thought to her womanhood by his helmeted marines.

In a splash of sunlight which shone through the clouds her white and gold robes glowed like another sun. Her long hair was a wild tumble of blonde curls down her back. He stared hard at her, and then she was lost to view, herded into the hold with the rest of the slaves.

She truly is a remarkable looking woman, thought Klaus. The kind of woman I have never seen the like of before. Something compassionate stirred in his soul and he stood at the rail wondering if he had seen her before. Was she an Atlantean noble woman captured by the Greeks? There was something about her...

Anything of value was appropriated from the merchant ship and then the stricken craft was cut loose. Satisfied, captain Meinbach watched as the wreckage promptly sank, saving his gunners the job of sinking it. To stray into Atlantean waters had sealed the merchantman's fate.

Now his crew would follow the prescribed procedure for interrogation and disposal of the captives from the stricken ship. He felt little knowing that the badly injured Uitlanders would be shot and disposed of in the ship's furnace after being interrogated. Atlantean law demanded that the Empire's secrets were kept at all costs.

"Make sure nothing is left afloat, nothing must remain of her," said Klaus to his first mate.

"Aye Sir," said the first mate clicking his heels. He turned and hurried back down to the deck to supervise the cleanup.

Klaus knew that all other human-like beings were merely ciphers; sub-human lookalikes to beguile the people of Atlantea.

Those young and strong enough would be kept as slaves. Their eventual fate was to serve the Empire working in the coal mines on the island of Erebos.

Atlantean humans were above the mainland scum. They were genetically advanced and pure. Their fair skin, blue eyes and dark hair set them apart from the swarthy skins of other, lesser, humans such as the Greeks, Phoenicians and Persians.

The Empire possessed the supreme inventions of steam and industry, including the recently discovered wonder of electricity which lit the great city of Atlantis. Captured slaves would never be permitted to return to their homelands to spread word of the great power and technology they had experienced.

Klaus decided to go and watch the interrogation for a while. It did not amuse him to see the Uitlanders tortured but it was his duty. To hear their cries and prayers as the political officers pitilessly extracted information had never sat well with him. But an Atlantean naval captain was required to be present at such things. Everything which occurred on his ship was his responsibility.

4

HELENA NOTICED THAT THE CREW of the black ship were a stern race who spoke little. When they did speak, it was in a guttural dialect. The words sounded a lot like Greek; but none she heard were friendly or kind. The men were unusually tall, wearing very plain charcoal black uniforms trimmed with silver braiding and red flashes. Those commanding had a blue braid around the collars. All had weapons they pointed at the survivors, the like of which Helena had never seen. Chased with gold, cylinders and cubes, long rod shapes with hand grips and sharp blades on the end. What were these things? Helena wondered. She saw her brave captain challenge one of the soldiers as she was propelled up the gangway. A huge grim man stabbed captain Agapitos in the stomach with the tip of his unusual spear. The crew of the *Hieglund* offered no help to the stricken man. He died soon after, convulsing with agonizing cramp, crying out in pain and none could comfort him.

As the ramps lifted she turned her head and saw the wreck of their ship slip beneath the storm swell.

"May all those souls find comfort in Hades," she whispered so that her captors could not hear. It felt like her lifeline with Greece had been cut forever. "I must be brave, I must be strong," she repeated over and over.

"Move," a gruff voice said behind her. A hand pushed her in the back and she staggered forward

Helena and her crew were herded down steel ladders through narrow, dimly lit passageways into a place which seemed purpose-built to hold human prisoners. Metal doors clanged shut. Guards watched them, but the wounded were left where they fell. None were treated with respect. Helena saw a crewman lying on the chill metal, his broken leg twisted under him. She went to his side and commanded another man cowering nearby to help her move him to a more comfortable position. He groaned piteously in pain, but sighed when they had laid him gently on his back.

"Thank you Priestess", he whispered. "Are we already dead? On our way to Hades?"

"I cannot tell you if we are indeed dead or alive," said Helena. "Yet I think we remain alive and must await the outcome of our imprisonment on this ship of demons."

"If you live, Madam, please tell Athena of Short street on the Acrocorinth that her husband is dead. I feel my time is upon me to take that final voyage." he whispered.

Helena fetched the man some water from a bucket by the door and was startled as a metal door on the far side of the hold was thrown open. One of her crew was grabbed and hauled roughly from the room. The door slammed shut with an ominous clang behind the guards. The random removal of men happened again at regular intervals; none returned.

While we are perhaps rescued, we are now slaves of a nation whose cold-blooded attitude exceeds that of the brutal Spartans, thought Helena sadly. I always thought of the Spartans as the most cruel warrior race; brutal in the extreme leaving their own children naked in the cold to fend for themselves. All they think about is war and combat. Always cruel and callous in their treatment of their helots. Yet these cold black uniformed men seem soulless; without any humanity at all. They chill me to the bone.

She sat beside the man with the broken leg, holding his hand. Finally the soldiers marched up to her and grabbed the man roughly. They began to drag him screaming from the cell.

"You brutes!" screamed Helena, as she tried to intervene.

"You will be next," said one the guards, shoving her aside. She fell heavily on the unyielding steel deck-plate. Pain lanced through her shoulder, but she remained silent, her fear now tempered with loathing.

5

THESE MEN WHO HAVE CAPTURED US, WONDERED HELE-
NA, RUBBING HER BRUISES; are they real men or servants of
Poseidon? What is to become of us? My crew have vanished
without trace. Why did they bother to rescue us? She bowed
her head and thought hard. I must not be afraid; these pitiless
men have treated us like animals. I realize they will not treat
those of weak character well. If I am to die, being dignified and
strong befits my status as a priestess. I must conquer my fear.
Showing strength and taking the initiative is perhaps my only
hope. She sighed deeply, as she heard the footsteps of the
guards approaching. She thought of her mother and her two
beloved sisters waving farewell to her at the pier in Corinth.
She recalled their smiles, the flowers that they threw off the
pier. Her throat constricted.

I *will* see my family once more, she vowed, if the Gods allow
me the grace to do so.

When it was her turn, Helena was led by two huge guards through the ship. Steam writhed about the corridors. Beams of blue and red light flashed upon them as they walked through the ship, lending an eerie mistiness to the chill echoing metal. Soon they arrived in a room made entirely from grey metal. Loud shushing sounds and a regular booming seemed to indicate the room was close to the mysterious force which Helena imagined must cause this ship to move effortlessly through the ocean without mast and sails, even against the wind. Was it some God given magic or were these men working with evil powers? Helena asked herself as she looked about the room.

In front of her there was a chair positioned under a bright light. Straps hung from the chair. Pools of blood spattered the floor around the chair. It looked like a slaughter house and Helena shuddered.

A tall man sat at the center of a long table. Other men sat either side of him, grim and hard looking. Their hair was dark, their skin pale against their dark uniforms. Death inhabited all their faces as if their souls had already left their bodies. Their mood seemed merciless and as black as their charcoal uniforms. Helena's feet felt like they were chained to the floor, for a moment fear ruled her heart and her limbs. Her escort pushed Helena towards the chair under the light.

I will prevail, she urged herself. She stood tall beside the chair and spoke to the men, hoping her native tongue would be understood by them.

"I see death in your eyes." she said loudly, staring at each interrogator in defiance. As if each knew shame his steel blue gaze could not hold her bold stare for more than a moment. Her escort began to force Helena into the chair. The tall fellow who sat at the center of the table raised his hand and barked an order. The men let her go and she stood straight and proud.

"I have no secrets. Ask me what you want to know and I will tell you freely. I am from a people who neither know your race, nor your language. Do you know mine?" asserted Helena.

"We understand you. Here are our questions. Where are you from?" said a man seated on the far left of the table in a harsh Greek dialect.

"I was born in Corinth and am a priestess of Apollo at Delphi. Before the storm blew us off course, we were headed for Ortygia. I was to officiate at the crowning of King Theron."

"You lie," said the man, flatly – as if by rote.

So how would he know if I lied? Wondered Helena. He likely had never been to Delphi, or to Greece. These men are so arrogant, so ignorant. She looked at him contemptuously.

"How could any of you possibly know if I lie or not? Indeed, how can I prove where I come from, or whence I was going?" Her anger grew as she spoke.

"Is this what you did to all my crewmen? Ask them where they come from and where they are going and then tell them it is a lie? To what purpose? If you wished us dead you could have left us to the mercy of the ocean. A leviathan of the deep had already damaged my ship and consigned us to the mercy of Poseidon."

"Enough of your superstitious nonsense foolish woman," said one of her interrogators. "Your Gods are of no help to you. We are civilized men who have no need of such fables."

A man pushing a trolley with many instruments on it came into the room from a door on the other side. Helena glanced at the bloody tools with which the trolley was laden and spat at her interrogators. Angry mutterings spread among the men at the table. Perhaps she had offended them? Certainly they had offended her.

"To what purpose do you amuse yourselves with tormenting innocent humans? You say you are civilized. Shame on you all for what you want to do to me. Are you cowards, who fear a woman so much you will torture her?" she cried, unafraid of these who looked like men but resembled cruel ravening beasts of legend in their actions. The men began arguing and shouting amongst themselves. Helena stood silent, her chest heaving with fury. She looked them in the eyes defiantly, should any of them dare to look at her for a moment in their incomprehensible deliberations. Finally the tall man seated in the center of the table ordered.

"Take this woman and confine her in my personal prison cell. I will dispose of her when I have no further use for her."

"Yes, captain." Her escort of thugs lifted Helena roughly by the arms and propelled her out of the room. They shoved and pushed her through the ship until they reached an ornate gold and silver decorated wooden door. Opposite it was a small black door with heavy bars across it. She was thrust into the cell and the door clanged shut with an unpleasantly final sound leaving her in cramped darkness.

6

KLAUS THOUGHT HARD AS HE WALKED TO HIS CABIN LATER THAT NIGHT. All the crew of the merchant ship had been interrogated and the injured disposed of. Only those fit for hard labor were left in the cells.

I wonder what I should do with the female captive? He wondered. She seems very civilized and her demeanor is more like Atlantean noble women than an ignorant Uitlander.

His orders were clear and explicit: to kill or capture all foreigners who strayed into Atlantean waters. All ships of foreign nations found within 100 leagues of his home shores suffered this fate. The crew's orders were followed to the letter; naval discipline was strictly adhered to unless the captain had good reason to do otherwise. Women were usually dispatched as their feminine wiles were a threat to the purity of the Atlantean race.

So why did I order this strong proud woman to be my personal property? He wondered.

He opened the holding cell and found her standing looking out at him, her green eyes wide but unafraid. He grabbed her arm and pulled her into his cabin. There he tied her with rope to a pole in the center of the large opulent room.

He looked at her closely. She was disheveled from the storm, soaked in salt water and she must fear for her life – but her eyes did not show it. No doubt she was thirsty and hungry, yet spirit radiated from her like light from the sun. Her white robes trimmed with gold were ripped, dirty and wet. His crew had left her adorned with her gold armbands and bracelets knowing that the captain was entitled to such booty. At this moment she should have been begging for her life but she matched his gaze look for look.

The truth is I feel unnerved by this woman. Damn it! Her green eyes, fair skin and hair worry me. Does she somehow have Atlantean blood running in her veins? He speculated, walking about the cabin, his hands clasped behind his back. Some people of the outer isles have coloring such as hers. If she is of our race, I should not kill her; I am, after all, a civilized man. Perhaps she is an enigma, a puzzle, sent to try my resolve or test my honor? All my life I have been taught to value the purity of race. Racial strength and purity are surely the only reasons the Atlantean race is so far advanced?

"Woman, where did you get your green eyes and fair hair? You are not like a Greek woman in appearance at all." Klaus spoke to her in her native tongue.

"Release me and I will tell you. Are you afraid of a mere woman?" She mocked him "I see you have a sword and other strange weapons on your belt and yet you seem to fear me. Why have you tied me up?"

Klaus was taken aback. It seemed natural to have restrained her, yet – she was right. I am a naval captain; I have no fears for my safety. She is a mere woman.

"I fear no woman," he snapped back. "If you promise not to try to escape, I will release you."

"Where would I go but to fling myself into the sea? The mercy of Poseidon is mercy indeed compared to yours," she raised her eyebrows.

Damn the woman! He thought. She disdains me and my mission, but I will show her my more honorable side. My father brought me up to be a man who respects women. Klaus untied the rope and pointed to a chair in front of his desk.

"Sit there and we will discuss your fate. Insult me and I shall throw you overboard myself." Klaus fingered the whale bone handles of his pistols as he sat and looked at his captive in silence. Perhaps he should simply shoot her and cast her into the ocean and be done with her? He was confused by his hesitation.

Am I merely beguiled by her beauty? Klaus wondered. I should act according to my naval duties. Damn this woman! The longer she lives the more I am torn between duty and honor. She appeals to something in me that demands I protect her. Is it simply her beauty? He stared again into her defiant eyes. She reminded him of a tall ship cutting through the waters; steadfast, strong, magnificent.

Helena sat in the chair as gracefully as she could manage. She returned the captain's hard gaze with a blazing stare of her own. Her mind considered and planned swiftly. This man seemed to think she had some of their blood running in her veins because of her fair complexion and green eyes. Maybe she could use this to her advantage? Race seemed important to him. If she were to claim a common ancestry to his people, would he spare her? Perhaps my grandfather provides a key to these fair skinned people? His lineage was a mystery, she recalled, and mother said he had the same fair skin as I do.

"You asked me where I inherited my green eyes and fair skin," said Helena, "my grandfather was shipwrecked on the shores of Greece, near the port of Corinth. He had green eyes and spoke a different tongue to our own. He spoke of a foreign city and ships with no sails. Over the years he became quite famous for his stories of strange wonders. Naturally his green eyes and fair complexion were passed on down through my family. My mother was fair, as I am, but with blue eyes." She held the captain's stare, saw shock in his eyes and felt a small victory. She lowered her lashes and fluttered them a little.

"I thought so," said Klaus confidently, marveling at his sixth sense about her. He crossed his legs and smiled. "Your grandfather must have been a fisherman from Atlantea. The fishermen of our islands are simple folk who continue to use sails and oars. Our steam engines are too large for such small craft. But their blood is pure and clean from the contamination of weak foreigners and their trade is necessary for our economy."

"If this is so, who am I to you? I am contaminated with blood which is not pure Atlantean." she asked softly, clasping her hands over her breasts, her eyes downcast, her lids fluttering as if over impending tears. I hope I'm not overplaying my hand. I don't want to him to think I am merely trying to seduce him. The purity of my blood is crucial to my survival.

"I don't know," Klaus replied in confusion. "The circumstance I find myself in regarding the possible capture of an Atlantean by one of our ships has never happened before, that I can recall. I need to take advice; I will discuss it with the ship's political officer. I am faced with an unusual dilemma; if you truly are of Atlantean descent I am duty bound to treat you as a guest. But if you are not of our blood then your fate will be either slavery or death."

"So my fair skin, hair and eyes – so different from the Greeks - are the reason you spared me?" she asked, looking him in the eyes once more.

"Yes, there is something about you which caused me to believe you are not a common Uitlander. As captain of the *Hieglund* I must follow my orders but also my conscience." He paused, looking intently at Helena who sat silently waiting.

"I will change your status to guest of the Atlantean Empire."

"Thank you, captain," said Helena, stunned at the sudden change of her status. She had been expecting to die, as the crew of her ship had no doubt already died at the hands of this cruel man.

"What has happened to the crew of my ship?"

"The injured have been disposed of; the able-bodied men are to become slaves of the Empire, working in the coal mines of Erebos Island." Now he had made a decision, Klaus felt a great sense of relief.

"My name is captain Klaus Meinbach. May I ask yours?"

"I am Helena of Delphi. Priestess of Apollo." She smiled proudly hiding her dismay at the news about the brave sailors from her ship. She was alive, that was what mattered for now. He stood at attention, clicked his heels and bowed his head towards her smartly.

"Madam, you shall find me an honorable and gracious host." Helena stood also and looked down at herself.

"These are my robes of office. I am afraid my garments are not fit to live in. Would you be able to provide me with something dry, clean and warm?"

Klaus nodded and walked to a polished gold device and removed the cover. He spoke briskly into the mouthpiece.

"Ensign Rache to the captain's cabin immediately."

"As commanded," a voice replied from a plate beside the mouthpiece. Soon a knock was heard on the door.

"Enter." A young man smartly dressed in the ship's uniform of black with silver trim entered and saluted.

"Find some spare clothes for the lady, ensign." ordered Klaus. "Get a spare uniform, or something from the stores, to serve her as clothing until her gown can be laundered and mended."

The ensign was about to leave when Klaus held up his hand.

"Wait until the noble lady gives you her clothes, then you will take them to the laundry."

"Yes sir," the ensign said. He moved to a position beside the door and waited.

Klaus went into his sleeping cabin and brought out a large woolen blanket from a locker under the bunk. He gave the blanket to Helena.

"Please disrobe and my staff will clean, repair and dry your robes. You may use the empty cabin next to mine as your quarters for the rest of the voyage. As my guest you have nothing to fear from me or my crew. I will however, post a guard on you. Regulations, I hope you understand?"

"Of course, and I give you my word as a noble woman I shall do nothing to challenge your authority." Helena went into the adjoining cabin and undressed; wrapping the blanket around her body. She picked up her bedraggled robe and returned to the main cabin.

"Thank you," she said to the ensign, who took her robe and left. Klaus clicked his heels and bowed as he would to an Atlantean woman of noble birth.

"Now I must tend to matters aboard ship madam," he said curtly. Helena smiled at his formality.

"You may call me Helena, if you like." she said modestly. Klaus noticed Helena's smile, how intensely vibrant it was; something he had not noticed in any woman before. Blushing slightly, Klaus spoke stiffly, awkwardly.

"You may call me Klaus, but only when we are alone. You must call me captain Meinbach in all other circumstances." He turned briskly on his heel and left the cabin.

7

HELENA BEGAN TO EXPLORE THE TWO ADJOINING CABINS. All the door handles were made from highly polished brass. The doors and panels were of beautiful timbers, colored russet, golden and brown. A porthole showed a view of the wake of the ship astern. Large waves from the storm still passed under the steamship, causing her to roll and shudder.

She found a room with a large bath, something she had missed terribly while on her ship. Greek ships made no allowances for having women aboard, or washing. There was an unusual white basin with a wooden seat over it. Hoping it was designed to be sat on she passed water into the basin. It looked like the right place. Now she wanted to empty the bowl but could see no way of doing this as it was fixed to the floor. There was a lever on the wall above the basin so she pulled on it to see what happened. There was a sound of running water then amazingly the dirty water was expelled and replaced with clean. Marvelous, she thought, a self cleaning water basin, I wonder what else there is to find? This is one invention they could have shared. A flushing toilet could hardly win any battles against them.

She investigated the bath; which had two faucets set into the wall over it. She turned one and cold water came out. When she turned the other hot water came out. Wonder of wonders! Helena gloated over this splendid invention. Surely a woman must have designed this bath complete with the hot and cold water, she thought. Fixed on the wall was a sheet of a shiny reflective substance reflected her so well Helena could see herself as if she had a twin sister before her.

Oh. I look a mess. I feel dreadful; my body is itching from the salt water. I have endured enough humiliation in front of the captain. I will feel better when I have bathed.

The water flowed freely and quickly, with careful adjustments she drew a deep hot bath. Upon investigation the bathroom cabinet held soap and other pleasant smelling oils which she put beside the bath. Dropping the blanket to the floor she stepped into the deliciously warm water and lay back until the water lapped her chin. Testing the oils and soaps she selected the nicest ones and added them to the bath water.

Helena soaped herself and sang a love song she had learned as a young girl. The water was so delightful she lay back and, despite her best intentions to be ready when the captain returned, fell asleep.

8

OUTSIDE HIS CABIN KLAUS PAUSED AND REMINDED HIMSELF THAT HE WAS CAPTAIN OF THE WARSHIP *HIEGLUND* and should not allow himself to be distracted from his duties. For the first time in his life a woman had a disarming and disturbing effect on him. Of course, when all was said and done, she was simply flesh and blood. But such flesh and what blood, his sub-conscious reminded him. The way she carried herself was very like his dear departed mother. He could always recognize noble women by their deportment and grace which were inborn and inherently identifiable to men of similar birthright, like himself.

Klaus went in search of the political officer Werner Schmitt. He found him sitting at one of the dining tables in the mess room, drinking East Indian Tea which their trade ships had brought from the Orient.

"How is the tea?" asked Klaus.

"Wonderful. I admire the trader captains; they trade with so many tribes around the planet, but have the skill to keep their trade ships just far enough offshore to keep prying eyes from discovering our wonderful technology," said Schmitt, smiling. "Someday I plan to get a commission on a trader."

"It is a double edged sword for me as a warship captain, Werner. Like most skippers it is my dream to command such a large oceangoing vessel like a trade ship. It is a pity they have to be large enough to carry all the small trade ships on their decks plus coal and freight for a return voyage. I love the nimbleness of the *Hieglund*, but commanding such a huge ship, taking her to far distant parts of the world pulls at the adventurer in me. It is such a pity the trade ships are so expensive to produce. We have many captains and so few trading steamers," said Klaus.

"I am sure given time you will reach a high position Klaus, and be able to choose your own ship. I have heard another is in the planning stages," said Werner.

"Well that is good news, we need at least six or seven steam traders, not the three we presently have. But I wish to discuss an issue with you - regarding a political matter."

"Of course captain," said Schmitt becoming formal.

"The woman we brought aboard from the Greek ship was delivered to me as my prize, at my request. I have interrogated her and I believe she may have Atlantean blood in her veins," said Klaus.

"Really? What brought you to this reasoning?" asked Schmitt.

"Firstly, her appearance. Unlike other women we have captured she is strong, she challenged us. This confidence is noble, very like my own mother. Helena also told me her grandfather was shipwrecked - washed ashore on the Greek coast. He had fair skin, fair hair and green eyes like hers. He talked to the family about ships with no masts. He was obviously one of our fishermen who had been blown off course and shipwrecked far from home. I know this happens every now and then. Our fishing boats are at the mercy of the weather."

"The old man would face the death penalty for such loose talk if it was true," said Schmitt.

"Maybe so, but Helena is not responsible for the sins of her forebears."

"Helena? Sounds like you have struck up a rapport with this woman, captain." Werner sounded sympathetic. "One must be careful not to allow emotion to cloud one's judgment in these matters," he warned.

"I am the captain of this warship and I shall do as I see fit!" Klaus frowned.

"Of course, I did not mean to imply you have been swayed by her," said Schmitt.

"No offense taken," said Klaus, "I have a mind to ask the Court of Genetic Purity to decide her fate. I cannot countenance the killing of a woman with our bloodlines without our law prevailing over the decision. After all, that's what the courts are for, are they not?"

"Of course captain. This is a wise decision. We will take her before the court and let them decide her fate. I shall have her put in the cells and post a guard."

"That will not be necessary Werner; she has given me her word of honor she will not escape. She will remain in my care until we dock at Atlantis. This patrol is nearly over. I will give the order to return this evening," said Klaus getting up. Before he left the mess room he ordered the steward to bring two meals to his cabin.

9

KLAUS STRODE UP TO THE BRIDGE and ordered the *Hieglund* set a course to return to the port of Atlantis. The navigator barely had time to say.

"Yes sir." before his captain left the bridge in indecent haste. The navigator winked at the helmsmen. The rumor that the captain was keeping a woman locked in his quarters had spread quickly around the ship.

Klaus nodded at the marine on guard outside his cabin, who stood holding a musket in front of him at the ready; he came to attention. Inside the cabin Klaus found no sign of Helena and was surprised to find her asleep in the bath. He stood for a long moment beside the bath considering the beauty of her white skin revealed to him dimly through the cloudy bath water. The one thing which prevented her from exactly resembling an Atlantean woman were her long blonde curls, which given her noblewoman attributes - could certainly be overlooked.

Klaus coughed. Helena awoke with a start, then in her fright and sleepiness slipped beneath the surface of the bathwater. She surfaced, spluttering and coughing.

"A gentleman doesn't surprise a noble woman while she is taking a bath," she said rather sternly, her cheeks flushing in embarrassment.

Klaus raised one eyebrow. "Well it is my bath after all, is it not?" Helena laughed and broke the tension between them.

"You're right. What a delightful invention. I would love to meet the woman who invented this bath." she said, turning toward Klaus, resting her arm on the edge. Klaus smiled, his stern expression vanished, and Helena saw a different man.

"I must disappoint you Helena, the bath was devised by a man. Although I have no doubt his wife ordered him to invent it." Helena laughed again, her joy loud in the small room.

"Now that I can believe. Do you have a cloth so I may dry myself?"

"Of course," Klaus drew a fine linen towel from his store cupboard. "Here is a towel, dry yourself with it," he said. A knock on the cabin door revealed a steward who gave Klaus a parcel; he entered the bathroom and placed the bundle on a bench near the bath.

"Your robes are now clean and dry."

"Thank you so much!" exclaimed Helena. Klaus turned smartly on his heels and left the bathroom.

10

HELENA DRESSED IN HER CLEAN ROBES AND LOOKED IN THE MIRROR.

"I almost look like my former self," she focused on the person in the mirror. "But can you pass yourself off as a noble woman, I wonder?" She pointed a finger at her reflection. "Helena, you must find out more about this stern captain and his secretive Atlantean Empire. Why do they want to keep their empire so secret? Yet they somehow manage to trade with other nations despite their obsession with secrecy. You must also stay alive for your mother and sisters and for Greece."

Her robes felt wonderful and she twirled in front of the mirror. She belched.

"Manners Helena," she reminded her reflection, and then sighed. "I am so hungry; I hope they have tasty food on this floating prison." Knock! Knock! The door rattled a little on its hinges.

"Are you ready for our evening meal Helena?" said Klaus from the other side of the door.

"Just one moment Klaus," she said as sweetly as she dared. Helena was warming to this game of cat and mouse, in spite of the danger.

Klaus had dressed for dinner in his finest dress uniform with a ceremonial sword in an ornately engraved silver scabbard. Helena looked him up and down; in his knee high soft leather boots with his dark hair slicked back, he looked a rather dashing sort of man. His sculptured unshaven chin instead of looking scruffy, seemed to emphasize a sensitive expressive mouth.

Helena arranged her wet hair on top of her head; this revealed her gold earrings and emphasized her sacred golden dolphin bracelets and priestess armbands. Her white robes fell softly over her lovely curves. Klaus offered his arm, she placed her hand upon it and he led her to the dining table, set with a delicious smelling hot meal.

Their meal was a roast duck, accompanied by fried vegetables and a small soft white grain which Helena did not recognize. A ceramic jug of red wine sat on the table with two goblets of pale green colored pottery. Klaus poured the wine for Helena and himself. Helena tasted it then coughed and spluttered her hand on her chest.

"What's wrong?" Klaus asked, rising from his chair.

"This wine is too strong for me," Helena said, patting her lips with a napkin. "May I have a jug of water? At home we always drink wine with some water added."

"Really?" Klaus exclaimed. "You do indeed come from a foreign country. We always drink our wine as it comes from the cask." He fetched Helena a jug of water from the bathroom. She poured some into her goblet of wine. Now she tasted it, breathing a sigh of relief and looked at him gratefully.

"Thank you, it tastes a great deal better with a little water." Helena smiled. Klaus sat down again.

"Tell me of your life as a priestess of Apollo." he asked. "I have always been curious about the lives of the Greeks. We know they are the most advanced tribe we trade with." Helena sipped her wine.

"It is an interesting life as Apollo's handmaiden. Our temple at Delphi is sacred to the Epsilon. The temple has a sacred cleft in the rock where the vapors of the Gods are emitted. The ancients say that Apollo slew the Dragon Python and cast him into the cleft. The Oracle - Sybil we call her, inhales the vapors and speaks the prophesies of Apollo to all the mendicants and pilgrims who come to Delphi seeking comfort, instruction and guidance from the words of the God himself."

"So there are many people at the temple?" he asked leaning back.

"Yes, many travel from the whole world to hear the Oracle speak."

"What questions do they ask?" Klaus was mystified by these primitive religious rituals. His people had no need of religious observances. Atlantean Law was their complete guide to all matters in life. Who would need more than the Law? Indeed the Law had guidance for all possible human needs.

"Oh many things; Will I get with child? Will the man or woman I love marry me? When will the hard times be over? What should we do next? Kings like Croesus, Princes and the leaders of many cities like Athens and Sparta seek the Oracle to prophesy when times are hard to ask for guidance. When they win a war as a result of the advice of the Oracle they build Treasuries on the path up to the Temple of Apollo," she replied smiling, "The Temple is very rich and we have the best of everything." She gestured gracefully indicating her jewelry and robe of the softest finest wool and linen weave with pure gold trim. Klaus smiled.

"So if I wanted to become a priest of Apollo and be with lovely priestesses like you, what would I have to do?"

"Oh you could never become a priest!" exclaimed Helena, "unless you were descended from a family of sailors. It is men of the sea whom Apollo chooses as his priests. So young boys of ten years are selected from our seamen and fisher folk to serve at the temple."

"I would certainly qualify," smiled Klaus. "My father was a navy commander and his father before him. My forefathers before them were ocean traders. I would be perfect for a priest of your God Apollo. However, I cannot understand why anyone would believe in such a vague and unreliable entity as a God."

"Perhaps," said Helena looking him in the eye, "There will come a day when you will remember this conversation; a day when you will wish you *had* a God to whom you could pray. A God to whom you could attach the hope of rescue, redemption, even of forgiveness."

Klaus smiled uncomfortably, the concept of redemption, the need to be forgiven; to be rescued from *anything* had never occurred to him. The need to reply was taken by a mess steward arriving. They sat in silence while he cleared away the remains of their meal.

Klaus produced a large ornately carved wooden pipe which he proceeded to pack with a strange but not unpleasant smelling herb. Then he took an elegant brass engraved box, flicked a lever and a small flame sprang up from the box. Klaus held the box to the pipe and sucked strongly on the stem. The flame played over the herb and it caught fire. The captain breathed in the fragrant smoke with every sign of enjoyment.

"What is that you are doing?" Helena asked, leaning forward curiously. She sniffed the smoke and coughed. It smelled acrid but interesting.

"This is a rare but delicious herb which our traders bring back from a far distant land where it is grown. The seed is very fine and the flower scent is sweet. We call it Tobac and I enjoy smoking it very much."

"May I try it?" she asked, reaching out her hand. "I am interested in everything my forefathers may have done. My grandfather did not mention that the leaves of a rare plant were burned and breathed into the mouth thus."

"Nay, dear Helena, you cannot partake of this plant or the smoke of it. Tobac is reserved for men in the navy. Women would look dreadful doing this." He took a deep puff of the pipe smoke and blew it out lazily; a series of smoke circles moved slowly upwards.

"A noble woman such as you must be above such things." He smiled into her eyes and she felt that perhaps she could relax with this man a little.

"How old are you, Klaus?" asked Helena.

"I am 32 years old, still a young man. The *Hieglund* is my first full command. Of course, I wanted to be a captain like my father." Klaus puffed on his pipe. "It's very sad but my parents are both dead now." Helena's brow furrowed in sadness. She went to speak but Klaus held up his hand and stopped her.

"They died together and I imagine that in their last moments they were happy."

"But – what happened to them?" Helena asked, clasping her hands together.

"My father had a small steam launch, a lovely boat. He and my mother loved to go on excursions to the other islands in our archipelago. It was on their return from Balcopine Island that the boiler, which powered their launch, unfortunately exploded. They were late back from their voyage and I took out our other boat, the *Meinbach II* and went looking for them." Klaus rubbed his face lost in the memory. Helena could see how grieved he was and her heart softened further.

"Finally, having searched the ocean in just the way the *Hieglund* searches for ships, we found the debris of the *Meinbach I* floating in the ocean, not far from Ruacana Island." Klaus took a deep breath. "So I am an orphan."

"It is very sad, and are you all alone?" asked Helena softly.

"I had no brothers or sisters and I have never met a woman I wish to marry, so I spend my time as captain of the *Hieglund*. I love my ship and my crew," said Klaus proudly.

"It is a tragic story," Helena said. "Yet my father died in a similar way. He was a strong caring man who was greatly loved by my family. When he was young he went to fight for Corinth against Athens. He survived the battle and came home with a few scars to tell tall tales about. When I was 15 years old, not long after I went to serve at the temple as a young priestess, I received a message which told me my father had disappeared while he was on a fishing trip. A great storm had swept through and he never returned." Klaus leaned forward and took her cold trembling hand in his big warm hands.

"If you had not rescued me today I would have drowned in the sea, just as my father did."

"You will be safe with me, Helena," Klaus said. He sounded reassuring and strong. However Helena had an intuition that this captain, no matter how bold, brave, or in charge he was on his ship, was perhaps not in charge of everything Atlantean. The xenophobic laws of his land would likely not bend to encompass a woman who, although fair of skin and green of eyes, was nevertheless a blonde interloper in a state which preferred those of black locks and blue eyes.

Delphi was cosmopolitan; Helena had experienced pilgrims from many lands and tribes. All were human, no matter what their skin or hair color or what tribe or city they hailed from. She did not understand these Atlantean people, and realized that while she could accept them, it was possible they would never accept her.

"I am tired now," said Helena, rising and stretching. "If it pleases you, I would like to go to my rest."

"It is late; I have enjoyed talking to you," Klaus agreed. "I will have time on the morrow for us to speak some more." He escorted her to the door of her cabin and bowed formally as she said good night and closed the door. Klaus waited for a few moments in his state room and then went on deck. He took a deep breath of the fresh sea air and stared up at the night sky. He began to pace the deck.

He felt tormented by his decision to spare Helena and what he was about to do. If Helena was found guilty of having an impure bloodline she would be condemned to death. Then he would bear full responsibility for her death; not only in law, but in his heart and soul. The vision of her face smiling at him from the bath that afternoon repeated over and over to him as the night went on.

The captain did not yet realize it, but he was smitten by the Greek woman. He was falling in love with an Uitlander; captain Klaus, the man who never fell in love.

11

FOR THREE DAYS THE *HIEGLUND* STEAMED a long zigzag course towards Atlantea, constantly on the lookout for foreign ships to be captured. Whenever his duties allowed, Klaus spent every minute with Helena. The crew became accustomed to seeing them walking together around the ship, deep in conversation. Helena was full of questions about the amazing technology the Atlantean's possessed. Their technology seemed like magic to her, except that these men were quite obviously not magicians. She decided to absorb everything she could.

"What are those long heavy sticks which make a loud noise and kill?" Helena asked. "I feel afraid of them."

Klaus looked up at the guard on deck above them, "You mean like the one the guard is holding?"

"Yes, one of those, what are they?"

"They are muskets; a mechanism which uses gunpowder, and bullets of metal to kill people at a distance. We also have these

—" from under his coat he pulled out a beautiful apparatus about as long as his forearm. It had a shiny metal tube, a whale bone handle with intricate carvings etched onto the hand grip. It also had many ornate metal moving parts. Helena put out her hand and felt its heavy weight.

"This is a pistol. With this a man can kill a man or beast, but only at close range."

"It is heavy, but beautiful. I can see the value in being able to kill at a distance by pointing. I have never been able to watch sword fighting to the death," Helena returned the pistol to Klaus.

"Will you teach me to use it?" Klaus looked at her with new respect as he returned his pistol to the holster.

"In my own country women are safe from harm, men are not a danger to them. But I see from the looks your men give me, that they would all happily kill me." Helena shuddered a little, "so I would like to be able to defend myself."

"Of course, if you wish it," Klaus said, "I can train you on the ship's foredeck," he smiled at her. "I enjoy shooting. In my youth I was a crack shot."

"Oh yes, I would like that." Helena smiled back. "When can we start?"

"We can begin this afternoon."

After the midday meal they strolled to the bow of the ship. Klaus showed Helena how to load the pistol with powder, pack it in, push in the lead shot and then fit the percussion cap on the breech block, then cock the hammer. Then he modeled how she should stand to take aim, then gently pull the trigger.

They shot at wooden target shapes which Klaus had attached to the handrail. Helena focused upon shooting the target of a small animal. She held the heavy pistol in her right hand, her finger on the trigger, and supported her shooting arm with her left. After deliberating upon her aim and the target finally she took a deep breath and pulled the trigger through. A deafening explosion caused her to scream, the pistol kicked and she stepped back. When she recovered, she found Klaus was applauding her. Peering through the smoke, she saw a large hole in the body of the target she had aimed for.

She is going to be a crack shot, thought Klaus, his admiration increasing. They practiced for over an hour until Helena's arm grew tired.

Standing on the open bridge deck, political officer Werner Schmitt, frowned sourly. He watched as his captain taught the Uitlander woman how to shoot. What was most disturbing was that she was becoming an excellent shot. He went to write his report to the Political Bureau. Werner could see the woman had bewitched the captain he loved. Foreigners were even more dangerous than he had been taught. I must tell mother about this, Werner mused to himself. Mother has always said we must keep foreigners out of Atlantis. I now understand why.

While Klaus was busy with the business of running his ship, Helena spent her time on the aft deck sitting in a comfortable chair enjoying the ocean air. She was determined to learn to speak, read and write the Atlantean language. Using a simple book which a crew member found for her, she began to read. Although the script was very different, the Atlantean language was very similar to her mother tongue, Greek. Helena was an accomplished scribe. She was used to speaking and writing in foreign tongues and found herself able to read many simple Atlantean words even though she did not understand the language properly.

Aware that Helena only had her priestess robes to wear, and that these clothes would be unsuitable for a woman to wear in Atlantis, Klaus had discovered there was a talented tailor aboard. Franz Topo was finishing two years of compulsory service in the navy. After measuring Helena, Franz had his captain's permission to raid the ships stores and was engaged in making her an outfit fit for an Atlantean lady of noble birth.

Klaus took Helena to view Franz using the machines for sewing. She stood, lost in wonder, watching the machine operate. The sharp needle pushed the thread up and down through the fabric – all the man had to do was push the fabric through the machine and it was stitched. She realized that with this machine, a single person could complete an ornate gown in a matter of days.

Like all Greek women, Helena grew up spending many hours at the loom, weaving fabric from wool and linen. Fabric was so precious that often their robes were created using ingenious methods from one piece of uncut cloth. All women spent every moment they were not growing food, caring for children and cooking; spinning fiber and weaving cloth. Helena wondered what Atlantean women did with all their free time.

Every chance she got Helena would talk to Klaus about every detail of Atlantean life. Klaus in his turn was fascinated by Greek village life, and the travels and people Helena had met with as a priestess of Apollo.

Slowly her fear of the captain and the crew subsided, to be replaced with wonder and amazement. How had the Atlantean's managed to develop their civilization in such secrecy? How can a people happily exist without any gods? Many times she was forced to examine her own beliefs as the *Hieglund* steamed closer to Atlantea; further and further from her homeland.

Klaus's stern countenance had softened. He patiently explained that Atlantea was an Empire. The Political Party ruled their state with a stern fist and kept a class system of Nobles, Engineers, and commoners in their place. Additionally, there were guilds. The Captains' Guild controlled the Atlantean Navy and commanded thousands of fierce marines. The Captains' Guild acted outside the law and was self policing. In Atlantea a man could improve his status by excelling at seamanship or engineering.

Commoners worked in the production factories, on the farms and lived in the cities or small fishing villages. Noblemen and woman lived in designated suburbs in the huge city called Atlantis. The commoners were the largest number of people, but depended on all the other guilds to keep their living conditions far above the rest of the world.

Hundreds of years earlier, their ancestors discovered black coal, which was burned to produce the steam needed for all their engines. The coal was mined by slaves, mostly captured seaman who had inadvertently strayed into Atlantean waters. The coal mine was on a nearby island, which gave access to a massive coal deposit, providing the entire archipelago with energy. Quite simply, it was coal and iron which enabled the Atlanteans to evolve their mighty technological civilization.

As the captain and his captive walked upon the main deck deep in conversation, Werner Schmitt often stood above them on the bridge and watched them with a scowl on his face. He predicted that Klaus's fascination with this woman would lead to no good.

12

ON THE FINAL EVENING BEFORE THEY WOULD dock in the port of Atlantis, Klaus and Helena dined as usual in Klaus's cabin. The steward had just cleared away the dishes when there was a knock on the cabin door.

"Come in," said Klaus. Franz, the tailor, entered the cabin with Helena's dress hung over his arm, wrapped in a linen sheet. Helena clasped her hands together in anticipation. Franz laid the bundle over the sofa and presented his creation.

Helena gazed at it, fascinated. The ship's stores had apparently stocked a great quantity of silky cream colored fabric, with enough matching lace to form a long full skirt with many flounces. Just the latest style in Atlantis, Franz assured her. There was a white linen blouse, with long ribbons at the throat which tied in beautiful bows. To be worn over the blouse was a brown leather wasp waist corset. To complete the ensemble he had made a beautiful jacket which buttoned transversely from throat to hip. The jacket had full sleeves at the top which gathered into long tight buttoned cuffs. Franz had also created a matching lace trimmed hat and found a small pair of brown leather riding boots which buttoned and had white spats for her footwear. Her strappy leather priestess sandals were not the kind of thing Atlantean women ever wore.

"Wonderful. Any of our women would be proud to wear this outfit. Even my own mother would have been proud to wear this." Klaus clapped his hands to show his appreciation of Franz's craftsmanship and resourcefulness. The captain reached inside his jacket and pulled a gold coin from his pocket. He tossed the coin towards his tailor, who caught it deftly, then bowed before he left the cabin.

"You must try on the outfit Helena, it looks fantastic," Klaus enthused, "I will record that man's name; indeed I will have him tailor my next uniform."

"Of course Klaus, give me a moment." Helena went into her cabin to change.

Klaus felt more excited than he had in a long time. Over the past three days he had become extremely fond of Helena. He was certain that when the Court of Genetic Purity saw what a fine specimen of a woman she was, and how perfectly like an Atlantean of noble birth she behaved, they would grant his request and allow her citizenship without raising any objections.

When she finally emerged from her cabin dressed in the skirt and blouse Klaus stood mouth agape. Helena was more beautiful than he had imagined any woman could be. He had been courted by many single attractive women in Atlantis. Yet never had he seen a woman as desirable as Helena was that night. Any man of his standing would be proud to have Helena on his arm in the great mall – or in his bed, he thought. Then, with a small start, he realized what he envisioned – how exotic, shamelessly sensual and lustful his thoughts were. But - he did not care one jot.

"How does this work?" asked Helena holding up the corset. Klaus smiled.

"Come here and I will show you." Helena stepped close to Klaus, who took the corset.

"Now raise your arms." Klaus positioned the boned soft leather around her slim waist, under her breasts. Then he began to tighten the corset using the soft woven cords at the back. He began to pull it very tight. Helena gasped

"Please tell me if this is too tight," said Klaus. "I know you are not used to a corset, however fashionable woman like their waists to look slim."

Helena was about to complain but decided if Atlantean women could stand to have their stomachs squashed into the back of their spines, well then, so could she. After all she was a Greek high priestess, able to endure much.

Helena buttoned on the jacket, and Klaus led her by the hand and stood behind her while she looked at herself in the full length mirror in his cabin. She admired the exquisite lace, the complex sewing, also the way Franz had made it to fit exactly to her female form. This civilization may have a lot to offer, she thought, re-tying the bows at her throat. In the mirror she could see the admiring smile of the captain as he looked at her. She turned, looked Klaus in the eye and smiled.

"Thank you, I..." but before she could say another word he kissed her with a clumsy kiss. She tenderly returned his passion, persuading Klaus with her lips and tongue to take a gentler approach as his arms wrapped around her slim waist. She placed her hands on his hips pulling him smoothly towards her body. Becoming aware of what he was doing, Klaus stiffened, drew his lips from her soft mouth, put his hands on her shoulders and gently pushed her away.

"I am so sorry." said Klaus, agitated, moving away. "I forgot myself, Helena. A ship's captain must never take advantage of his guest in any way. I beg you to forgive me." He clasped his big hands together compulsively. To hold her body against him was his dearest wish. Yet naval etiquette decreed that, while captain of his ship in the midst of a voyage, he must not.

Helena wanted to reassure him that his kiss was most pleasant and welcome. In her culture open shows of affection were normal. Yet something made her hold back. She saw shame on his face and decided not to step close to him again. She wanted to put her arms around his neck, and say 'I forgive you Klaus, please kiss me again,' which was truly what she wanted. He was so cold, almost supernaturally controlled compared to men she had met in Greece. In her mind's eye visions of the maenads and worshippers of Bacchus drinking wine around bright warm fires, making love under the chilly winter full moon and following the orgiastic mysteries of Pan in the caves behind the temple at Delphi flashed, a colorful distant memory. Helena drew a deep breath, reason conquering her awakening passion. The customs of his race should be attended to, respected.

"Of course, captain," she said mastering herself. "We made a momentary mistake. The moment has gone. Let us forget that it happened." She held up an ornate flat brass and leather wallet, which was attached by a swivel device to a clip on her corset. Helena opened the magnetic fastening to find inside a variety of instruments.

"Now, sir, please tell me what these are for?"

Klaus took the object from her and laid it on the table.

"It is known as reticule. A strange name and I cannot tell you the derivation. Let me show you what it is for. The first compartment has utensils for eating. These are of silver, much the best and most hygienic of metals. Then here," indicating an empty slip pocket, "is where you keep your Atlantean ID tablet. I hope that very soon you will have one of our beautiful silver tablets with your name on it."

He went to his desk and opened his own more masculine reticule and showed her a slim silver tag stamped with his Genetic Purity number and his name in ornate text. Helena marveled at a society which required all citizens to carry an engraved tablet to identify them. But then, she thought, anyone without an ID tablet with the right number and name on it was permitted to be killed or enslaved. Certainly an ID tablet made it easy to identify people.

"Now this is a view scope." Klaus drew out a complex apparatus and unfolded it. "You place it on your head thus." He arranged the array of slim wires and glass lenses on her forehead.

"Each lens may be used to see through. This and this - allow viewing up close, of very small things. This telescope here -" He gently moved a brass tube with glass pieces at each end down over her right eye. "Allows you to see in the far distance with great detail." He stood back, admiring the effect of the view scope arranged on her hair.

"Oh... I see..." Helena murmured switching the lenses up and down on their tiny brass swivels. "A very useful device for enhancing vision and what is this?" she asked, drawing out a flat gold colored rectangular device which seemed featureless but for some curvy runes enclosed in boxes along one edge. Klaus took it up and began to turn it showing her the different parts.

"This is a communication device. We call it a fonier. One of our most brilliant engineers designed it to be powered by the sun. See this shiny panel here? You expose this to the sun for an hour to make it work for an hour. It is very short range, perhaps a mile or two. With these symbols you may control how to use it. Begin and Stop are this key; Call and Select 1, 2 and 3. Three other communicators can be contacted by one of these at any time. If you wish to change or add another person, then an existing contact must be removed from the memory of your fonier." Helena turned pale and took a deep breath.

"This is – well, it's magic." she paused, speechless. Klaus placed the fonier in Helena's hand and pressed a symbol marked on the corner of the device. A delicate chime sounded from his reticule which still lay upon the desk. Klaus moved across the room, pulled his fonier out and depressed a different symbol. He spoke into his device. His voice came loud and clear from the golden device in Helena's hand. She was so surprised she almost dropped it and gave a little scream.

"Helena," said Klaus through the device. "There is a pattern of dots on one side of the fonier. If you speak close to the dots I will be able to hear you, just as you can hear me."

"Hello – Klaus?" said Helena, trembling hearing her voice issuing from between Klaus's hands. She fell down on the sofa and fainted right away. Klaus hurried to her side, found she was still breathing and called the doctor on the ship's com system. His voice was anxious and quite unlike a voice the doctor had ever heard from his captain.

After a few moments Helena returned to consciousness. She was very quiet; the new technology had overwhelmed her. The doctor and Klaus conferred quietly in Klaus's cabin.

"You must remember, captain, that this woman is from a simple society, where devices such as ours have never been seen, and would appear to even the most intelligent of men as magical. Helena has survived a storm. She has survived the annihilation of her crew and the prospect of dying herself. Now she is adjusting to life in a nation utterly foreign to her own. I am not surprised that she has fainted." The doctor gave Klaus a small packet.

"This is a strengthening tonic. Make sure she drinks a teaspoon of this dissolved in warm water twice a day."

Klaus mixed the tonic and encouraged her to drink some. When she felt better Helena asked politely.

"Now captain would you please read to me from your library? I have a great thirst for your language and I wish to be fluent in it as soon as possible." she arranged herself gracefully on the sofa.

"Of course Helena. I have an excellent book which details the construction of the *Hieglund.*" As he searched his personal library for the book, Klaus did not see Helena roll her eyes in disappointment. When he returned with the book and saw her upturned smiling face he knew he was right in his choice. The poetry book he had contemplated reading from was plainly too superficial for her studious mind.

As Klaus read her the tedious details of the construction of the steam warship Helena wondered if these people ever did anything frivolous, creative, romantic or fun. She was accustomed to poetic stories celebrating the great deeds of heroes, Gods and their minions, but then, Atlantea was godless and likely distinguished no heroes. She sighed softly.

13

HELENA LOOKED IN THE MIRROR ONE MORE TIME to admire herself in her new outfit. She enjoyed the way it looked, and she was getting accustomed to wearing the tight corset. On her feet she wore the boots and spats which peeped out shyly from under the full skirt; her hair she wore down in flowing blonde curls over her shoulders. Klaus had sent a steward to her quarters to inform her they were about to steam into the great city of Atlantis within the hour. Satisfied she knocked on the door and asked the guard to follow her out on deck.

Directly ahead, she could now see a colossal volcanic island which seemed to emerge from the sea like a growing thundercloud; such was the speed the *Hieglund* steamed at. Helena ran to the bow and stood on a small deck set right in the prow of the ship. From the cone of the volcano she could see a slim stream of smoke lazily unfurling like the smoke from Klaus's pipe. Further down the shoulders of the volcano dark green vegetation grew. The island had large forests which grew down to the sea cliffs on the coast.

A polite cough came from behind Helena as she stood smelling the sea air. When she turned a junior officer bowed and handed her a helmet set with lenses at the front.

"When you wear this, noble woman, you will see far into the distance." He assisted Helena to don the helmet. He flipped several of the lenses in front of her eyes. Magically the island swooped closer. She moved the lenses away from her eyes and the world was normally distant again. She had no idea how the helmet worked but work it did and she looked again and was spellbound at what she saw.

"Compliments of the captain," said the officer, bowing before returning to his duties.

As the morning haze began to burn away Helena saw on the lower slopes of Atlantea the most amazing sight she had ever witnessed. A huge grey and brown city of high pointed stone towers appeared which spread along the top of the cliffs, and fingers of the city climbed up onto the mountain slopes beneath a high cliff. Then the harbor of Atlantis appeared, protected by a mighty curving stone breakwater taller than the mast of the largest Greek warship. Either side of the harbor entrance stood two white stone buildings of enormous proportions. Atop their lofty spires stood great flashing lights of red and green, visible for a great distance. These towers would dwarf any building in Corinth with their enormous size and magnificent scale. With the assistance of the viewing lenses she could see men moving about in the towers behind windows which were taller than several men in height. How could these towers stand without falling in a storm? She wondered. They must be incredibly strong. As the *Hieglund* steamed inside the breakwater she put down the helmet. Now they were close enough and her eyes could feast on the landscape and all its wonders without assistance.

Helena was enthralled; she stood soaking in the changing vistas of the city which could be her new home. The *Hieglund*, which only a few days ago was the largest man made thing she had ever seen, was now dwarfed by the amazing scene which unfolded before her eyes. If only my mother and my sisters could see this, she thought. If I told them without them being here to see if for themselves they would never believe me, *never*.

Many ships were in the harbor. Some had smokestacks while the smaller vessels were sailboats with colorful sails. It was a busy scene, boats sailing in all directions. Sea birds flew overhead squawking and wheeling above the boats. Many seabirds dived for fresh scraps as the fishing boats cleaned their catch from the night before. Helena breathed in large puffs of air as her nose twitched to a myriad of interesting smells flowing out from the docks and the great city beyond.

Large barges were moored at the quays; their decks stacked with timber, or corrals of live animals. Bales, boxes, and baskets of food were unloading or loading. Smells of steam, coal smoke and hot oiled machinery assailed her nostrils but they did not take over her senses. She was too interested in all that was new, as well as that which was familiar to allow it to overwhelm her today.

Countless aromas – spices, and herbs; tobac and tea flooded around her. Smells of cooking wafted in the breeze. Overall the salty smell of the ocean combined to create a symphony of odors which reminded her just how hungry she was.

Our stories of great Olympus City of the Gods do not come *close* to the magnificent reality of Atlantis, she thought. Maybe there was a God of Technology who had decided to share his blessings with this Empire?

The quays were constructed from a grey stone which was very smooth and uniform in color and texture. Great pillars disappeared down into the seabed to support the huge docks. There were gangplanks devised so they could be lowered from the quay onto decks to accommodate different heights of the tide. Big steam ships were tied to these piers. Waves surged around these vessels as the wash from the *Hieglund* flowed in to the shore.

One steam ship dwarfed even the *Hieglund*. She had four great chimneys to the *Hieglund's* one. Helena had to bend her head far back as they passed this ship just to see it all. She could read the name written huge and high up - *Valkyrie*. On her many decks a mass of people were scurrying about. Tiny men stood on small wooden platforms suspended from the scuppers of the ship painting her black hull. The *Valkyrie's* proportions were such that it was almost impossible to believe that mere men could have built such a gigantic vessel. Surely their God of Technology himself must have helped or interceded in such an undertaking, she thought. On the deck of this colossus were stowed several merchant ships similar to the vessel she had been rescued from. Now she began to see the lengths the Atlanteans would go to hide their technology from the rest of the world.

"That is your secret," she said to the wind and birds. "You use our own ships to trade with us but they need only to return to their mother ship to unload. Then aboard her, you are returned to Atlantis." How simple, simple but effective.

Suddenly the huge ship made a trumpeting sound like the battle horns of ten thousand warriors, causing Helena to jump out of her skin and hold her hands to her ears. The *Hieglund* answered with her own trumpets hidden somewhere below and much steam coming out of vents in her chimney. Men cheered and people on passing boats waved excitedly. Helena realized this was a welcome for the *Hieglund* after her patrol at sea.

Wagons of massive proportions moved about the docks, not pulled by oxen or horses but driven by men. Some were towing a train of several laden carts. Smoke and steam hissed and billowed from the wagon chimneys. All this from coal and hot water, she thought, I wonder how it came about?

Two small steamboats came alongside now, one at the stern and one at the bow. They began to push the *Hieglund* slowly towards one of the empty docks. Ashore a large group of men were waiting for them and a large steam wagon with many carts of the black coal piled high stood waiting. All of the steam breathing machines, big and small, ran on parallel metal rails. Helena looked up to where Klaus was directing things from the bridge. He saw her and waved, then turned away as a crew member approached him. She waved back but she was sure he didn't see her.

The *Hieglund* bumped gently against the gray docks and ropes were thrown from the seamen to the men on the wharf. The battleship was secured in minutes. Helena marveled at the speed and efficiency of the seamen. It was incredible to watch how a ship so large could be handled so adroitly using only small pushing boats. The marines of the *Hieglund* cheered and tossed their caps into the air. They were answered loudly by the people on the docks. Gangplanks were lowered and the men from the quayside swarmed aboard.

Helena lifted her gaze to the mighty city beyond which tow-ered over the huge docks of the port. The first unusual thing which took her fancy were a profusion of cylinders which moved as if floating amongst the city's towers. When she looked closer she could see these cylinders were supported on huge cables. The cables connected to docking ports which protruded from the upper stories of the tower buildings. Helena stood with her mouth open trying to take it all in. She saw the regular move-ments of small steam trams on rails laid in the city streets. These trams transported people around the city. Unbelievably, the trams traveled as fast as a horseman might canter, riding their rails on the wide city streets. Beautiful gardens of flowers and green shrubs were everywhere she looked. What a city. It was so outstanding!

Strains of music, rhythmic and strong drifted from the city to her ears. She could hear the babble of many voices, the hoot-ing of steam whistles of many tones and the shushing of steam engines close by and far in the distance but all clear in the morning air.

And the people! So different they were from the olive skin and thick curly black hair of the Greeks. Fair of skin, with dark hair while some had light colored hair but not as light as her own. Most of the women were dressed in outfits like hers. Long ruffled skirts, some narrow and clinging to the body, others full and flounced. Jackets and blouses of bright complimentary or contrasting colors. Always, under the jacket and over the blouse was worn a corset which pulled in the waist and emphasized the breasts. Some women wore simple sun hats; others had flowers and feather decorations in their simply arranged long straight dark hair.

Working men and women wore blue, gray or charcoal uni-forms; extraordinary caps and leather or metal helmets fitted with lenses, spyglasses and other equipment adorned their heads. The men wore breeches with layers of colored shirts and stout boots. The smartest men had knee high boots of brown and black leather. Helena could not believe the colors they were so vibrant and alive.

She saw people crowded in eating houses, sitting, talking and eating. Helena felt eager to join the colorful friendly throng and see close at hand all the wondrous sights of Atlantis. Surely this was the greatest city in the world and it seemed to extend as far as the eye could see.

14

KLAUS SENT A SEAMAN TO ESCORT HELENA to her cabin with instructions to prepare to disembark. He was busy with much paperwork to complete before the new crew boarded the *Hieglund* and the ship was provisioned for another patrol. The current crew stood ready awaiting their orders to go ashore. The deck hatches were being removed and up on the dock, steam cranes equipped with huge opening buckets like the mouths of dark monsters began to empty the coal wagons and swing across to drop the coal into bunkers in the bowels of the ship.

Klaus had called the political officer, Werner Schmitt to the bridge. Now he must attend to Helena's bid for citizenship. A naval captain was empowered to apply for citizenship for any useful person his ship might capture or rescue at sea. Of course, all of the people Atlantean ships captured were Uitlanders, and therefore applying for citizenship for any of them was a rare occurrence; slavery was their ultimate destiny.

"Good morning captain, a flawless docking, congratulations," Werner said smoothly, smiling and clicking his heels. "My sister Rainia would be pleased to have you attend her birthday party on the fifteenth. I was supposed to invite you sooner but other matters came up during our voyage and I forgot." He bowed towards captain Meinbach.

"Thank you for your kind comments Werner. Why of course I shall attend your sister's party. I shall bring Helena with me so she can see how we have fun in Atlantis. Your sister is well known for her beauty and her parties."

"She will be delighted to hear you will be there captain, she especially asked for you to attend," said Schmitt. Rainia, like many local maidens, had the handsome eligible captain in her sights as a potential husband.

"Now I must ask for your advice, Werner. I am not certain of the procedures of the Court of Genetic Purity concerning Helena of Delphi. You know I am convinced she is of our blood and worthy of citizenship but truth to tell I do not know where to start. The law courts, lawyers and their skullduggery are beneath me as a naval captain. However, if I must consort with their kind I need to know the standard procedure, from your point of view, as our political officer."

"You do realize the woman is actually a foreign prisoner, an Uitlander and must be arrested and charged with being a person of non-Atlantean blood," said Schmitt.

"Of course I do, but she is under *my* care Werner. We can do the formal charging anytime. I intend to petition for her personally," said Klaus, sounding tense.

"Yes of course captain," said Schmitt, "but we must obey the law. I'm sorry; I must take her to the Central Empire Prison to be charged." Klaus jumped to his feet.

"What! That place is only fit for criminals and the slave scum we drag in from the sea." he shouted. "Helena is clearly of high birth. Any woman from any race simply could not learn our language in the short length of time she has. Helena cannot be anything but of noble blood. She will damn well stay with me under my protection. I shall pistol whip any insolent government official who lays a hand on her."

Schmitt cleared his throat. He was fully aware that the Captain's Guild was the mightiest in all Atlantea and the guild membership were not to be trifled with.

"Captain, I am sorry but the law is the law – even for a captain of the Atlantean Navy. We must think of a strategy to help you achieve your goal to have Helena recognized as the noble woman you believe her to be," said the political officer gripping his hands together behind his back.

"Some well placed shots in the heads of a few government buffoons will make my intentions clear enough," said Klaus grimly, checking his pistols and appearing to Werner as if he fully intended to carry out his threat. Schmitt had already decided he was not about to be that particular government official.

"How about I approach the chief magistrate, he happens to be an acquaintance of mine, to get the paperwork started. I will arrange to have the woman – I mean Lady Helena, placed in your care until there is a date set for a hearing." suggested Schmitt.

"You're a good sensible fellow Werner, and I am indebted to you," said Klaus warmly. "You shall not go unrewarded. My report on our voyage will be of great help to you. Although why you choose to work with the Political Department swine, who possess neither courage nor any scrap of honor escapes me. If you wish it, I could recommend you for a place at the Naval Marine Corps Academy. The marines are a great service. They need men who won't flinch when there is blood to be spilt." Klaus handed Schmitt a folder containing the report.

"You're very kind captain; it is a great honor to serve the marines. Alas I have bad knees, the result of an accident in my youth, and I fear I would be rejected by the Corps," said Schmitt.

"Bad luck Schmitt. But 'tis worth a try – the Political Department is beneath you." Klaus briskly put on his cap and jacket. "Now you must excuse me, Werner, I am going to take Helena shopping, to find some shoes and clothes to suit her station. If you wish to find her, she will be a guest at the Meinbach estate. Tell the Political Department representatives to be polite towards her or they shall answer to me personally." The two men bowed formally towards each other, clicked their heels, and Klaus strode out of the bridge toward his cabin.

Schmitt almost ran to his cabin to collect his kit. He knew the chief magistrate owed him a favor; also his friend had a taste for fine teas. He adored the smell and taste of fragrant foreign leaves. Werner happened to have acquired a collection of special teas during his years as the *Hieglund's* political officer.

He was soon sitting in a steam tram compartment planning a strategy to benefit Klaus and Helena. While the tram clattered and puffed toward the gray government buildings and the court house, Werner decided his plan must present as little risk as possible to himself.

15

LOOKING AT THE GREAT CITY OF ATLANTIS, Helena felt like a tiny ant standing at the foot of a gigantic foreign ant hill, but instead of being hesitant or overawed she took Klaus's arm in high spirits. They walked up the gangplank and along the busy dock towards the city. Frequently Klaus had to hold Helena back from the rails to prevent an approaching steam tram from running her over. He waved a finger at her with a broad smile like a father chastising a child but Helena was too excited to care. It was all so new to her and Klaus was enjoying the wonders of his city revealed anew to him by his beautiful visitor's curiosity.

A steam tram halted beside a roadside terminal where passengers of all kinds were waiting patiently for it to arrive. Klaus guided Helena towards the rear doors. Helena held tightly to Klaus's arm as they boarded. Rows of wooden seats filled the length of the tram. The tram was nearly full; working men and women in uniform, mothers with children and elegantly dressed teenagers. At one end, seated in a separate enclosure the driver operated the tram using levers and brakes. At the rear of the tram, enclosed in a steel cab, the stoker kept the furnace fired.

Helena heard a whistle blow and the tram began to move ahead with a slight jerk as the steel wheels took purchase on the track. The city of Atlantis was set out in tiers of streets covering the gently rolling foothills above the port. A bell was rung and the tram made chuffing noises as it lumbered slowly up a gently sloping street which led into the city center.

Helena was breathless from the sights they passed. The skyscrapers which had seemed huge from the docks now loomed as large as mountains. The tram moved slowly along the bottom of a deep canyon between the buildings. The streets of the city were wide to allow the steam trams, steam wagons, riding horses and those on foot to pass without fear of collision. Helena looked up and saw flying trams suspended on cables passing back and forth far above them. She felt fear thrust through her, imagining the dreadful damage below if one of those flying cylinders fell to the earth.

"I'm scared, Klaus," she whispered, squeezing his arm and shutting her eyes.

"What are you afraid of?" he asked.

"What if one of those things fell down?" Helena gestured to the sky. Klaus peered out and up. He looked at her, smiled and patted her hand.

"There is no need for concern, Helena; the sky trams are very safe. They were built many years ago and are very strong." He pointed out the window. "Strong towers support the cables, which are made from the strongest steel twisted together many times. The sky trams carry people from building to building. Many people never set foot on the ground in Atlantis. They don't need come down from the towers to live a full life."

As she continued to watch the scenes on the street Helena saw people riding strange metal contraptions which had a large wheel as tall as a man at the front, and a small wheel at the back. These machines had a seat upon which the rider sat and handles on the front which the rider used for navigation. Each rider wore baggy pants, a leather waistcoat and a leather cap. Attached to the peaked hat were a collection of lenses fitted to goggles. Helena giggled. She watched the riders as they rode along jiggling unsteadily, their legs pumping pedals which seemed to drive the machines along.

"Klaus, I have never seen such wonderful things and all these people. Atlantis is truly amazing!" she exclaimed. Klaus sat beside her calmly, enjoying her delight.

"It has taken countless generations of focused effort and much sacrifice to lift ourselves above the simple world which all other humans live in; to invent, build and make use of all our machines and ideas," said Klaus. "Our forefathers decided a long time ago that we would not let anything deter us in our goal to develop a society with technology at its core."

"I want to see everything." said Helena. Outside the window an elegant carriage drawn by four beautiful black ponies came into view. It clip-clopped by with shiny glass windows and polished brass lamps gleaming in the sunlight. It was driven by a handsome uniformed driver; two marines armed with muskets stood at the back.

"Even the horse drawn carriages are a delight and make our simple carts look so clumsy," she said, clasping her hands together. The carriage stopped and the marines quickly moved to open the door and a superbly dressed couple emerged from the carriage. She was attired in a lacy pink flowing dress with a grey leather corset and a matching pink parasol. He wore a stiff grey tricorn hat, a full white shirt with a tailored grey leather waistcoat and matching pants. His highly polished boots came up to his knees. On his lapel a gold steam engine badge gleamed. The marines began to follow them as an escort as they made their way down the street.

"That couple are so elegantly dressed," she exclaimed. "Why do they have marines as guards?"

"That man is a member of the Engineers Guild. I saw his gold steam engine badge on his lapel," said Klaus. "They rarely venture into our shopping district from their own part of the city and when they do they are assigned a guard of honor to escort them."

"Who are the engineers? What do they do? Are they in danger that they need an escort?" Helena raised her eyebrows.

"Our engineers are the reason for our great knowledge. Some of them are descended from the great Reinhart, founder of our engineering technology. They live in a separate part of our city and work incessantly creating new and wonderful inventions for our convenience."

"So, they are your equivalent of our Gods? You seem to honor them in a special way. They are different from the other people of Atlantis. Perhaps Hephaestus the God of fire and metalworking has blessed them particularly," she smiled and cocked her eyebrow at Klaus.

"Uh – I am lost for an answer – for the moment," said Klaus smiling at her. It is good to see that Helena is so taken with our civilization, he thought. Most primitive Uitlanders we test with our ideas cannot cope with even our simpler technologies, but Helena seems to be embracing everything. A chime sounded from Klaus's reticule, he pulled out his fonier and pressed a symbol. He held it to his ear; Helena could hear a faint voice coming from the instrument.

"Thank you Mercer," said Klaus, "I shall be home this evening with a lady guest. Prepare dinner for two, and the best guest room." Klaus pressed a button to end the conversation and returned the golden instrument to his reticule.

"That was my housekeeper," he said. "She is preparing for my return. I'm sure she will enjoy meeting you."

Helena smiled at him. These instruments could save a great many mistakes and energy. The fonier made sense, a messenger did not need to be sent on foot to inform Klaus's housekeeper that he had returned to Atlantis, and to give her Klaus's instructions. The possibilities were exciting, although Klaus had told her he thought these rich man's toys were unlikely to catch on with the rest of the populace.

With a loud clang and a hissing of released steam the tram stopped in a colossal city square. Set about the paved space were large ornate fountains featuring leaping dolphins and strange open mouthed dragons entwined around a volcano from which issued steam. Tall trees, seats in the shade and flower beds led the eye to glassed-in stores selling all manner of goods. Klaus and Helena stepped down from the tram and moved towards the nearest store front.

"Oh Klaus look at all those dresses and shoes. They are so different but so grand," said Helena "I want to look at them." She pulled on Klaus's arm pointing towards a shop which glowed with beautiful fabrics, bags, shoes and ribbons. Willingly he followed her, delighted by her exclamations of joy at her discoveries.

"Choose what you want Helena. You must have some new shoes and some more outfits. You can't wear the same one all the time, no matter how beautiful it is," said Klaus grinning broadly.

Helena bought skirts, elegant long dresses, petticoats and corsets, complicated lacy underwear, hats and shoes. Klaus insisted she purchase a riding outfit with breeches, and he chose some exquisite jewelry for her. The jeweler's had an effulgence brighter than the other stores. This was because Atlantean jewelry glowed with beautiful colored lights. The jeweler, charmed to have someone new to explain the phenomena to, demonstrated how the jewels became brighter in the direct sunlight. He explained in a coarse guttural Greek that the gemstones stored and reflected back sunlight and even moonlight.

"Something the engineers have invented but I have no idea how they did it," Klaus remarked.

"Oh, so sea captains do not know everything then," Helena quipped. Klaus laughed, and Helena liked what she saw. A laughing smiling Klaus was quite a different man to the cold officer she had confronted days before.

Klaus seemed to have an inexhaustible supply of gold coins in a leather pouch at his waist which he was happy to spend on things for Helena.

She carried her parcels, and when she could carry no more, Klaus bought a shopping cart which she drew along behind her. Elated, Helena found one shop after another to entice Klaus into. The happy pair walked and shopped on into the afternoon, neither noticed the buildings were becoming smaller, shabbier and the stores not so enticing. Inadvertently they had wandered into the seedier side of the city.

When Klaus noticed two rather shabbily dressed men beginning to pay them attention, he took Helena by the hand and turned down into an alley between some scruffy buildings. He motioned for Helena to be still and as the men came around the corner she noticed there were knives in their hands. Klaus put his hands on his pistol grips.

"Stop!" he commanded loudly, "I have been watching you misfits for some time; did you honestly think you could best me with those puny vegetable knives? I shall give you time to withdraw and no more will be said."

The older man held his ground, looking stern. The younger man dropped his knife on the cobbled street. He left it there and looked at his companion as if for guidance. Helena saw they had gaunt faces and a desperate look about them.

"I see one of you has the sense to know when you are bested, but you sir, are a fool," Klaus bellowed at the man holding his knife in front of him.

"Do you intend to shoot me out here in the street do thee? And me armed with such a small knife," hissed the older man as he advanced upon them, step-by-step, his eyes locked on Klaus's purse.

"I am breaking no law having a knife. But you cannot go threatening people with your pistols, no matter who you are. The law is the law. For a small fee, which would be of no consequence to you, we would gladly withdraw." The beggar's tone was placating, persuasive.

"Aye, I bet you will, you impertinent swine," replied Klaus. The thug was now only ten paces away.

"I give you warning, if you advance any further – I shall shoot you and I will not shoot to wound."

The man stopped, lowering his knife, his shoulders stooped in a show of submission. Helena thought the danger was over.

She glanced at Klaus's face. He was frowning, the tip of his tongue protruded from his mouth, his eyes were narrowed and he was totally focused on the man ahead of him as if he knew something she didn't. His hands gripped his pistols, ready to draw.

The thief drew back his arm and threw the knife straight at Klaus's throat. Klaus stepped aside and as the knife flew past his right shoulder he drew both pistols. The thug produced another much larger knife from inside his coat and ran at Klaus, his knife upraised.

Klaus brought a pistol to bear on his target. The thug hesitated for a moment, amazed at the speed at which the barrel was pointing at him. Klaus fired a round which hit his assailant square in the forehead and flung him backwards. His body collapsed with a thud onto the alleyway. Blood flowed out onto the cobblestones. Helena screamed in fright. The younger man, not wishing to share his companion's fate, turned and fled. If Klaus was upset he failed to show it.

"One of the disadvantages of some shopping areas of Atlantis, Helena, is that gutter trash are allowed to wander freely. They thought we were an easy mark." Klaus began to reload his pistol.

Three men dressed in dark blue uniforms and each holding a drawn pistol ran around the corner. They stopped running when they saw a naval captain, a pistol in his hand and a bleeding body in the street before him.

"Here are the Political Police arriving en-mass, too late of course, and of no use what-so -ever." Klaus said loudly and then aside softly to Helena. "Say nothing, my dear, I shall deal with this."

"Captain, what happened here?" asked the most senior of the officers.

"This man attempted to rob us at knife point and has paid for it with his life. Justice has been served." Klaus stated curtly. "I suggest you dispose of the body promptly and quietly."

"Usually we have an inquiry into these matters, sir." remarked a younger officer.

"I'll handle this," said the older officer tapping two gold stripes on his sleeve. "We have other matters to consider, sir. We saw a man running off after a shot was fired. Was he an accomplice?"

"Yes he was. They were attacking us with knives to steal from us. The man you saw escaping had the good sense to withdraw and is likely still running. I have been at sea commanding my ship for several weeks; this is my first night ashore. I do not wish to spend it writing out reports. If there are no more questions, my lady and I will bid you all good day." Klaus took Helena's arm and they walked towards the nearest steam tram station towing their shopping cart. If the PP officers had more questions they failed to ask them. They watched in silence, gathered around the stiffening body of the dead thief, as Klaus and Helena walked away without a backward glance.

Helena had seen death many times even though she was young. She was learning now that Atlantean sea captains like Klaus Meinbach were above reproach and ordinary citizens would be best to step aside rather than confront them. Perhaps the sea captain *could* save her life? Maybe, some day, she might see her family again. Unbidden tears flooded her eyes but she did her best to hide them from Klaus.

They ate at a restaurant selecting the fresh crayfish and steamed fish fillets served with delicious fruit sauces and an array of exotic vegetables produced on the island of Ruakana. As they relaxed and drank wine, Helena saw a sparkle in Klaus's eyes she had not noticed before. When he spoke of the sea, his adventures with pirates, the captures he had made, and what it was like sailing the oceans of the world, his smile was that of a boy. His sea blue eyes were expressions of his adventurous soul. Helena's fear of him was gradually changing to respect for this captain whose life was so different from her own.

In the dusk they caught a steam tram to the Meinbach estate on the outskirts of the city. It chuffed its way through lighted streets passing many brilliantly lit houses. Helena peered out at the scenery, and exclaimed that she could see neither lamps nor candles at the windows of the houses. Klaus explained that in Atlantis they used something called electricity for heating and lighting the houses and the streets.

"So what is this grey stone which all your buildings are made from?" Helena asked.

Klaus chuckled. "We make this stone, by mixing a lime substance called cement with stones and water. We can pour it into a mold of any shape. When it is set and dry it is as strong as any stone. If metal rods are built into the cement it becomes many times stronger." So, this man-made stone and metal was why the Atlantean's towers could be so high and yet so strong. Helena marveled at Klaus's extensive knowledge of construction, but he laughed saying that all young boys knew these things.

The steam tram passed fewer and fewer houses as they approached the outskirts of the city. The houses here seemed to be those of the wealthy, with wide frontages featuring gates flanked with pillars; flowering gardens, lakes and ponds. Every estate had well tended orchards and vegetable gardens. Tall, graceful trees of all kinds grew along a broad avenue. This became a wide paved road which headed down to the coast and ran along the edge of a rugged low cliff top. Trees grew scattered along the side of the road facing the coast and many beautiful homes were set on prominences further inland. Helena noticed white sandy beaches as the road wound in and out of natural coves and through tunnels hewn through the tough volcanic rock. After an hour of this pleasant journey Klaus pulled on a rope ringing a bell to let the driver know he wanted to alight at the next stop.

A beautiful tree lined driveway was the approach to the Meinbach estate. The smell of the tall pine trees and salt laden air reminded her of home. They heard the steam tram whistle, the bell clanged and it resumed chuffing along the coast road. As they walked up the driveway Helena could hear the noise of waves breaking on the shore and after a short walk the house came into view. It was a three storied mansion which, although constructed of concrete, seemed grander than Apollo's own great marble temple.

"Well, here it is. My family home," said Klaus as they struggled up towards the front steps of the house carrying all their purchases.

"I think its magnificent Klaus, and is this all yours, a mere sea captain?" Helena was all admiration.

"My family have been sea captains for generations. In the scheme of things a sea captain is the most exalted rank. We are one reason the people of Atlantca are so rich. We provide the Engineer's guild with materials we bring back from all around the globe."

Helena thought for a moment and realized Klaus meant the world, when he referred to the globe. She laughed as she set out to correct his mistake.

"Don't be silly Klaus, everyone knows the world is flat otherwise we would all slide off the low side."

"You have much to learn Helena," chuckled Klaus. "We once thought as you do, but we have discovered the world is round.

Very large and spherical. It is so huge an element called gravity keeps us from being sent into the black void of whatever is beyond us." He stopped and pointed to the stars.

"Did you know each one of those is a distant sun like ours but so many leagues away we cannot measure the distance? That's how we navigate using the stars. But come, it is getting late, we will have a late supper and I will show you to your room."

Servants opened the door and Helena found the huge house flooded with light from the cascades of brass and glass electric lamps in each room. Their purchases were taken to their rooms. They dined on freshly cooked meats, with warm bread and rich creamy butter.

"I have a tradition which I inherited from my father," said Klaus. "As soon as I arrive home from the sea I like to go hunting on the high plain. After so many days at sea I like the exercise and my household needs fresh meat. That is my plan for the next two days. Can you ride a horse?"

"Of course I can. I am an accomplished rider, although I do not tend horses." Helena felt excited, "I am very tired but I would love to see something of this amazing country, I hope it is as beautiful as your city."

"I will be up early, but you may sleep in a little." They stood. Klaus kissed her fingers gently. "Good night, may you have sweet dreams. You are safe from all dangers here at my estate. If you need anything my room is next door."

Helena found sleeping garments laid out upon a massive beautiful bed. She washed in a spacious bathroom which had a bath of her very own in it. She nestled into the sheets and covers of the bed and was surprised how soft and comfortable it was. She realized that for now, despite what had happened to her in the past week, she was safe and in a world of unimaginable luxury. She longed to try on all her new clothes. She had never owned so many things before in her whole life.

The morning could not come soon enough.

16

WERNER SCHMITT KNOCKED on the office door of magistrate Louis Kampf. He was greeted by a man servant. "Tell him Werner Schmitt is here to see him on matters of urgent state business. The magistrate is a personal friend of mine."

"If you will give me your coat, sir, I will inform him you are here," said the servant bowing low. "Please make use of the facilities in the lounging room." The lobby led to a comfortable wood paneled room furnished with sofas and low tables. Werner sat down, recalling many pleasant hours spent there.

"Would you like some tea or refreshment?"

"Yes, thank you, I will. I know Louis has some fine beer. How about a pitcher of his best lager and two glasses? I know he will approve."

"Yes sir." The servant hurried away.

Louis entered the room. Behind him the servant was carrying a tray with the beer and glasses which he put down on a table and promptly left the room. Magistrate Kampf was a tall, handsome man whose once black hair had changed to a becoming silver. He was wearing a long red silk smoking jacket over his charcoal suit, suggesting he had ceased work for the day. He shook Werner's hand warmly. Then he poured two large glasses of cold beer and gave one to Schmitt.

"So how are you? How is life in the navy?" asked Louis, making himself comfortable in a chair opposite Werner.

"I am well, but I have a problem which, if not handled properly, could lead to a serious political incident. It involves a naval captain, my captain actually." Werner sipped his beer. There was tension in his voice.

"Klaus Meinbach? The Navy's newest hero. You are treading on dangerous ground," said Louis, a tone of warning in his voice. "The Captain's Guild does not tolerate interference in naval matters. They have no qualms in shooting errant law-makers and officials who tread where the Navy believes they should not."

"Yes, I understand Louis; however this is not particularly a naval matter. It involves a matter of which is at the heart of our law and the reason we have a navy. For centuries we have shunned all Uitlanders and have maintained our bloodlines free from contamination."

"That is a different matter Werner. The naval authorities have always been onside with the Department of Genetic Purity on this. The DGP has never had to cross swords with the Captain's Guild on such matters either. You are not suggesting that Klaus Meinbach is from an impure bloodline surely?"

"Oh no, he is as pure as you or I, Louis. I will explain. On our voyage we captured a sinking Greek merchant ship. A storm had destroyed it, we captured the survivors. You know more slaves are urgently needed in the coal mines." Louis nodded, and refilled his glass. "This was not an ordinary merchant trader but a royal ship carrying a Greek High Priestess. We found she had fair skin, golden hair and green eyes – not common Greek features you will agree?"

"Aye that is true. Usually they are swarthy, with thick long black hair," said Louis. "So what did Klaus do? I thought he was usually a soulless bastard, and disposed of all Uitlanders without any hesitation."

"So he was, I assure you, somehow she has convinced Klaus she is of Atlantean blood through her grandfather who was apparently ship wrecked and possibly one of our fishermen. Helena of Delphi is rather beautiful and does look and act like our noble women-folk, except she has golden hair. She must have bewitched Klaus, as he has much more than a passing interest in this woman."

"Surely captain Meinbach may choose any of the captives for his own use? I cannot see it being a particular problem. I'm sure we would all like to have a retinue of attractive slave concubines." Louis said smiling.

Werner sighed heavily and refilled his beer.

"It is a family problem to me. My sister Rainia has set her sights firmly upon marrying Klaus Meinbach, and my mother is determined the match will go ahead. This Greek woman is now an impediment in that endeavor."

"Klaus has been a single man for a long time. Mother has been waiting for Rainia to come of age before arranging the match. He knows nothing of their plans. My mother is pinning her hopes on Rainia's birthday party to achieve her desires and unite our family with the Meinbach family."

"I see, so this woman has cast a spell of some kind on Klaus and you wish her to be removed from the situation?" Louis smiled, "A simple matter, Werner. I will have her arrested, charge her with being an Uitlander, arrange for a speedy trial and a quick hanging." Louis refilled his glass.

"No! That's the last thing I want. You don't quite understand my predicament, Louis." Werner's agitation increased. "If you send bailiffs to Klaus's estate to arrest Helena of Delphi Klaus will shoot them out of hand. My captain has a large appetite for violence. He is often the first man to board enemy ships and he enjoys fighting hand to hand with swords or even knives. He barely uses his pistols. The crew of the *Hieglund* think of him as some kind of God, despite the fact we have no Gods."

"True enough," murmured Louis. "All of our people who know captain Meinbach consider him to be a hero, and an excellent fighter."

"Were I or you to be seen to slight him in any way, the crew would not think twice of attacking us en-mass and killing us immediately. The marine detachments are even more fanatically loyal to him than the crew."

"Then what do you want *me* to do?" asked Kampf shrugging his shoulders and lifting his hands in a gesture of helplessness. "It seems we cannot do anything to rid Klaus of this Uitlander wench without being shot or beheaded."

"We can certainly lay charges with the DGP but get her remanded into his custody. That is what he instructed me to do. Then we can get a court date set which will give me time to uncover and expose her for the fake Uitlander filth she truly is.

However, at no time must he suspect my intentions," Werner said brusquely.

"Yes Werner, that plan is a good one. I know the court proctor at the DGP and can get this woman remanded without her ever appearing. Then it will be the DGP who will get the focus of Klaus's resentment. We will simply be seen doing our duty as excellent citizens in a fair and transparent manner."

"Thank you." Werner's relief was pronounced. "Politics is the art of prevarication whilst appearing to tell the truth, don't you think?" he mused, able to relax at last. He lifted his glass towards his friend with a grateful look of celebration and drained it.

"We must live in the real world. These decisions of a delicate nature, particularly where your mother is concerned - must be handled with considerable expertise, my friend." Judge Kampf smiled, "Now putting discussion of politics aside is it possible for you to get me more of that excellent exotic tea?"

17

KLAUS WAS UP AT DAWN ORGANIZING THE HORSES and the servants. Their hunting party was to stay overnight on the high plain, an uncultivated plateau high above the city which was a part of towering Mount Aoxomoxoa, the huge volcano which created the island of Atlantea. Klaus wanted Helena to witness for herself the incredible view of the city of Atlantis from the edge of the high plain.

Several large strongly built ponies were presented for Klaus's inspection. He lifted each leg carefully, feeling tendons for knots or bumps, indications of possible lameness problems ahead. The ponies had been bred by the Meinbach family and were almost as big as the riding horses favored by horsemen on the flat cultivated parts of the island. His blacksmith followed behind him making sure the clinches on the iron shoes were tight. The smell of the small coal fired forge, and the sound of his hammer reshaping shoes rang out in the still morning air. The hustle and bustle of the servants stowing tents into saddle packs, cleaning leather harnesses, everything arranged as it should be, pleased Klaus. He thought of his crew on the *Hieglund*, each man knowing his job and attending to it with pride.

Klaus selected for his mount a four year old coal black stallion called Ox. The pony shone and his long black mane had been groomed until it felt silky to the touch. Finally he chose three other ponies, all mares. Two would be remounts, to be attended to by the servants until needed. These horses were proud looking animals, heavily muscled with robust constitutions and great courage. The climb to the top of the plateau followed steep rough tracks and the sure footed ponies were the best mounts for these conditions. Klaus was not concerned about the arduous climb, but he hoped Helena's riding skills were up to the journey.

The hunting party included servants, who walked the distance to the camp site leading the saddled remounts and two pack donkeys carrying the tents and supplies. Two hunting muskets were strapped to the rear of a pack with butts facing skywards and covered to prevent dust getting in. One of the servants was responsible for carrying this pack complete with spare rounds and powder.

Walking back to the house for breakfast, the frosted grass crunched under his boots. A frost was usual for this time of year. The morning air was crisp and cool in his lungs and the rising sun spoke to Klaus of adventure. He looked up at the tall cone of Mt Aoxomoxoa which dominated the skyline to the East.

This will be an interesting trek, he thought. I have a feeling Helena will reveal more about herself than she might care to show otherwise, I would like that. He smiled. Getting to know

Helena was the most interesting process he had ever experienced.

Helena wore the new riding outfit Klaus had bought her to their early breakfast. This consisted of tight breeches tucked inside soft tan leather riding boots, a thick soft linen long-sleeved blouse, and a dark brown jacket made from the softest deer leather on the island. A leather sun hat with a wide brim completed her outfit.

Helena was used to riding bareback, so the deep seated leather saddle with thigh pads and wide stirrups was easy for her to use. Klaus wore similar riding clothes, with leather chaps over his breeches. His musket was carried in a scabbard strapped to the rear of his saddle. His saddle bags were packed with food and he had a water canteen strapped to the pommel. His sidearms were a large hunting knife in a sheath on his belt and his pair of single shot, long barreled, naval pistols in holsters.

Helena thought he made a dashing figure as they walked their horses to the rear of the estate. She noticed many workers tending to rows of grapes and orchards of lemons, apples, oranges and some exotic trees she had never seen before. They rode for an hour which Klaus calculated from a mechanical sundial carried in his shirt pocket. Helena was astonished at the many convenient inventions the Atlantean's used, but she adapted quickly. She didn't ask Klaus how his sundial worked since she had discovered he would launch into complex explanations of the inventions which confused her even more.

Klaus reined his horse in and waited for Helena to ride up beside him. The two ponies nuzzled each other's necks looking for a salt lick. The trail was gradually rising; it was a well used route to the high plateau. The lush lowland vegetation was becoming sparse as the topsoil became thinner.

"How are you handling the ride, Helena?" asked Klaus.

"I'm fine," Helena said, smiling at him. "This saddle is so comfortable – and the stirrups are excellent. I have such a strong seat it would take a lot to dislodge me."

"That is good." Klaus said, patting his mount's neck. "The trail gets steeper now. Soon we will dismount and water our ponies. Then we walk for half an hour and ride for one, this way the ponies will last until we reach the plateau. We can rest then and wait until my servants bring up the remounts."

Both ponies were content to walk briskly until the trail steepened where it wound through a forest of tall trees. Helena enjoyed the rising sun on her neck. Her mare showed her contentment by dropping her head and settling into a steady pace. Helena rode on a loose rein; the calm tractability of her mount filled her with confidence.

Klaus reined his horse in and dismounted at the mouth of a narrow path. "Come, dismount and follow me. There is a stream nearby." he said.

Leading the ponies they followed a rough trail that meandered through the forest. Helena marveled at the varieties of trees, many of which she had never seen before.

"Klaus, the trees here are so different. I recognize some, but others look unusual."

"The trading captains have brought back seeds of many trees and plants. Lower down the soil is good and we have plenty of rain and sunshine so most species do well on the island." Klaus halted and pointed, "Look, there is an oak tree, found on an island far away in the cold North where the people paint themselves blue."

"Your ships trade with a lot of cultures, I never knew the world was so big," said Helena.

"We have ceased trading with the blue tribe. They are too much trouble. Like most primitive tribes and Uitlanders they are very stupid. Always fighting amongst themselves although their island is sparsely populated."

"Is that why your culture has become cut off from the rest of the world, Klaus?"

"Yes, we have a far more advanced culture. We have discovered that most humans are nothing more than advanced apes. Atlantean people are far more intellectually, genetically and technologically developed than any Uitlanders."

"Apes?" asked Helena, wondering if he regarded her as one of these ape creatures.

"Oh, I forgot! You probably don't know about apes. They are a very hairy animal that has some human characteristics. Now, here is the stream, let's water the ponies."

"I'm a Greek – an Uitlander to you. Does that mean I'm also a hairy ape?" Helena asked, feeling offended at this attitude.

"Of course not!" said Klaus emphatically. "Perhaps I have been ignorant of the truth. I have never met a Greek like you. Yet our scientists and forefathers have taught us that all foreigners are low creatures with poor genes, not to be bred with."

"So you have never questioned these rules? In our culture we are taught to think, to ask questions. There is a large sign at Delphi carved on a wall of our temple 'The unexamined life is not worth living'." she said, leading her mount to the stream.

Their ponies eagerly drank from the clear waters of the stream swishing their tails and from time to time stamping a hoof in the water. They knew from other journeys there would be no more water until they had climbed to the high plain.

Klaus rubbed his chin. "Well said, Helena," he said, stepping back from the stream. "You have given me food for thought. Let me consider the matter for a while."

They relaxed in silence, holding the reins while their ponies drank. Helena smiled a secret smile to herself. Maybe I can teach this arrogant captain to think for himself?

"Helena, I must warn you that there are dangerous animals on the high plains in addition to the wolf packs," said Klaus.

"Shouldn't I have a weapon then?" She asked, a small frown of concern passed over her face.

"I agree. I have a spare knife in my saddle bag. I'll get it for you." Klaus opened one of his saddle bags. The knife was in a leather scabbard with a stout leather belt. "Put this on, Helena. I have kept it ever since I was a boy. The belt is now too small for me, but it will fit you."

Helena strapped the belt around her waist and experimentally pulled the knife out of the sheath. She tested the keen edge and thrust it back in.

"Thank you. I can protect myself now."

"There is another predator on the high plain and it is much more dangerous than wolves. We call it the Poisonous Dragon," said Klaus.

"Poisonous like an adder?"

"Not like a snake, exactly. A bite from the dragon will create a wound which festers within hours. You will die a horrible death, unless the limb or infected part is cut out straight away. They are dirty, foul smelling beasts who prefer carrion to live flesh. They have no fear of men and will attack us if hungry."

"What do they look like?" asked Helena, shuddering.

"Like a large lizard with four short legs, a broad muzzle and long tail. Some are longer than the height of two men. They run for short distances and are surprisingly fast for their great size," said Klaus, "The dragons are solitary creatures, and live in caves or underground burrows. I have not seen one since I was a boy."

"They sound frightening." Helena looked about her with a new alertness.

"Many think they are dying out. I doubt very much if we will see one, but I thought you should know, just in case" He turned his head. "Ah, the ponies are finished, now we can return to the main trail."

As they returned to the main trail, the rest of the hunting party, who were on foot came up behind them. Helena found herself looking a lot more carefully at the terrain around her. The thought of huge smelly dragons caused her to touch the hilt of her knife over and over for comfort.

"Are you ready for the hard part of the climb?" asked Klaus. "If so, let's remount. Give the ponies their heads, they know the way."

So they allowed the tough ponies to set the pace. The sturdy animals began the climb with renewed vigor, as if eager to reach the top.

Soon Klaus and Helena rode in single file along a narrow path which zigzagged up a steep slope between tall clumps of boulders and scruffy trees. Far above Helena could see the edge of the plateau. Nervously she checked out all the caves and holes amongst the boulders, just in case any were a dragon's lair.

Klaus's pony was more robust, he forged ahead. Helena had to urge her mount to keep pace as best she could. They continued the routine of the ride, riding for an hour and walking for half an hour until by noon they gained the plateau. They watered the ponies from a stream fed by the mountain snow on the far off volcanic peak. Klaus hobbled the ponies' front legs so they would not wander far, but could graze with ease.

They washed in the stream and splashed their faces with the frigid water. Klaus unloaded his saddle bags and set out a meal of fruit, cheese and fresh bread upon a large, flat rock. Contentedly they sat and ate, looking up at the gigantic cone of Mt Aoxomoxoa which disappeared into the ever present clouds which clung around the summit.

The soil on the great plain was poor, the grass dry and coarse. Several species of small hardy trees managed to survive the challenging volcanic conditions. The panorama from their vantage point was stupendous. Now Helena could see that the plateau formed a vast plain encircling the mountain. Waterfalls cascaded down the steeper slopes feeding streams which led to water holes. Herds of deer and small buffalo moved about the plain. Truly, it was a hunter's paradise.

Great eagles and birds of prey were floating on thermals high above. Their wild calls often broke the silence. As they sat quietly, Helena noticed pheasants and grouse scuffling around in the scrubby undergrowth.

"Does anyone live here, Klaus?" asked Helena.

"No. It is forbidden to build here, only temporary shelters are permitted. It is a place men may hunt and boys can become men. The high plain is a sanctuary for wild animals, something Uitlanders would never understand."

"It's wonderful, the plain seems endless." Helena, stood and dusted off her breeches. She ignored his disparaging comment this time, absorbed by the wonderful vista surrounding them. Klaus showed Helena how to use her view scope and she spent an hour lying on her stomach on a small hillock admiring the changing vista with childlike wonder. The day was so perfect and the wildlife so abundant. A constant parade of deer, herds of pigs, and buffalo visited two large water holes and grazed the plain below her. She noticed a pack of wolves relaxing and playing in the shade of a grove of trees.

Now the servant leading the remounts appeared and handed the reins over. Klaus instructed him to stay with the first two ponies and to meet them at the prearranged camping site in the late afternoon.

The riders mounted their fresh steeds and rode south east towards the base of the mountain. Klaus's quarry was the long horned mountain goats which lived on the high mountain slopes. He intended to get one for dinner. They rode close to herds of deer. The timid creatures scattered as soon as the riders were sensed. The day was hot now; Klaus and Helena removed their jackets and tied them on the rear of their saddles. Their fresh mounts were keen to run on the plain so Klaus and Helena let them gallop. Helena tied her hat to the pommel of her saddle and her long fair hair flowed out behind her. Klaus found himself watching how well Helena could ride. Her strong lithe figure riding easily at a canter stirred feelings in him which were equally enjoyable and mystifying.

Soon Klaus reined in his mount and held a finger to his lips. He pointed to a rocky outcrop above them.

"There are goats up there," he whispered. "I just saw them move! I remember there is a large pool nearby where we may leave the ponies to graze. Then we will climb on foot up to where the goats are."

They walked the ponies slowly to the pool, allowing them to get their breath and cool down. The ponies were unsaddled and hobbled and began munching happily on the vegetation. Klaus carried his musket over his shoulder and they climbed up a rocky hillside which supported only the hardiest of grasses and mosses. Klaus stopped behind a massive boulder that must have been dislodged many years ago from the upper slopes. He beckoned to Helena and she quietly walked to join him. In the shadow cast by the boulder they drank from water flasks and waited. There was enough vegetation near to attract Klaus's quarry, the big horned mountain goats. He loaded his long barreled hunting musket carefully. He would only get one shot, so he made sure the ball had a good load of powder behind it.

Helena was content to look over the plateau and watch the deer and other grazing animals using her view scope. Klaus tapped Helena's shoulder and pointed up the mountain slope. A group of shaggy haired mountain goats were picking their way down the mountain towards them. A huge billy goat with massive horns led the way. Behind him was his herd of females with kids of all ages. Helena watched them with keen interest, scanning with her view scope.

Klaus laid the barrel of his musket in a small cleft between some rocks. Taking careful aim he waited until the herd came within range. He had already picked out his target. Silently he aimed at his intended victim allowing some lead for distance and the slight breeze. Now he was completely focused and slowed his breathing. The goat stopped to pick at some lichen.

Boom! The sound was like thunder to Helena. She jumped at the sound, alarmed; she had forgotten the awful sound guns made. Goats ran in all directions leaving no time for a second shot as the quarry were soon out of sight. A goat, maybe a yearling, lay still about a hundred and fifty strides away up the slope. Excitedly Klaus pointed out the prone form of the goat to her.

"Why didn't you shoot the big one?" Helena asked after the ringing had stopped in her ears.

"Because he is the breeding male, his old meat would be smelly and tough to eat. Hold this while I go to fetch our dinner," said Klaus handing the musket to Helena. He began to climb up the rocky slope.

18

THE MUSKET BLAST AWOKE THE DRAGON. Small golden eyes with red vertical pupils opened slowly. A glossy black tongue as long as a man's forearm slithered out, tasted the air and sensed smells of prey close by. The ancient reptile rose on gnarled legs, standing on feet which supported claws longer than a grown man's fingers. One of the few remaining dragons of Atlantea, it had not eaten for almost a month. The smell of fresh goat meat was too compelling for it to remain hidden in the underground lair. Dust rose from the floor of the dragon's den and a ghastly stench accompanied the reptile. As it moved, piles of bones and corruption remaining from old meals were noisily shoved aside. The dragon crouched slightly, and then moved ponderously up a low tunnel to the surface. Bright sunlight made it blink but the radiant warmth gave power and flexibility to sluggish muscles. Then the dragon slowly moved out onto the hunting grounds of the high plateau.

The glistening black tongue tested the air for a scent trail to follow. The dragon's mouth was full of rows of serrated teeth designed to tear and cause a ragged wound. As evil as these teeth appeared, they were not the reason the dragon's prey died, once bitten. The reptile's mouth hosted a species of virulent bacteria which would cause any wound from the teeth to become septic. Within hours a bitten animal would suffer massive infection and die of blood poisoning within a day.

Patiently the dragon would track a bitten victim slowly, by the smell of suppuration. The long forked tongue flicked out, to taste the air and sense the putrefaction caused by its bite as if it were a signature. The dragon would gradually close in on the fevered prey. There was never a need to hurry since it preferred meat as putrid as possible.

The hungry reptile continually tested the wind. Picking up the scent of a slain goat, the dragon began to stalk the intended meal. The scent was close by. Instinctively the giant reptile kept low to the ground, its mottled brown skin blending in with the drab underbrush. The powerful tail was still, lifted off the ground, making almost no sound as the hunter closed in on the prey. The smell of fresh meat excited the beast. The scent led up a steep slope where it found a pile of bloody entrails. These it hungrily swallowed whole. This food gave energy and it rested a while digesting and gaining strength. However, like many reptiles, the dragon was capable of eating nearly seventy percent of its body weight. Now, appetite intense, the lumbering reptile followed a strong scent of blood down a rocky slope.

Wherever the odor of meat led, the dragon would stealthily follow.

When Klaus reached the fallen goat he took out his knife and slit the throat and turned the carcass, hanging it to let the remaining blood drain out. Then he opened the belly and cleaned out the entrails. The musket ball had passed through the chest of the animal. Then he tied the hocks together with a leather cord and carried the goat down the slope to Helena, slung over his shoulder. He took the musket and offered Helena the butt.

"Hold this, please," he said then he slid the barrel between the bound legs of the goat and picked up his end of the gun. With Klaus in the lead they carried the carcass between them suspended on the rifle back to the horses still feeding where they were hobbled beside the pool.

It was a large natural rock pool, shaded by huge volcanic rocks, full of cold sparkling clear water. They laid the goat carcass in the shade by the rock pool.

"Can you swim Helena?"

"No, but I can float a little. I am not very confident in deep water," replied Helena.

"Well if you can float you can swim. Let's enjoy the cold water. We are hot and dusty. I know this pool. The water isn't as deep as it looks," said Klaus undressing. He put his clothes, knife, musket and pistols on a dry rock beside the pool. As he slowly waded in Helena watched, admiring his strong muscular body. He stopped when the water was up to his chest.

"The water is beautifully cool, Helena. Come in and I will teach you to swim. Don't worry you will be safe with me." He smiled a dazzling smile, as his blue eyes flashed a warm invitation to her.

Helena undressed. She was accustomed to swimming naked and felt proud of her body. At home in Corinth they frequently swam and washed nude, openly enjoying the water and fun. Seeing Klaus enjoying himself splashing about in the pool gave her a confidence she otherwise wouldn't have with a man she did not truly know. She let the hunting clothes fall to the ground and stepped out of them.

Klaus admired her lovely pale peach skin and pert breasts with her curly blonde hair tumbling like spun gold around her shoulders. His gaze traveled down to enjoy her long sensual legs as Helena cautiously stepped into the pool. The cold water sent tingling shivers through her body. She made little screams and gasps, but once she got used to the cold water she walked in up to her breasts. Klaus swam to her and she splashed water over him. He laughed and splashed her back. Klaus dived under and swam around her legs and then popped up, laughing and flicking the water out of his hair.

Helena lost her footing and slipped towards Klaus. He caught her to him and held her close. Softly, gently their lips met, their breath melded and for a glorious moment they were one. Their warm skin pressed close, the chilly water emphasizing the delightful heat of virile flesh.

Helena shuddered and sighed; she relaxed in Klaus's arms. She knew she could trust him now. His touch felt wonderful, strong, masculine, and right for her. She allowed her legs to twine with his, the cool water allowing a closeness which on land she would not have trusted.

Holding her close, Klaus knew that this woman, wherever she was from, felt absolutely right for him. Now and forever. He blushed all over and found her body twined about him like an eel. He laughed and kissed her soft lips again and again, then he murmured in her ear in a soft tone that surprised Helena.

"Now dear Helena, you must learn a little swimming." She smiled at him and they moved slowly apart, hands holding hands, eyes holding eyes – green linked to blue.

Then he began to show her the rudiments of swimming, first on her back then on her stomach. They were having so much fun neither noticed the dragon as it rounded the rocks near the pool.

The dragon heard splashing in the pool and crouched in the shade, testing the wind for scent. It smelled two new kinds of animals. This time it lowered itself almost flat to the ground. The dragon's poor eyesight made out two animals splashing in the water. Prey lay close to it on the ground, but the fresh meat in the pool could be made into future feasts. The cold reptilian brain thought ahead to the next meal.

The dragon wasn't afraid of water; long ago his kind had perfected swimming while hunting in the streams and pools of the high plain. The animals swimming in the pool had a soft delicious smell. Swimming creatures were often vulnerable. Now it crept slowly to the brink of the pool near the swimmers. Hidden in the shade of the rocks the dragon slipped gently into the water. His long tail propelled him effortlessly through the water.

Klaus stood legs braced apart, toes splayed out on the bottom of the gravel pool. His arms cradled Helena's body, supporting her while she lay on her back kicking her feet.

"That's it! Kick with your legs and lay your arms by your sides palms down. You will float as well as move through the water." Klaus saw a look of horror appear on Helena's face. "What's the matter?"

"There," Helena croaked in fear, as she pointed between her legs.

Now Klaus saw the huge dragon head with unblinking golden eyes like lamps swimming steadily towards Helena. He swept her up in his arms and, mustering all his strength, threw her towards the edge of the pool.

The dragon's head and shoulders exploded from the water, pursuing Helena's flailing legs. The jaws as long as Klaus's arms snapped shut with a sickening click. Foiled in the attack on Helena the reptile lashed out at Klaus with a vicious swing of the tail. Klaus managed to put his arm up to ward off the blow, but was knocked under the water. The water was clear, with his eyes open Klaus saw the dragon turning towards him, short legs paddling furiously. Now the beast came straight at Klaus, the thick black tongue flicked in and out, golden eyes focused on him.

Momentarily Klaus saw a vision of that foul mouth clamping onto his arm. He could not get away by fleeing, so he dived under the dragon, rolling onto his back on the bottom of the rock pool. His eyes were wide open as the dragon swam right over him. Klaus realized with horror that he was not the target of the dragon at all!

Helena ran through the chest deep water as fast as she could. She heard a loud splash and looked behind her. Klaus had disappeared but the dragon, with only its broad head showing above the surface, was heading straight for her at a terrifying speed. The water was a cold wall holding her back. She pushed as hard as she could, but the dragon was gaining on her. She gasped and raced to take those precious steps to gain the shallows. Yet what protection was the dry land? She was naked and vulnerable, her soft flesh could be torn open any moment by the monster behind her.

The reptile was almost upon her. She heard it panting as the water rippled around the shoulders and muzzle. She sensed the huge mouth as it opened to reveal rows of serrated teeth covered with foul smelling mucous. Helena drove her legs as hard as she could. She must escape this awful beast, she must!

Crouching on the bottom Klaus thrust upward. He swam for all he was worth after the dragon as it pursued Helena. The tip of the tail whipped through the water in front of him, eluding his grasp for long moments. Klaus lunged and grabbed the scaly tail, then planted his feet and pulled as hard as he could. The huge reptile snapped at Helena's legs and missed as it was dragged backwards in the water. It exploded into action, thrashing in the water, rolling over in an attempt to free himself. Klaus could not hold the tail, it was too strong. The dragon broke free and swam again towards Helena's retreating legs.

Helena leaned forward toward the shallows, gasping; expecting to feel sharp teeth crushing her leg or claws raking her back. But the strike never came. She looked around and to her shock the dragon was only a short distance away, swimming strongly at her. Helena's feet found new traction, she had reached the shallows. Now she could run! Gasping, pushing her legs to go faster and faster, feeling the water splashing her thighs, then her knees and finally her ankles. She sprang out onto the shore and turned to look. The dragon had ceased pursuing her and turned to seek a new victim, Klaus!

As Helena fled from the pool Klaus slammed his palm down on the water as a signal of victory. The victory was short lived. The dragon seeing it had been thwarted, now turned his huge body towards Klaus. Two unblinking golden orbs of death which connected a simple brain to the urge to hunt now looked at Klaus. Uttering no sound, the creature swam towards him, thick mucus dribbling out the side of the huge mouth. Stinking breath came puffing from the big nostrils above those awful teeth.

"Helena!" shouted Klaus "Get my pistols! Run to the other side of the pool." He pointed, "I'll meet you there." He turned, took a deep breath and dived back into the water. He swam as fast as he could to the other side of the pool with the dragon in pursuit.

Klaus's pistols were a few paces away, on a flat rock with their clothes. Helena grabbed the holster belt which held the weapons and ran around the pool. She saw Klaus swimming with a strange overhand stroke which propelled him through the water with amazing speed. The head of the monster was a mere twelve paces behind him; she could not tell if the dragon was gaining. Their speed seemed identical. The far side of the pool was a steeply sloping clay and pebble cliff. A flat rocky ledge protruded about a yard above the water. Klaus was making for this part of the shore. If he could get to it she could give him the pistols – but how? The bank was high behind the rock and she could not see an easy way to get down to it.

Her chest heaving, Helena ran swiftly and stood on the top of the cliff not sure what to do as Klaus swam towards her. Klaus reached the shore, climbed out and reached up to the rock. The dragon was only two yards from his feet. He put one hand up onto the ledge, then two, and kicked hard hauling himself up onto the rock ledge.

"Take the pistols out. Pull back the hammers to cock them." he yelled to her, turning as the monster swam up to the ledge and began scrabbling at the clay wall underneath attempting to climb up.

Helena pulled a pistol out of the holster; the weapon was much heavier than she remembered. She was trembling and panting. With her left hand she pulled back the hammer.

"Now what?" she screamed.

"Aim at the dragon, just as you did at the target, then pull the trigger," instructed Klaus as calmly as he could. The dragon's huge head was just under the ledge, its long claws dug into the soft shore. Klaus took hold of a small shrub growing out of the bank above his head and anxiously tried to haul himself further from the reptile.

Boom! The pistol fired - the round plunked harmlessly into the water beyond the dragon.

"Aim lower!" cried Klaus. "Use the second pistol. Hurry!"

Helena bent down to pick up the second pistol. The dragon scrambled up onto the rocky ledge. Klaus shrank as far away from the predator as he could, holding onto the plant for support. The dragon made a low hissing sound, the mouth opened and the long black tongue flicked out towards Klaus.

"For pity's sake, shoot!" he cried, as the reptile crouched like a tiger about to spring.

Helena supported her arm on a rock and focused. She must not miss the beast this time. She took a deep breath and pressed the trigger. Boom! The second shot was deafening. A bloody wound appeared across the dragon's back as the bullet plowed a furrow through the creature's hide. Instead of disabling the reptile, this wound infuriated it. Now the dragon spun about, trying to relieve the pain. The rock ledge set in soft clay moved, then completely dislodged. The ledge tumbled into the water, taking the dragon deep down into the water with a fall of clay and rubble. Klaus was left hanging, holding onto the flimsy shrub, his feet scrabbling for purchase on the slippery clay and pebble cliff.

Below Klaus, the dragon surfaced and charged the bank again, digging long claws once more into the clay bank. The long heavy tail swished frantically in the water as it used every means to propel itself up towards Klaus's dangling legs.

"The belt, use the belt. Pull me up. Hang onto the end of it, tight," called Klaus, his voice hoarse.

Helena pulled the leather belt from the holsters, tucked her fingers into the buckle and lay on the edge of the bank. Below her Klaus clung to the shrub with one hand, his knees braced on the bank, while he reached up to grab the belt. Below him the monster was leaping and snapping with jaws wide enough to bite a man in half. It made hideous hissing and grunting sounds as it scrambled and splashed. More of the soft bank splashed into the water below Klaus, he was slipping down towards the water.

At last he felt the tip of the leather belt touch his upraised fingers. He grasped at it desperately. He pulled as hard as he possibly could. Helena felt his weight come onto her arms. He was so heavy. Her body began to slip forward. She opened her legs, dug her knees into the soft soil as hard as she could. Her arms felt like they were being torn from her shoulders, but she hung on grimly to the belt buckle with her eyes tightly shut. She could not bear to look down. Klaus's toes gained purchase in a flaw he discovered in the cliff. He pushed upwards digging his feet into the narrow crack. He released his grip on the plant and dug his fingers into a high crevice. This took the awful weight from Helena and quickly he pushed himself up towards safety. With the help of Helena's free wrist; Klaus hauled himself up onto the top of the bank.

They lay there for a moment in each other's arms, breathing hard. Time stood still.

"Oh Klaus!" she whispered "I thought you were lost. What if it had bitten you?"

"Thank you, dearest Helena. Fortunately, it bit neither of us. I owe you my life and I promise I will repay my debt to you." Klaus sat up and peered over the lip of the cliff.

"Look, the dragon is leaving." They watched the dragon swim to the low side of the pool, drag itself out and walk slowly away. The bullet wound had taken the beast's appetite away. Now it sought the comfort of a dark burrow. Klaus helped Helena to her feet and dusted her off.

"Are you unhurt?" he asked.

"I think so. My shoulders and arms ache but they will be all right." Helena replied. "Aren't we a mess?" She indicated their muddy, scraped naked bodies.

"We are indeed, but at least we are alive and unwounded by that beast." Klaus picked up his pistols, belt and holsters.

"I must teach you how to shoot properly. Come, it is time to leave this place, we have trespassed on the dragon's territory for long enough."

They walked hand in hand to find their clothes and fetched the ponies. The cool pool water washed off the mud then they dressed and ate some fruit. Klaus strapped the goat carcass to the back of his saddle and reloaded his pistols in case the dragon decided to return.

Together they trotted towards the setting sun and the campsite. Klaus promised Helena the greatest view in the world. She was content to look over at his smiling face, outlined in the setting sun. It was the face of a man who cared for her enough to have saved her life twice. For her at that moment, he was the greatest view in the world.

19

THE SUN WAS DIPPING TOWARD THE HORIZON by the time they had ridden to the edge of the plateau. The ponies had lost their initial enthusiasm for the ride and slowed to a walk. This speed suited Helena, who was suffering the tiring effects of a long day in the saddle.

Not far ahead Helena sighted three tents laid out in a row with a fire blazing like a beacon in the fading light. The sky was shades of red, and orange becoming a soft purple as the sun slid below the ocean horizon. Beyond the tents the land fell away. As the sun set they drew their horses to a halt. Not far away was the edge of the cliff and far below the great city of Atlantis began to twinkle in the dusk. The street lighting and electrics lit up the great buildings and houses, side by side, the modest and the fantastic revealed in golden lights.

Helena thought she could be looking at the mythical city of Olympus, the dwelling of the Gods; such was the beauty and majesty of the scene a thousand feet below them. Clinging to the coastline in each direction, the city pushed out past the great docks and spread out toward grand estates, and then finally dissolved into farmland. The towers at the mouth of the harbor were glowing golden. The sea was silver, blue and gold. A warship was patrolling the horizon, the smokestack emitting a long trail of smoke. Along the coast road she could see the steam trams chuffing, the lights from the trams twinkling in the setting sun.

In all her life she had never dreamed the world could hold such wondrous things. She felt overwhelmed by everything she had witnessed over the past few days. Tears welled up in her eyes. She dismounted and stood by her pony's head. The horse nibbled her forearm and champed the bit causing it to jingle. Helena felt an arm slip gently around her waist; Klaus looked down at her, smiling.

"It's the greatest view in the world to me," he said proudly, looking into her green eyes, admiring the glow the setting sun painted on her silky skin and how it turned her hair into fiery strands of red gold.

In this moment Helena was no longer a Greek priestess of Apollo, she was simply a strong loving Greek woman, looking into the eyes of her rescuer and protector. Klaus smiled and wiped a tear away from her cheek with the side of his hand. He leaned his head down and kissed her mouth softly, then firmly. It was the perfect time, the perfect place and Helena kissed him back. Her lips moved softly under his, her whole body drank him in.

Two lovers kissed on the edge of a plateau above the most mysterious, most perfectly amazing and beautiful city in the world - Atlantis. They were still kissing when the light faded completely and they were silhouetted by the full moon which rose behind them. Beyond were the numberless bright stars of the heavens which looked down on them with divine approval.

"Oh Klaus," said Helena "Do you feel the majesty of this place? It's wild, almost desolate, yet up here on the high plain I feel at one with the Gods."

"Aye, this place is wild, but it is a place I come when I am troubled or need to get away from the affairs of commerce and war," said Klaus, taking her hand. "I am glad to share this special place with you, Helena. Come, let's go to our camp, I will order the cook to prepare our evening meal." They began to lead the horses towards the tents.

"There is a natural hot spring nearby where we can bathe. Beneath us there is great turmoil. The mountain has been known to spit fire and brimstone some years. But in the quiet times, as now, steam, fumes and hot water where we can bathe are all that remains." They walked hand in hand towards the beckoning firelight of the campsite.

The servants served a delicious meal of potatoes, wild goat stew and a sweet apple pie. Then Klaus accompanied Helena to the hot pools, the electric light he wore on his head illuminating a valley which steamed in the cool night air. The pools of clear hot water bubbled up out of fissures in the rock steaming and hissing. Helena had to be careful as some of the water was almost boiling. They tested the temperature of the pools and found that near where the steaming water poured down in a misty waterfall over the edge of the cliff, the water was a perfect temperature. They took off their clothes and lay talking softly, relaxing in the heat. Klaus found his hand holding Helena's in the warm, soft water.

Helena was tired; the hot water eased her bruised and saddle sore body. But it was late when she retired to her camp bed in her own tent. She thought about her captain, the big man who was at once cruel but also kind; whose big strong body had never tasted defeat. She felt the stirring in her heart of love's early blossom. These things comforted her and concerned her at the same time. What was Klaus thinking as he lay in his bed tonight? She wondered. Did he share the emotions she was feeling? She hoped so – perhaps his kisses meant he cared for her. Perhaps, despite all his indoctrinated superior attitudes towards her race, he could have strong feelings for her? Surely inside him there dwelled a boy who loved the sea and riding his pony on the wild plateau; a boy who could love a woman like her.

20

RAINIA SCHMITT LOOKED AT THE GOLD edged birthday invitations piled on the hall table, about to be delivered by her mother's servants to the Atlantean elite. She felt excited, for the first time in a long time. I so want this to be a success, she thought, I long for my 20th birthday to be the start of my romance with him. She sighed and visualized captain Meinbach, her tall handsome dancing partner, holding her tight. Rainia and her mother Ada had chosen the dance tunes from the happiest, most romantic dances their culture had ever composed.

Rainia remembered seeing the captain for the first time in his dress uniform; her heart fluttered like a flag in a storm. Her brother Werner had introduced her to Klaus Meinbach at the commissioning of the new battle cruiser *Hieglund*. Amongst so many others he stood out like the twin towers that guarded the entrance to Atlantis.

Over the past four years Rainia had begged Werner for every scrap of information about his captain, and demanded that Werner persuade Klaus to attend her party. Several of his officer comrades were also invited and some from the marines including his own lieutenant from the *Hieglund*.

She rang a small bell and two servants dressed in green and gold uniforms, her family colors, walked into the room and stood before her.

"Deliver these. I don't care how long it takes, I want them delivered today."

"Yes noblewoman," they replied in unison. The messengers quickly gathered up the invitations, read the addresses and realized this would be a long day.

"Darling, you look wonderful." Rainia turned as her mother entered the hall. Ada Schmitt could trace her ancestry to the first inhabitants of the Atlantean archipelago over 800 years before. The blood of the genius Reinhart who started their civilization on the road to technological greatness ran in her veins. She swept down the hallway into the living room. Dressed in long flowing skirts and a tight corseted bodice; with her face powdered, full lips painted she possessed the great beauty of her bloodline. A beauty she had passed on to her daughter.

"Thank you mother." Rainia followed Ada. "I have sent away the invitations. Oh! I do hope Klaus will come to my party and leave that Greek woman he has adopted at his estate."

"Greek woman?" Ada said, "I know not of this woman." Her voice took on a harsh indignant tone.

"Didn't Werner tell you mother?" asked Rainia, "This last voyage the *Hieglund* took a Greek merchant ship and captured a high priestess on it. Werner said she has convinced Klaus she has Atlantean blood through her grandfather and he intends to petition the courts to get her citizenship."

"Ridiculous notion!" exclaimed Ada crisply. "For her to be conceived her grandfather must have consorted with Uitlanders. How anyone would want to breed with those sub-species of humans truly horrifies me."

"I think she has cast a spell over Klaus, mother," continued Rainia. "Werner was going to take her to the republican prison and Klaus reacted rather angrily towards him for even suggesting such a thing. I hear she is quite beautiful, with golden hair," said Rainia, smoothing her full skirts.

"Well, we must feel sorry for Klaus. By anyone's standards, he should have married by now. He is far too fond of adventuring and hunting on the high plains. His patrols at sea take up too much of his time. He needs a good woman, an Atlantean woman, to bed him. He needs *you*, Rainia."

"Mother what are you saying?" Rainia exclaimed, shocked at her mother's language.

"Oh, don't be so prissy girl. A man of his status and breeding who deflowers a maiden would of course stand by her to save her reputation. I for one would demand it, and your father would too if he were still alive," said Ada. She picked up a hairbrush and started to brush her daughter's hair.

"Rainia, you are a woman now, and Klaus is not only rich but famous. He needs an heir; he is the sole scion of his ancient bloodline. This line is perfect to breed with our own. If I was younger I would seek him as a husband myself." Ada's hair brushing was brisk.

"Oh don't say that!" exclaimed Rainia, horrified. "Klaus is so much younger than you."

"Rubbish girl. I am as much older than he, as you are younger." Ada laughed, "I warn you, use this party to make Klaus Meinbach yours by any means because if you do not, there are plenty of woman in Atlantis who will!"

21

IN THE MORNING, after a delicious meal of goat stew, Klaus and Helena rode ahead of the main party on fresh mounts. Because the walking was so much easier downhill, the ponies could manage the whole journey back to Klaus's estate.

Morning mist was slowly rolling away off the high plain. Cold air bit into their lungs as they rode at an easy amble. Small puffs of dust rose at each footfall and clung to the ponies' long fetlocks. They were minuscule moving figures in a vast wilderness. Above them loomed the great silent volcano, the peak hidden in morning mist.

As the sun rose higher, the mist cleared. After riding for an hour and walking their mounts for another half hour, Helena decided to spice up the ride.

"Race you to the edge?" suggested Helena, her eyes sparkling as she remounted her mare.

"Helena, be careful. The drop at the edge of the plateau arrives quickly and you might not notice where the slope falls away." warned Klaus, one foot in the stirrup as he was about to remount.

"What's the matter big man, scared? The winner is the first to enter that copse of trees at the edge of the plain." Her arm indicated a dark smudge on the horizon. Then she laughed spurring her horse forward. The eager pony squealed and hit the ground in a flat run. Klaus laughed, swinging himself into the saddle.

"You obviously don't know me well enough." He yelled to the fast disappearing rider. His pony, a larger heavier animal, seemed up to the challenge and commenced the chase at a gallop towards the edge of the plateau.

Helena was fortunate to have a light, swift filly as her mount. She was finer boned and possessed of greater speed than Klaus's mount. Helena and her mount flew across the plain sending clods of earth and dust flying backwards toward Klaus who could not match that high speed. Galloping into a wide ravine she surprised a herd of grazing deer. They fled in all directions as Helena's pony ran among the startled animals. She marveled as the deer, sensing her closing in on them, switched direction in a heartbeat; leaping the low brush in a bound. Her smile widened as she relished the mayhem she caused. Klaus had to slow to avoid some of the herd who were dashing frantically in his direction. For a moment he became engulfed in a maelstrom of twisting and turning bodies, his senses obscured by the choking dust and thundering hooves.

Helena leaned forward and touched the neck of her mount.

"Run," she yelled to her filly as the thrill of the race energized her spirit. "Show how we woman are the true leaders of the pack." She laughed and looked behind to see Klaus, who was obviously not enjoying being covered in dust, looking ahead with an intense stare.

They ran on over the rough plain following the trail. Klaus's horse shied as a flock of wild fowl was disturbed by Helena's passing. The big birds exploded up from the brush with a loud beating of wings and screams of alarm, but he retained his seat. Now Helena's lead was a hundred lengths or more. Her horse still seemed strong and eager but she was not sure of the distance to the edge. The well used trail was clear and easy to follow but she noticed Klaus was happy to settle into a more sedate gallop. Had he lost hope of winning or did he know something she did not? He had a lifetime of local knowledge.

She thought she recognized a low barren hill with a single large tree on the top, bent over by years of strong winds. The trail wound around and over the hill in a leisurely manner. Beyond this hill was the copse of trees.

"Yes," she cried, "the end of the race is in sight." Her lead was enough that she eased her mount to a slower clip. This race is over! She thought triumphantly. Poor Klaus, she would have to be magnanimous in victory. The roan filly appreciated the slowing of the pace; white foamy sweat appeared on the pony's neck where the reins rubbed her. Helena was an experienced rider but not such an experienced horsewoman as she thought, so she failed to notice that her fillies' courageous spirit was masking increasing tiredness.

Klaus noticed Helena start up the gently winding trail. He laughed and leaned forward in the saddle to pat his big steed's neck.

"She has yet to learn the art of navigation my friend. She is about to learn that the fleetest vessel is no match for a master of distance."

The big stud, bred for power and strength, not speed, lowered his head. As they approached the hill Klaus stood in the stirrups leaning slightly forward over his mount's neck. The pony began a vigorous driving canter straight up the side of the hill. His iron shoes drove deep into the soil, sending great clods of earth flying up behind him. It was hard work, but up he went, straight as an arrow. Even low bushes did not deter or slow him. Klaus balanced himself slightly forward allowing his mount to apply more purchase with his powerful hindquarters and used his voice to urge him on.

Helena looked behind her and saw Klaus had disappeared. She rode on, wondering where he was. Then she heard a slapping of leather and grunts of exertion from Klaus's steed.

The man has deceived me! He has held his pony in reserve to take the steeper direct route over the hill. What a delicious beast of a man he is! She slapped the reins on her horse's neck and called out for help from the Gods.

"Apollo, hear me!" she cried brightly.

Victory was still within her grasp. Her mount flew up the rough earth trail breathing hard. Helena leant into her left stirrup as she rounded the final corner reaching the crest of the hill. She saw the clump of trees in the distance which marked her finish line. Her mouth was dry but she had no time to drink from her water bottle.

Her gaze darkened as she noticed Klaus's big horse was now ahead of her, running at a quick canter. Her filly pricked her ears when she saw the other pony and sprinted after him at a full gallop. Helena's blood was up, sensing the race was no longer hers.

When her pony faltered for a stride she kicked her onwards, shouting encouragement. Her filly stumbled, Helena urged her harder. She would not be denied. The filly dug deep to her brave heart, the gap closed but now the finish line was approaching fast. Klaus turned and, riding with one hand, doffed his hat. His smile was broad, enjoying his tactical move, which had out-foxed her.

Helena's fighting spirit was ignited. Ahead she saw a glimmer of hope. They were about to go past a large mound of earth. The trail cut through a small twisting ravine which would force them to a slow trot at best. She felt the hill beckoning, taunting her with a whispered promise of success. Maybe she could use Klaus's trick by simply running up and over the hill and so regain the lead? She attacked the side of the hill, her pony snorting; sweat flying from her mouth into Helena's face.

She thought she heard Klaus cry

"No! Helena, no!" But she was committed to her course now, and even if the God Apollo had appeared in front of her, he would not have dissuaded her.

The filly staggered as she valiantly tried to keep up her pace. Looking ahead Helena realized why Klaus called out a warning. The ravine made a sharp dog leg to the right. Now in front of her she had a choice of plunging into the ravine or making a mad leap to clear it. Unfortunately the other side offered only a steep scrubby bank as a landing zone. Klaus was now almost below her. Helena saw his tormented face as she spurred her pony to make the jump of her life.

Muscle and sinew tightened and released in one tremendous effort. Helena felt as one with her filly as they flew over Klaus's head and landed on the other bank amongst the low scrub that grew from its sides. The pony's legs buckled at the impact and her weariness began to betray her. The filly whinnied and tried to scramble up the bank. Helena slipped her feet from the stirrups to dismount. For a moment rider and pony were in jeopardy of toppling backwards into the ravine. Helena screamed in fear, she could see herself and her mount crashing to the path below in a moment.

Klaus's big black stud appeared at her side taking great leaps to get there. Klaus swept Helena from the saddle with his left arm and swung her up behind him. He grabbed her pony's bridle and slowly guided the filly downhill to the path. Klaus used his own pony's strength and size to anchor the slide of their mounts down the bank locked together. Smashing through scrub and bushes on the way, the ponies slid and staggered down the bank, until finally they stood panting and snorting once more on the trail.

Klaus flung one leg over the pommel of his saddle and dismounted. He reached up for Helena and she fell into his arms. He didn't speak for a long moment as he looked at her. She took a sobbing breath. Then he kissed her with all the passion of one who thought his love had been about to die. His stoic persona crumbled, falling all around him like a shattered egg shell.

"Helena, promise me you shall not show such disregard for your life again. I could not bear to see you leave me in such a way."

"I am sorry Klaus! I became enamored of winning in the moment." She took another sobbing gasp. "I fear I may have broken my pony's wind with my wild riding," she said looking at the flanks of her heaving, sweat soaked filly.

"Do not worry on that score, my dear Helena, this filly is one of my best stock. She is bound for the broodmare paddock and has many years of roaming the high plain in her yet. Our race is over, we must walk the horses now. It will take some time before they regain their wind. Come, take my hand and we will cross the finish line together." She smiled and slipped her arm around his waist.

"Let's walk like this for awhile," she said, looking up at his handsome profile. Obligingly Klaus slipped his arm around her waist and clicked his tongue, the tired ponies followed them.

Klaus laughed good-naturedly when Helena slipped free from his embrace at the last moment and ran across the finish line into the copse of trees. She held up her arms in triumph, laughing. He ran forward and caught her up in a passionate embrace.

22

HELENA WAS FALLING ASLEEP IN THE SADDLE by the time they reached the Meinbach estate that afternoon. Several times Klaus had shaken her by the shoulder as she slumped forward. Finally they reached the stables and handed the reins of their tired mounts to the servants to attend to. They enjoyed a light meal and Helena soaked in a hot bath before retiring for an afternoon nap.

Klaus perused the correspondence which had arrived while he was at sea. He saw the gold edged invitation from Rainia Schmitt and looked at the ornate card for a few long moments. He knew it would be taking a risk socially and in every other way to attend the party with Helena. It risked her being abused, spat upon or worse for being an Uitlander, yet his reputation was such that – surely, anyone *he* felt was suitable for introduction to Atlantean society *must* be accepted. His word was enough. He stiffened his shoulders and his chin. It was about time Atlantis learned that worthwhile people lived outside the closed cell of their island lives.

Two hours later Klaus awoke Helena and told her of the party the next evening and suggested they find something for her to wear. They carefully searched through all her new clothes and his mother Angelina's clothes looking for something elegant but understated, which would perhaps not display her radiant golden locks as brightly as the rising sun they resembled. Madame Meinbach's clothes fitted her well, including the ornately constructed brocade corsets.

"We must have been a similar size," said Helena as she twirled in front of the large mirror in the luxurious dressing room.

"Indeed you are my mother's size. I had not considered it before this moment. She was regarded as an elegant woman by Atlantean society. I kept her clothes in remembrance of her after she died. I cannot part with them just yet." Klaus had a warm look in his eyes as he looked at Helena. She smiled at him, her glowing green eyes like a warm buzzing spell bewitching his senses.

The bureaucratic ice in Klaus's veins was dissolving as he grew to know this strong willful Grecian beauty preening in front of the mirror. The long skirts and corsets, the ornate hair ornaments and high heels of Empire fashion suited her well. His heart beat fast, his body throbbed with desire. Despite her Atlantean blood being diluted with Uitlander blood he was extremely attracted to her. Kissing her was deliciously intoxicating.

Klaus was surprised at himself. Helena interested him like no other woman. There were many women of equal beauty, endowed with power and wealth, who sought his attention in the past four years since he became the *Hieglund's* captain. None enchanted and thrilled him like this foreign woman he had plucked from certain death in the sea.

"I will teach you to dance before we attend this party," said Klaus as Helena swished her full skirts and giggled at her image in the mirror.

"Dance?" she said. "I already know how to dance; we have many dances at Delphi. How do you dance in Atlantis?"

"We have the gasuotte, the zalz, the untet and wilyfox. All must be mastered before I can take you with me to the party."

"Really?" she asked, looking at him seriously. "I always believed the worshippers of Dionysius were the ones who truly danced and they have no need of lessons."

"Indeed." Klaus was uninterested. "In our society knowledge of these dances are taught to all children of the upper classes. Slaves and fools never need such education, of course." Helena smiled.

"Of course. Our slaves do not get taught the finer elements of social life. They are tools for use, not for teaching inessential entertainments." She twirled her skirts again and took some happy dancing steps across the room.

"So when do my lessons begin?" she trilled happily. She felt almost recovered from the stiffness and tiredness she had suffered after their hunting expedition and looked forward to the party.

"Now if you wish," said Klaus. "Follow me." He was in his informal clothing today, dark red trousers with a black stripe and an elegant deep-blue shirt, which emphasized the azure of his eyes. Helena followed him into the formal living room, where he went to a peculiar instrument which sat upon a side table. He pressed some buttons on the machine and a joyful strain of rhythmic music filled the room. Helena looked about in surprise, seeking the musicians who were playing music, but could see none. She rushed to Klaus and looked at the instrument.

"How do you make this music?" she asked breathlessly, excited. "I can hear ten musicians but I cannot see them. Is this a kind of Atlantean magic?"

He laughed and pressed a button on the top of the instrument which stopped the music.

"No indeed. It is a machine we call an audi. It is a way of playing sound so we may hear and enjoy it at any time and also recording music or voice at any time I wish."

"Oh. How amazing and astonishing. So you have the dance music in the audi?"

"Yes I do." he confirmed warmly, looking down at her. He enjoyed her delight in Atlantean inventions. "Now listen to this," he said pressing another button. The look on Helena's face was one of total astonishment as the sound of Klaus and herself talking about the audi filled the room. She put her hand to her mouth and laughed delightedly.

"Oh Klaus, how amazing!" She clapped her hands and danced a little jig.

Klaus pressed another button, the voices stopped and the dance music began again. He stepped up to her and took her hands in his.

"Time for dance lessons," he said. "Put your left hand up on my shoulder - so. And hold my left hand thus - in your right. Good, now we step with our feet. Beginning - one two three - one two three, around in a circle - so."

They spent several hours on the dance lessons until Klaus was sure that Helena, who was a quick and able study at the new dance steps, would be able to keep up with the other women at the party. For the group dances he ordered his upper servants to provide dance partners. It was a delightful evening and Klaus found himself smiling all the time, without realizing that for the first time in his life, he was truly, deeply happy.

Helena was sleeping when the messenger arrived late that night. Klaus paid him and opened the letter.

23

HELENA FELT A HAND ON HER SHOULDER tugging her from a delightful dream of riding a pony on the wild plains. She looked up and saw the smiling face of Klaus standing beside the bed already dressed in charcoal pants, his pale blue shirt unbuttoned at the collar.

"What is it? Why do you awaken me so early Klaus? Surely we don't need any more dancing practice this early in the morning?" she murmured, peering out the window which barely glowed with the dawns early light.

"No, of course not, you are already a delightful dancer my dear. I have news! We must dress quickly. We have been invited to a very special gathering," Klaus's face was animated and he grinned with excitement.

"When did you hear this news?" asked Helena, propping herself up on a pillow.

"A courier brought the invitation late last night. I didn't want to wake you as you had retired for the night," said Klaus.

"This is an invite from my friend Dieter Meier. He is the foremost of our brilliant engineers." He held up a thick folded card with mechanical diagrams printed in blue upon it.

"Do you know this man personally?" asked Helena, thinking Klaus was indeed a handsome man and when he was as happy as he was now she became blissfully happy as well.

"Yes, we were at university together but he is a few years older than I. Dieter is different from most Atlantean men, he is a bit of a rebel you might say – an unusual but likeable genius. He has liberal ideas and at times has faced censure from the Politicos. But his brilliance as an engineer silences all his critics. The engineer's guild is held in the highest regard in our country, next to the Navy in fact, so the Politicos are forced to ignore his most outlandish statements."

"You make him sound exciting! I can't wait to meet him Klaus! Shall we eat before we go?"

"Yes, I have the servants cooking now. Bathe and dress please. The servants have laid out your travelling clothes for you in the bathroom. Hurry now! Dieter can be very impatient."

Klaus kissed her forehead, turned and ran from the room like an excited boy. Helena found her bath already full and she bathed quickly in the scented water. Hung on a stand was a pretty pale blue dress she had purchased the first day in Atlantis with a dark blue satin corset; matching gloves, a pale blue be-ribboned hat and a pair of dainty black leather shoes whose tips shone like mirrors.

Klaus was waiting for her pacing the floor in the foyer dressed in his captain's uniform, carrying his hat under his arm. He looked up when he heard her and smiled

"You look beautiful darling, the most *noble* of noblewoman. Now we must away at once to catch the tram."

"What about breakfast?"

"Oh, I forgot about the food. I will ask the servants to pack our meal in a basket and we can eat on the steam tram," said Klaus and called his housekeeper on his fonier.

They hurried down the drive and caught the steam tram which stopped almost right outside the main gate of the estate; and were soon eating a delicious breakfast as they chugged through the hinterland past all the vast estates towards the city. It was the dawn of a beautiful day.

"Klaus I can see the spires and towers of Atlantis even though we are far away, the sun is lighting them up," said Helena who had her head partly out of the window. She sat back.

"Now exactly where are we going?" she composed her hands on the stem of her parasol.

"We must pass through the city to get to Volkesgarten; the forbidden zone."

"The forbidden zone? It sounds dangerous, will we be safe? Are you armed?" asked Helena, staring at him. Klaus smiled and opened his coat to show off his pistols in their holsters.

"I rarely travel without them my dear. Our destination is Volkesgarten, the domain of the engineer's guild. It is known as the forbidden zone because of all the secret work that is undertaken there. Most of our wealth goes towards their research and development work. Only engineers and their especially invited guests may ever enter Volkesgarten. I have been several times to visit Dieter. His workshops are the grandest of all, wait and you will see." He grinned in anticipation.

"Oh I am excited! I want to see everything I can." The tram entered the city passing through grand squares and past towering buildings. Sky trams moved silently so high above, their cables were barely visible and they seemed to float in the sky. Helena became silent as she gazed wide eyed out the windows; awed again at the impossible magnificence of the elegant buildings.

The tram slowed and stopped at many stations. After a while everyone had disembarked until only Klaus and Helena were left.

"Why are no more people getting on the tram?" asked Helena.

"I have paid the driver to stay on this line all the way to the forbidden zone. We will be the only passengers from now on until we change at the Colossus."

"What's the Colossus?" Helena was looking out the window enjoying the noise and hubbub of city life. Bicycles ridden by men and women moved sedately past other steam conveyances on rails. Horses cantered by on horse paths, crowds thronged the squares and shopping streets.

"I guarantee you will know it when you see it," said Klaus. "It will be a nice surprise for you."

"The colors of Atlantean clothing amaze me Klaus. Where do all the bright colors come from?"

"Now the answer to that, I do not know," he said, "I have never thought about the colors of clothes."

The steam tram suddenly switched tracks to another line, Helena let out a small cry of fright.

"I didn't see that coming, we are going so fast. It's a wonder that people know to stay clear of the tram lines. Ooh! Look at those fountains." Klaus smiled, enjoying the delightful wonderment on Helena's face.

They were now past the city center entering the Eastern suburbs where the rich and noble people lived. Behind a large carefully tended flower garden a high carved marble fountain burst into life. Water spouted into the air at a great height then cascaded down into many layers of ornate bowls.

"I can see a rainbow in the water," said Helena "It's the hand of the Goddess Iris."

"Not really," said Klaus, "It's merely the sun's rays shining through the water just like any rainbow. The colors are -"

"Oh Klaus, stop it! With all your scientific talk; can't a simple Greek girl worship her Gods for a moment?" Klaus laughed and slapped his thigh.

"You remind me of a young girl seeing the world for the first time. All right, I will promise to stop all scientific talk. You will get enough from Dieter I expect."

"Is Dieter handsome like you?" Helena smiled wickedly.

"Oh, well if you think *I* am handsome, you will be impressed with Dieter. Let's just say he never has any problem with the ladies. He is handsome - much more so than I am. I'm sure he will find you the most beautiful noble woman in all Atlantea just as I have." he grinned and raised his eyebrows at her. Helena laughed.

"You can be so sweet at times Klaus, I like you much more when you are in this mood."

"Dieter is an orphan or so he says, from one of the outer islands. Hmmm - Come to think of it he never really talks about his life before we were at university."

"By the Gods! Look ahead of us. Sweet Apollo!" exclaimed Helena. Klaus looked out at the scene ahead.

"Oh you mean the bridge? It *is* wonderful. That is Colossus. We must stop before it to have our identity checked. At the other side of the bridge is the start of Volkesgarten."

"I have never seen such a huge bridge. How did they build such a thing?" Helena stared at the huge steel arched bridge which straddled a deep jagged rift in the hill which extended all the way to the smoking volcano above. It seemed to Helena as if the Gods had torn the land apart; rent open like a loaf of bread.

"Well first they -" he hesitated. "Sorry Helena no scientific talk, remember?" Klaus smiled and raised his eyebrows. "The tram stops here at the end of the line. We must disembark now. Dieter said in his invitation that he would arrange our transport to his workshop. Come, take my arm, and prepare to be amazed."

Helena was warming to this adventure and clung tightly to Klaus's arm as they walked down the steps to the platform. A sergeant and two marines were waiting there and they saluted Klaus before the Sergeant spoke.

"Good morning captain. May I see your invitation and identification please?" Klaus handed over his silver identity tablet. The sergeant inspected it and compared it to his clipboard information.

"That's all in order, captain; now the noble woman's tablet please."

"She has not been issued one as yet," said Klaus, "She is a guest of mine; I will accept all responsibility for her."

"My orders here are quite specific captain. I..." There was a sudden whistling sound which grew louder. They looked to their left as a sleek, shiny metallic tram approached the station from the other side of the bridge. Apart from the hiss and whistle the tram was almost silent as it stopped beside the platform in front of the public tram.

A ramp descended from the metal skin of this new tram and came to rest gently on the platform, creating an open doorway from which a distinguished, tall, broad-shouldered man wearing a tailored grey suit of fine cloth walked down the ramp towards them. An intricate gold steam engine badge gleamed on his lapel.

"Klaus my old friend! So good to see you," he said in a thick accent. He crushed Klaus to his chest in a bear hug.

"Hello Dieter, good to see you again," said Klaus laughing; hugging Dieter in return. He disengaged the embrace

"This is Helena." He gestured for Helena to come closer. The big engineer bent over her hand and kissed it with soft warm lips.

"My, what an attractive woman you are. Klaus told me he had a friend he wanted to bring along, but never did I suspect that friend would be someone like you. I am delighted to meet you," said Dieter boldly, his long brown curly locks fell forward over his intense grey eyes which drank her in as he held her hand for a long moment. Helena tingled all over and smiled at him.

"Now we must away," he said briskly. "I have so much to show you, it is great to see you again Klaus. What have you been up to?" he winked at Klaus whose grin failed to cover his flushed cheeks.

The sergeant cleared his throat. "Sir, the lady doesn't have any identification."

"Oh, I will personally vouch for her sergeant. Any friend of Klaus couldn't possibly be an enemy of the state. We will take full responsibility for her."

"Very well sir you may continue," said the sergeant, "I was only following my orders."

"You are to be commended," said Dieter. "Your loyalty won't go unnoticed." The sergeant saluted.

Helena followed Dieter and Klaus up the ramp into the sleek tram. Inside she noticed large long black boxes either side of a passage way which ran lengthways along the tram.

"This way," said Dieter walking to the end of the tram where he entered a glass covered driver's compartment. "Saves time turning the tram around, having steerage at each end." he said, "Take a seat Klaus. Helena please sit beside me while I drive. Klaus has seen all this before."

"Thank you Dieter. My, this seat is really comfortable, so luxurious compared to what I am used to," she said as her body was engulfed in the soft seat.

"Nothing but the best in my tram," said Dieter casually as he released the brakes and moved a red lever forward. A low hum came from beneath them and the tram accelerated across the bridge. Helena looked down into the chasm far below.

"What caused that tear in the earth? It looks like it was done with such violence?" asked Helena staring out at the deep chasm to her left.

"It is a fault line, caused when the earth below moved violently. The island of Atlantea was weakest here and was torn apart as easy as you would tear paper. But that happened many thousands of years ago. Klaus, I have a surprise that will astound even you, my friend – I know you have high expectations of me," said Dieter as they exited the bridge and sped along the steel tracks at an alarmingly high speed. Helena found herself gripping the sides of her seat very hard as they approached a curve in the tracks. Dieter noticed her anxiety,

"Don't worry Helena; we are not even at three quarter throttle. You are as safe with me as if you were seated in your own home." He had such a reassuring smile Helena found herself relaxing and began to enjoy their headlong flight which was passing a circular building supported by elegant pillars surmounted by a dome. This building was surrounded by gardens and then by contrast they passed several drab red painted warehouses.

Dieter slowed the tram as they approached a huge colored glass and steel framed station house where several trams were sitting beside the platform. Dieter tapped a button on the control panel and the steel tracks ahead moved to one side and the tram clicked and clacked onto another track which led toward a magnificent high-domed windowless building set amongst mown grass and manicured gardens. The track approached this edifice down an avenue of handsome trees with dark glossy foliage and huge white flowers blooming abundantly amongst the green foliage. The fragrance of the blooms surrounded the tram and Helena breathed deeper with delight.

"Welcome to Volkesgarten. Home of the Engineer's Guild and my humble abode." Dieter opened his arms towards the view and Helena now noticed this area was inhabited by many people. There were beautiful gardens; a great row of huge warehouses painted in many primary colors and beyond them Helena glimpsed houses arranged in neat streets. She thought of Corinth and the jumble of comfortable but small stone and earth houses, the narrow ancient streets which wound in convolutions amongst the houses and she realized that this town of Volkesgarten had been planned and created by engineers with one purpose in mind; the creation of things all magnificent.

"Is this building ahead really your home?" Helena pointed, her eyes and mouth open in disbelief, wondering why these engineers needed houses the size of the Temple of Olympus.

"Well – it's my workshop." Dieter said. "My living quarters are somewhat smaller. I need this size of workshop because my latest project is rather large."

As they approached the building a door large enough to admit the tram slid open in the wall and Dieter piloted the vehicle inside and came to a halt beside a platform.

"Come on," he said, "we are due to attend a viewing of another engineer's invention before I show you *my* surprise."

Beyond the platform was a large space filled with mechanical devices attended by many men dressed in grey coveralls. Noises reverberated deafeningly around the enclosed space. The true size of the building could not be seen however as a wall blocked off the bulk of the building from view. A door at the far end of this wall was guarded by two marines. Dieter walked rapidly past the machines heading for the end of the platform where large double glass doors showed gardens and a path beyond. Helena had to run to keep up with his energetic strides. Dieter led them out onto the path; only Klaus didn't seem to mind the frenetic pace.

Gardeners in green coveralls and wide brimmed sunhats looked up as the trio emerged into the sunshine. A man with a steam-powered blade trimmed bushes while others raked leaves and tended flower beds which were laid out in the shapes of machines and tools.

"What is behind the guarded door?" panted Helena.

"A surprise, a rather big one," said Dieter smugly. "You will see it later. One of my engineer comrades is to unveil his latest creation and custom demands we other engineers attend even if only to see it fail miserably - as is the case sometimes. Come, come."

They followed the tree lined pathway toward a collection of domed buildings and workshops. As they walked they were joined by throngs of people moving in the same direction. Many of the men were accompanied by ladies dressed in gorgeous dresses with their hair arranged in many exquisite styles. Helena wondered if her own simple long haired style would be considered somewhat bohemian by these beautiful creatures.

She also noticed that not all the men wore golden steam engine badges; but those who did tended to drop their gaze when they approached Dieter, as if he had an authority over them which they acknowledged in this subtle way.

By the time they reached their destination, a large domed building with many high glass windows, the crowd had swelled to several hundred. Helena noticed marines patrolling the area in small groups, the official silver badges on their polished metal helmets glinting in the sunlight.

Excited chatter echoed from the high walls of the auditorium as the invited audience took their seats around a circular stage. Once everyone was seated there was a respectful silence until a short balding man, dressed in a white coat over a purple suit; with a wild array of view-scopes attached to his cranium, walked onto the stage. The crowd erupted into spontaneous applause. He bowed and waved his arms extravagantly at a large object covered in a blue velvet cloth which rested in the center of the stage.

"Good morning. I am Willum Shatzke. Today I introduce to you my latest invention: the electric harmonizer!"

"I wonder what it does?" whispered Helena to Dieter. He smiled.

"I know what it is - since I helped with the wiring; but I won't spoil the surprise for you Helena," said Dieter in a low whisper.

"I should have done something with my hair today, but we left in such a hurry I had no time," said Helena touching her long flowing curls with the tips of her fingers. "I look quite shabby compared to these other women."

"You look wonderful Helena, you are by far the most beautiful woman in the room," said Dieter flashing a broad, unabashed smile at her. Helena blushed and cast a quick sideways look at Klaus, who smiled at her and patted her hand. Helena was surprised how at ease she felt completely protected by the handsome powerful men sitting on either side of her.

On the stage the inventor clapped his hands, as an elegant brunette woman in a simple white silk dress glided smoothly onto the stage. She removed the velvet cloth. Helena sighed in amazement along with many in the crowd as a huge stringed lyre was revealed. The instrument was as tall as the musician and made from glistening golden wood decorated all over with flowers of gold leaf. Gleaming strings of silvery wire connected the uprights of the lyre, many more than the humble hand held lyres which Helena was familiar with in Greece. Scattered applause and whispers filled the hall.

"I present to you my electric harmonizer and the artist you are to hear today is noble woman Althea Kestler."

Willum waited for a moment as Althea seated herself beside the instrument and picked up a slim bow-like object. She fidgeted about for a moment on the seat then nodded that she was ready. The engineer went over to a large box and turned some dials. There was a crackling and humming sound for a few moments then silence as he made some further adjustments.

The woman drew the bow over the strings of the harmonizer and a wonderful melodic sound erupted from what seemed like the walls of the auditorium. She began to play a musical score with an exquisite melodic harmony. Helena closed her eyes and swayed gently to and fro as she became wrapped up, entwined in musical wonderment. Althea played with a touch and finesse which could only come from years of practice and Helena fell completely under her spell. The strangest thing, thought Helena, is when I close my eyes it is as if there are many instruments and musicians playing, not just one.

Finally the musical piece came to a wondrous climax. Althea stood and bowed gracefully. The crowd stood enthusiastically; clapping, stomping feet and cheering while Althea and Willum bowed many times to the applause. Dieter leaned over and spoke loud enough to get Klaus's and Helena's attention.

"Let's leave now. There will be endless speeches and a boring lecture from Willum about his electric harmonizer. Come, come." Dieter gestured for them to leave and they excused themselves as they walked slowly out from the cheering throng to a side aisle.

They left the auditorium swiftly. Helena almost running as she followed Dieter's huge strides.

"That was the most amazing thing I have ever heard!" Helena said to Klaus as they hurried along after Dieter. "I would love to play an instrument like that!"

"I will get you a prototype to learn on but first we must win the court case against you," said Klaus, cocking his head at her. She frowned and sighed.

"Oh yes, I forgot." Klaus and Helena strove to keep up with Dieter but by the time they reached the entrance to his workshop Dieter was standing waiting for them, his hands twitching and his lips compressed.

"Come in, come!" he said. He held the door open for them and followed them in.

24

HELENA GASPED IN ASTONISHMENT at the sheer unbelievable size and dimensions of the space behind the door. The roof was higher than a strong man could throw a small stone and was covered in girders and beams arranged in a complicated web of steel. The flat concrete floor was bare and in the center rested something massive covered in a huge sheet of black cloth.

"What is under there? It's simply enormous! Is it a new kind of steam ship?" asked Helena standing on her tip toes, peering at it.

"Your guess is close. It is a vehicle for travel, but not a kind of travel that you or Klaus could ever imagine." Dieter walked towards it, leading them, his head held high.

"I am not one for long speeches. Klaus, as my oldest friend, I wanted you to be the first outsider to see my latest and perhaps greatest invention. Please stand here." He halted and waved his hand, pointing to a place on the floor.

Helena and Klaus stood and waited, looking up at the huge black-clad object with wide eyes as Dieter briskly approached a panel in the wall and moved a lever.

Far above them something metallic began clanking. Fine wires attached to the top of the sheet began lifting the fabric up, gradually revealing Dieters engineering masterpiece. There was a sharp intake of breath and a long "Oooohhh!" from Klaus and Helena as an extraordinary silver melon-shaped craft was revealed.

Klaus took Helena's hand and walked with her around the machine, their eyes busily inspecting every part. A large fin extended out from each side of the silver melon. At the narrowest end was a collection of rudder-like fins. Underneath, it rested upon a glossy black, silver and glass tube shaped structure. At the rear of this they saw a dark maw of metal blades. As they walked around the gondola towards Dieter they passed a brass-bound door set into the side and then looked into windows where they admired the luxurious interior of four red seats, wooden tables, a telescope and a control panel of red, green and orange lights and levers.

Helena reached up and cautiously touched the glossy silver covering. Her fingers found it felt soft, smooth and warm to the touch. A humming emanated from the machine. Then Helena noticed the gondola was not resting on the floor but was in fact floating at least six inches above the ground. She gave a little scream and held Klaus's hand very tight.

"Do you see that?" she remarked, her voice high and strained, "It does not touch the ground! What is this? Some kind of magic from Hermes?"

"No, I'm sure it is some magic of Dieter's, I cannot explain it." Klaus turned to Dieter, a small frown creasing his forehead, "How is this happening? You have showed me many an invention in our time as friends, but never such a thing as this. It is floating like a boat on the ocean, yet in the air. It is incredible Dieter! How have you done this?"

Dieter stood stroking the gondola of the silver and glass machine as a horseman strokes his favorite steed. Helena wondered if he slept in his workshop with it every night.

"I call it a Cloudship," said Dieter "It's a ship designed to float in the clouds. Yet I think it may be more useful to us than something which floats without direction." He stood back and waved his arms at the silver melon shape. "The Cloudship will be a transport and can explore foreign lands, and track their ships. Maybe we can catch birds and bring in loads of trade goods from lands far away."

"But how can it do this?" Klaus had a deeper frown on his face. "Floating on the ocean is obvious, but in the air? Impossible. How would you maneuver it?" Dieter laughed and slapped a hand on his thigh.

"I know, it's amazing isn't it? The large silver aerodynamic balloon above us is filled with voltsgassen, a gas which is lighter than the air you breathe and causes this machine to have little weight. This gas I discovered venting from a fissure not far from here on the side of Mount Aoxomoxoa. I collected the gas and filled a huge balloon with it. Then over the last two years I experimented with the unusual properties of this gas. I discovered that if I alternated an electrical charge through it, the gas became hotter and electrically active. I then invented a way of making use of this extra energy which now drives the gas turbine - right here." He patted the side of the large metal tube behind the cockpit. Then he drew their attention upwards.

"See those ducted fans?" He could not hide the excitement in his voice; he seemed like a happy little boy. "They pivot in all directions – I'll show you." Dieter motioned for them to come closer. He opened the door, climbed a small ladder and sat in the pilot seat at the front of the machine.

"Look up and see - when I move this control lever those tubes on the balloon move." He demonstrated the positions of the lever and Helena noticed the four small tubes progress slowly from facing downward to being angled backwards and then they moved around pointing forwards.

"Yes - those tube things, I see them moving," said Helena. "What do they do?

"I have this engine," he waved his arm at the back of the cockpit "It makes a powerful wind which is directed out of those tubes. Using this high powered blast of wind I can make the Cloudship go up, down, forwards and even backwards." He waved at the fins attached either side of the fuselage, "These wings help control the ship in flight so that I can make turns and steer accurately to my destination."

"Oh Dieter, you make things so easy to understand," said Helena, "But I think your machine is truly only a magnificent flight of fancy. Anything as large as a temple is not likely to fly by a mere mortal's efforts. If it really does fly I want you to take me up in it and show me that it works – and without the intervention of Hermes the messenger of the Gods." Dieter threw back his head and laughed heartily.

"A challenge is it? Klaus! Do you hear Helena? She has challenged Dieter Meier to prove himself."

"Well, I have never known you to turn down a challenge in your life!" said Klaus, "But even I, with my education in machines, cannot see how something as large as your Cloudship could fly and surely it will be unwieldy in any but the calmest airs."

"Perfect! Outnumbered and scorned," said Dieter. "I shouldn't do this but I care not for the politico's and their absurd obsession with secrecy. Right! Both of you up the ladder. Klaus, you sit beside me and I will show you a few of my tricks!"

Helena hurried up the ladder, Klaus right behind her. They settled themselves in comfortable seats as Dieter engaged the starting mechanism. A whirring sound was swiftly followed by a low whine which began to increase in intensity as Dieter added power pushing a lever forward. The Cloudship began to vibrate, then the whirring settled down to a deep harmonious hum which was quiet enough to allow conversation in the closed cabin.

"Quiet isn't it?" said Dieter "A trick using some of Shatzke's harmonics which have more than one application." Slowly the Cloudship began to rise. Dieter was busy moving levers, words were no longer needed.

Klaus and Helena sat slack jawed in utter amazement looking out the windows at the moving scene outside. The craft rose until it almost touched the high ceiling then, as Dieter manipulated the steering ducts, the nose began to turn and completed a circular survey of the interior of the cavernous hangar. Now the pilot allowed the craft to descend again until it rested just above the floor. Dieter moved more levers and the muted sounds of the turbine died away.

Klaus and Helena applauded their pilot. Dieter stood and bowed in front of his seat.

"Thank you, thank you," he said grinning.

"That was incredible, you have certainly astonished me to-day," said Klaus "But have you tested the Cloudship in windy weather?" They disembarked and Dieter closed the door.

"In truth I have tested it only in light weather, secretly at night, and it performed very well. But it is still experimental," said Dieter as he again operated the lever that lowered the covering sheet.

"It has great promise," said Klaus, his voice deep, his stare longing.

"I am sure you will see more of it. Now come with me, I have a gift for each of you." Dieter led them beyond the Cloudship, to a strong brass-bound metal door. He unlocked this with a series of three ornate keys and led them into his private office. Helena looked around the large light room enjoying the chaos of paperwork, drawings and interesting artifacts which littered the many wood and metal shelves, cupboards, half open drawers, tabletops; chair seats and the floor. Through a partly open door she could see a tumbled bed and living quarters next door. I was right, she thought, he *does* live with his Cloudship.

Dieter handed Klaus a large leather satchel, they murmured together as Helena walked about, her lips in a soft smile. This man needs a mother, she thought.

"Helena," Klaus called her to them.

"I am so glad to have met you, my dear," said Dieter. "I wish you and my old friend Klaus all the best. If I thought it would help your case, I would come to court to plead for you myself." He held a small square device in his hands; it seemed made of polished gold but was a great deal lighter when the inventor put it into her hands.

"This is for you, dear lady. Something to remember me by."

"Thank you, what is it?" Helena asked turning it over. The shiny golden box was carved all over with beautiful twining vines, leaves and flowers.

"Perhaps you can give it a name," said Dieter. He opened a compartment on one side. It was empty and lined with silvery metal mesh.

"Please Helena, go out into the garden and choose a flower of the sweetest scent you most enjoy. Place it in this compartment and swing the lid closed. Then bring it back to me." Helena looked up at him, her mouth open, her eyebrows raised. Then she shut her mouth and obediently took the box out into the garden. She returned having selected some star jasmine blossoms which she placed in the compartment. She showed Klaus the flowers in the box, then shut the lid.

"Now shake the box back and forth ten times," said Dieter. Helena did as she was told and then looked at him, askance. The box made no noise as she shook it.

"Turn the box over to the other side and open that side." With some difficulty Helena pushed open a latch and a closely fitted door sprang out. Inside was a small vial of clear oil attached to a tiny spigot.

"Take the vial out carefully," said Dieter his mouth curved in anticipation. Even as she lifted out the vial Helena realized what the machine did.

"Oh!" She exclaimed, "Oh how wonderful! The machine captures the scent of the flowers and imbues it into the oil." She could smell the odor of the jasmine blooms radiating from the vial of oil. Her fingers now smelled of sweet fresh jasmine blossoms and when she lifted up the vial the room filled with a delicious summer scent of jasmine.

Dieter smiled and gave her another box.

"This box is full of spare vials of oil. You will need them. The device will capture the scent of anything placed in it, and will concentrate the odor in the oil so you may smell the scent again and again. Or use it as perfume for your skin and clothes." Helena looked up at Klaus as tears filled her eyes.

"Oh Klaus, what a wonderful invention. Every woman would want one of these to create her own perfumes." He put his arms around her and kissed her cheek tasting her salty tears of joy.

"Thank you Dieter," said Klaus, "we are very grateful to you for these unique and wonderful gifts. If ever there is anything I can do to repay your generosity you have only to ask." Dieter kissed Helena's hand, clicked his heels and nodded to Klaus.

"Go and be happy," he said, beaming at them. "And remember, always take out the scented item that you put in the device, Helena. Remember too, it will capture the scent of *anything*." Helena opened the main door of the device and found to her surprise that the jasmine blooms were reduced to a fine dust which fell from the compartment.

As Klaus and Helena rode in the tram on the return journey back to his estate, Helena turned the device over and over in her hands.

"I wonder what he meant by capturing the scent of *anything*?" wondered Helena aloud, her lips pursed as she turned the box over and over. Today, she thought, I have seen things which could only exist in Mount Olympus, the home of the Gods. Atlantea is a wonderful civilization, but also the most frightening place in the world. I have seen enough scientific miracles today to last a lifetime.

She relaxed next to Klaus, as a final worry passed through her mind. I do hope things go well for me at the Schmitt party tonight. Helena squeezed Klaus's hand and leaned her head on his shoulder, oblivious to the coming and goings of the great city outside the window; her mind on more pressing matters.

25

HELENA WAS AWED AS KLAUS WALKED HER into the elegant, brightly lit portico of the Schmitt mansion. The Schmitt family was long established in the Atlantean archipelago and tonight all their wealth and opulence was on public display. Built of pitted red stone, from the volcano of Makemo Island, the entrance to the enormous mansion was fronted by ten tall pillars rising to an arched roof high above wide stone steps. Polished black floors lead to large warm rooms full of golden light. Helena could see the flashing colors of dozens of people socializing inside.

Three people were gathered to greet the guests. First, Frau Ada Schmitt elegantly dressed in a matronly deep blue dress covered in acres of frills.

"Klaus welcome," she trilled. "How wonderful to see you."
again. You are like our own family!" She greeted him warmly,
clasping his hands in her fashionably gloved grip.

"Thank you for the invitation, Frau Schmitt," Klaus smiled
back, not quite as warmly. He turned,

"Please meet my ward, Helena; a noble woman born in
Greece." Klaus raised Helena's delicate leather gloved hand,
bringing her forward. Her beauty shone as a sunlit cloud on a
rainy day.

"You are very welcome. Anyone with Klaus Meinbach will
always be welcome at my home," said Ada. Yet Helena noted
that Ada's eyes were cold and did not look her in the face.

A lovely young woman dressed in a brightly bejeweled, low
cut golden gown which shamelessly revealed her milky white
breasts, turned toward them and gave Klaus a brilliant smile.
She fluttered her dark eyelashes. Her long glossy black hair cascaded down over her left shoulder from a sparkling electrical
ornament attached behind her left ear which flashed every color
of the rainbow.

"Oh Klaus, my dear, how lovely to see you again." Her voice
was soft and seductive.

"Hello and happy birthday Rainia. Please meet Helena. I
hope that my ward will soon be declared a true noble woman
and then you and she might be friends." Klaus's voice was cool,
almost paternal. Rainia clasped Klaus's velvet coated arm with
both her hands and clung to him while looking adoringly up
into his face.

"Oh Klaus, I would do *anything* for you," she cooed. "Please,
may I beg you for the first dance this evening?" Klaus looked
down at her and laughed.

"I would decline," he said, "since I have my partner here on
my arm and she dances divinely, however, since it is your name

day I shall break with protocol and give you just one dance." Rainia squealed with joy like a little girl and clapped her hands as if in triumph.

"Oh thank you Klaus," she said brightly smiling. Not a moment's glance was spared on Helena. "I will be in your arms soon." the girl's eyes lingered on his face.

Klaus moved on to be greeted by a young man in a military styled velvet suit with silver braiding. He seemed familiar to Helena.

"Captain," he bowed a little too deeply.

"Werner, thank you for your hospitality on this special evening," said Klaus. Turning to Helena he said, "Do you remember my Political Officer from the *Hieglund*, Werner Schmitt?" She held out her hand and he kissed it while not looking at her at all, just as the others of his family had. Somehow this young man seemed sly, as if he were a liar, a snake; perhaps a poisonous toad. Helena recalled him from her first hours on the *Hieglund*. He would not care if she were dead. She was nothing to him. Helena shivered as a chill ran down her spine but she smiled at him, dissembling the warning in her heart.

"Pleased to meet you again Werner, in happier circumstances."

"A delight, madam. I do apologize but I must attend to our other guests." Werner turned abruptly away from them.

Helena placed her hand firmly on the captain's arm, he put his hand on top of hers and squeezed it reassuringly as they moved slowly through the reception rooms. Every part of the house was furnished lavishly. There were many ornate rectangular seats covered in the most delicate shades of soft silk velvet. The walls were wainscoted with rich red timbers. Abstract paintings featured here and there. Electrical lights in orange, red and gold cascaded from the walls and white plaster ceilings like the glowing blooms of exotic orchids.

Lovelier than these were the women, dressed in exquisite low cut corseted gowns of every color imaginable. Their hair was styled in complex arrangements of ornaments featuring animated electrical and mechanical toys and puzzles. Their gallant male companions were tall, dark haired, often bearded and wearing equally impressive formal suits of many different designs. Helena found the display of wealth overwhelming and ostentatious. It reminded her of when the rich Thebans visited the temple at Delphi to give thanks for their latest success in battle.

Gold and silver metals decorated everything with geometric patterns. The styles of nature do not intrude upon these people's thoughts, mused Helena. She looked at all the luxuries and wished to trade them for simple Grecian appreciation of acanthus leaves, grapes, the human form or the simple circular white marble Doric columns of her homeland.

These people only see and value things of the mind, she thought. Mechanical inventions are their way of life. Nature, religion, love - these precious things have no place of importance here on this island. They work to preserve their way of thinking and hide the advantages of their inventions from other humans. They would rather be isolated than risk change, which an understanding of the spiritual, or honoring of the love and connection between dissimilar peoples, could cause in their hearts.

Klaus escorted Helena amongst the party goers, speaking to many people, whilst introducing her. All were polite and none were friendly. It was as if she had a disease. It was awful to recall, but the truth was that she had been rescued from certain death by the crew of the *Hieglund*, only to be assessed for immediate death by a panel of men on the ship who were present for that purpose. Those men had the power to put their captives to death or condemn them to a slow death in the coal mines as if they were mere beasts of burden. They did not have an option to adopt their captives as citizens of Atlantea. Helena now remembered the scene on the *Hieglund*. Werner had been one of the death review panel, as had Klaus. She shivered despite the warmth of the evening air.

Klaus brought her some punch from an opulent display of food and drinks spread amongst large glowing arrangements of flowers on great tables in the main reception room. She sipped a sweet, pink foaming liquid in a goblet which seemed to be made of spun silver but the taste seemed tainted as if was made of some other metal. She smiled her thanks at him, he took her arm.

"There are men here I want you to meet," he said. "Come with me," He led her to a group of men, most of them tall and imposing. The older men had beards and curled up moustaches, very dashing fellows. Klaus addressed them as they walked up to the group.

"Greetings my friends and fellow captains ashore." They greeted him with great enthusiasm, shaking his hand, clapping him on the shoulder.

"Congratulations on the excellent slaves you brought ashore," said one, a man of about Klaus's age. "Do tell us about this one. Are you considering making her your concubine? Some of us have, you know - taken Uitlander women for our female slaves." Klaus smiled, moved closer to Helena and took her arm.

"No indeed. I believe Helena is at least half Atlantean. Observe her fair skin, her eyes of green. Apart from the color of her hair she resembles one of our pure-blood noble women." He turned to Helena, "Please forgive Lennox here, he is a brash fellow and has a harem of concubines. I believe they are all he thinks about." The other captains in the group roared with laughter. Lennox blushed, but looked Helena up and down with hungry eyes.

"Well then," asked another, "What is your plan? You should have put her to death long ago if she is not to become a slave. The politicos' policy is that we shall not breed with Uitlander women, otherwise they seduce us and cause us to weaken our blood lines with undesirable types."

"It's a shame," interrupted Lennox hastily. "I cannot see why we should ignore the other races of humans. As a trading captain I have seen a good deal of the world. Other humans may be more primitive in technology than we are, yet they all have their own skills and strong points. Why else would we need to trade with them?"

"Be careful what you say now," cautioned another whom Klaus had introduced as his friend Kurt Wagner. "We are in the house of Schmitt and they always agree with the politico party line, whatever it is," he lowered his voice. "Personally I suspect them of recording all our conversations tonight and sifting through them tomorrow for anything subversive - and here you are Klaus, bringing an actual Uitlander into their own home!" He clapped Klaus on the shoulder and laughed long and loudly. "Old Herr Schmitt will be turning in his grave tonight!" Klaus laughed.

"I found Helena resembles an Atlantean woman so closely I could not in all conscience destroy her, as I have done with many other Uitlander women. Helena seems to be closer in race to us than any other woman I have seen. To me, it felt like I would be murdering my mother, or my sister. This week I shall request a trial to ascertain her bloodline. If her claim is valid she may become a full citizen. Do I have your backing, gentlemen?" A chorus of affirmations rang out among the captains.

"We are the Naval Guild, we will back you as you have backed us in all things," declared Kurt, "We are stronger than the politico party and have no desire to run Atlantea, nor a wish to administer her laws. We also have to be above the law and decide for ourselves and our men; mariners who live in very different circumstances than all the others of our proud race, what is right and best for us."

"Aye! Hear, hear! You have that right!" echoed around the tight group of marine adventurers.

"Good luck, little lady," said Kurt, taking her hand and kissing her knuckles with warm lips. He looked her in the eye, "If you ever escape the clutches of Klaus here, look me up." His dark blue eyes were sincere.

The other men laughed again, their comments teasing Klaus, and Helena smiled.

"Thank you sir," she said. "I would like to make friends here in Atlantis. Your country is a very different place from my home. I would like to be happy here." She could see that the captains of the ships were much more liberal minded and open towards her than the general populace. She felt as if she could be among friends with these captains.

"What nation are you from?" asked a young mariner, "I am captain Zeldin of the traders, perhaps I have been to your home port."

"I am a priestess at Delphi," smiled Helena, "Corinth is our nearest great trading port. It is near the coast where my grandfather came ashore after his shipwreck. We always thought his talk of ships moving without sails or oars was a madness he had. Now I realize he was an Atlantean fisherman or perhaps a trader like you."

"Aye, my lady, I have indeed sailed and traded in those waters, although they are far from our shores. Our fishermen and traders do venture there in sail boats from time to time to buy excellent wine and olives. The shores can be dangerous, especially during storms."

They spoke warmly for some time. Helena about her disastrous stormy voyage and captain Zeldin spoke of his travels while Klaus stood by talking with the other captains. Soon loud dance music began in the next room. Rainia rushed to their group giggling happily and caught Klaus by the arm.

"You promised me the first dance!" she squealed.

"I shall be back soon, Helena. Then we shall see how beautiful *your* dancing is." He bowed to Helena and looked down at Rainia. He listened to her prattle with avuncular duty plainly on his face as they walked toward the dance floor.

26

HELENA FELT STIFLED – IT WAS HARD TO BREATHE restrained in her corset. The long trailing dress of deep red and gold was limiting her freedom to walk, to dance and step out as she was used to. While the sea captains were friendly, she felt uncomfortable with these dark haired people around her. Many of them looked at her suspiciously, some with blatant hostility in their eyes. Her hair was hidden by a deep red silk mantilla embroidered with pearls, yet it was impossible not to feel like an outsider. The truth was, she *was* a foreigner. The women of Atlantis were obviously taught to dislike foreignness of any kind. None of them approached to speak to her, and if she caught them looking at her and smiled towards them, they haughtily turned away.

Helena asked a servant where the lady's rest room was and found her way there. She shut herself in one of the stalls and shed a few quiet tears, feeling stressed and alone. She realised that despite Klaus's obvious power and strength, his plan to make her a citizen based upon her appearance and word alone was most likely not going to work.

A group of women entered the anteroom chattering. Helena could hear their voices clearly from her seat. Although the Atlantean accent was thick and guttural it *was* a Greek dialect. Helena smiled. They probably think they invented Greek, she thought.

"Oh, I don't know how Klaus Meinbach can bring an awful Uitlander slave to our private gathering. I simply shudder when I see it!" a shrill voice exclaimed. "I can smell that awful jasmine perfume she wears everywhere!"

"Yes, they are ugly and dirty. I find them *disgusting*. My slaves who come from that part of the world are all dreadful. You cannot trust them to do anything right. Of course they speak a horrid dialect of Atlantean. That Greek gibberish is a bastardization of our own beautiful language." Another voice cut in, Helena recognized it as Ada's and heard her say,

"I am going to make sure that conniving Greek slut disappears." Helena shuddered as if struck with a sudden chill.

"How are you going to do that?" asked another, younger voice.

"Oh I *will*, never you mind how. I have friends. I don't ask for favors often but when I do... I want Klaus Meinbach for Rainia. I will not have him waste his good Atlantean seed on that foreign trash."

"You really do not need to do anything," said another woman soothingly. "I'm sure the judges of the Genetic Purity Court will do what is right." In the ballroom the music increased in volume.

"Come, the dancing is going on without us!" said the younger voice gaily. The women moved off.

Helena sat with her head in her hands. When she finally felt ready to venture out into the party again she could not find Klaus anywhere. She walked, lonely and afraid, through the lower floor of the house. Ada came up to her smiling and friendly.

"I see you are enjoying our beautiful home, my dear," she said, taking Helena's arm. "Come this way, I want to show you the balcony." She pushed through some thick curtains out onto a balcony which overlooked the bright lights of the city. There was a small shriek and Helena turned to see Klaus standing on the balcony with Rainia's arms around his neck. His face was masked by the darkness.

"Oh mother, you frightened me!" cooed Rainia, "Klaus and I were only kissing. I hope you will forgive us?" She turned her face back to his, stretching up as if to kiss him again.

Helena cried out in horror, this was a final insupportable insult from these awful people. A pain she could not endure. She turned, picked up her skirts and ran from the party. She shed the tight high heeled shoes before she reached the slippery black marble floor and ran barefoot into the night. Tears flowed down her cheeks. Death in the ocean was indeed preferable to being Klaus Meinbach's woman.

Ada Schmitt turned to Rainia and Klaus.

"Klaus, I have long wished for your family and mine to be joined by marriage. Now is your opportunity." she said warmly, grasping hold of the curtains to return the lovers to privacy.

27

HELENA RAN TO THE END OF THE STREET and hesitated, unsure where to go, or what to do next. She saw a warmly lit steam tram approaching on the shiny metal lines it used, and waited to board it as soon as it came to a stop. Above the chuffing of the tram and her panting sobs she could hear distant shouting but she ignored everything. She wanted to get as far away from the party as she could. Chimes came from her reticule but she had forgotten what they meant.

Glad the steam tram was empty she scrambled up the steps and huddled in a corner of the conveyance, her hands over her face. She simply couldn't bear the awful foreignness of Atlantis and she desperately wanted to run up the path to her childhood home and have her mother and sisters hug her to them with love.

Klaus ran from the party.

"I'd rather face a boatload of rabid Persian pirates than these damn conniving women! Curse them all!" he exclaimed as he hurried down the street. He saw Helena running down the street ahead of him. He called out to her "Helena! Stop!" but she did not seem to hear him. Or maybe she knew it was him, and preferred not to know him any longer?

He tried calling her on his fonier, mashing his angry fingers on the button to call her repeatedly, but there was no answer. Why would she answer him? He had never shown her how to use the device and now Helena was afraid, upset and alone. He raced down the road, his elegant dancing boots slithered and slipped dangerously on the pavement. He saw Helena board the tram and he cast about for some way of following it, cursing under his breath.

I have been deceived by that damn Schmitt woman, he thought. This whole party was simply a sham, a subterfuge to get me to put myself in a compromising position with her daughter. I didn't even have the common sense to see I was being treated as a gullible fool and lured into a trap. No doubt Ada will now be appealing to all her guests to witness my betrothal to her daughter. They are all witnesses to my stupidity! His face twisted in a bitter grimace. I believed there was goodwill between Werner's household and mine. How wrong I was.

Klaus ran along the street after the rapidly disappearing tram. He was almost exhausted when he met a household servant leading a horse. It lacked a saddle but was a strong mountain pony, the kind he knew well. Panting he stopped, caught hold of the reins and said

"Halt, my man, I have urgent need of this horse. Take my card to your master. Have him send to me in the morning for payment for the animal." Seeing Klaus's elegant, expensive clothing and the gold embossed card the servant did not hesitate to hand over the reins. Klaus threw himself on the horse and kicked it in the direction of the steam tram which had disappeared around a corner in the distance.

Helena was awakened from her misery by Klaus sitting beside her, scooping her up into his arms and kissing her tears away. The tram had stopped, it seemed, and people were gathering around gawking at the scene. She was too miserable to care, except suddenly his strong arms were around her and she felt safe.

"Oh Klaus!" she sobbed into his jacket, "Go away. If you want that girl go and have her. Do not deceive me with your charm, your beautiful eyes and your kisses."

"Helena, Helena," his voice was soft, persuasive. He lifted her chin and looked into her eyes. "Will you please come home with me, please?" Remembering Rainia's lips on his strong mouth, Helena's lips trembled and she turned her head away. Klaus stood, lifted Helena firmly in his arms and stepped off the tram.

"Go on your way!" he called to the driver. Helena was trembling, in cold, fear and hurt. Klaus knew from his dealings with horses exactly how a tender young filly should be treated; with kindness and attention until she calmed and gentled. She wrapped her arms around his neck and so, carrying Helena, he took the reins of the pony's bridle, and began the long walk home to his estate.

It was not long before her pride came to Helena's rescue and she insisted upon walking. Klaus did not know she had bare feet until she began limping from a stone bruise. Then he lifted her up onto the pony's back and she sat astride, the huge skirt billowing around her.

They walked in silence. Why does he not speak? Wondered Helena, if he will not speak then neither shall I she decided.

The scenery changed as they trudged out of the city, the estates began with fields, vineyards and orange groves. Their silence was broken by the sound of a steam tram whistle.

"Let me help you down Helena. I will leave this pony in a field for the night."

Helena dropped her eyes as Klaus swung her down to the ground. She could hear the sound of the hissing steam tram as it rumbled toward them.

Inside the tram they sat in silence once again. The warm country air spilling through the open window failed miserably to warm the coldness which had invaded Helena's heart. How I wish I had drowned on the ship instead of being picked up by these godless, heartless Atlanteans. Death in the ocean would have given me peace, instead of a hopeless relationship with a man who doesn't really care for me. He could simply shoot me out of hand if I displease him. Helena sobbed silently, thinking of the cruel things said and done and, worse, not done at the Schmitt party.

They alighted and walked up to the doors of Klaus's mansion; still no words were exchanged. Two sets of eyes looked away, two minds remained closed unable to find any words that would give ease to the other. Helena ran to her room and locked the door.

Klaus gave the servants orders for food and other comforts to be left in the dining room and that they were not to be disturbed. Then he knocked on her door.

"Please Helena, let me in."

"*No!*" came her reply, muffled by sobs and a pillow.

"If you do not allow me to speak to you in private so the servants cannot hear I shall have to use force to break open the door." Silence was his answer. After waiting a few minutes Klaus's booted heel smashed the lock and the door slammed open. Helena cowered on the bed, staring at him, her face pale and streaked with tears.

Klaus pulled her upright to face him. Strong fingers gripped her shoulders. Helena's chin was lifted and he looked her in the eyes. His blue eyes blazed bright.

"You will listen to me now, Helena. Pay close attention to *all* that I say. I am not a liar, nor do I intend to deceive you." She choked, tears flowed down her cheeks. Summoning her courage she looked straight at him, her green eyes flashing with anger through the tears.

"You left me alone at that awful party and then the hostess led me to where you were hidden in the curtains kissing her daughter!" Klaus looked a little abashed and took a breath. He stood back and held out his palms.

"I can explain that."

"*Really?*" Helena's breasts were heaving. "This will be interesting to hear!"

"Yes I - I was dancing with Rainia and after the dance she led me to the balcony to show me something new in the garden she said. Before I knew it she had pulled the curtains behind us; then she threw herself at me and kissed me."

"You did not seem to be protesting about that."

"I was shocked by her forwardness. Women in Atlantis wait to be asked for a kiss by the gentleman in question. A girl like Rainia is putting her reputation at risk by throwing herself publicly at a man like me. Truly, I did not respond to her. It was all a plan to get me away from you."

"I ..." Helena gulped, "Perhaps that is true. I heard her mother say that she wanted you for her daughter and that you were wasted if you were going to be with me. Then she was nice to me and led me straight to where Rainia was kissing you." Two more sobs racked her chest, as she thought of that dreadful moment. Klaus frowned thoughtfully.

"It seems they planned for Rainia to throw herself publicly upon me. So I would be forced to marry her, because her virtue would be compromised. To preserve her family status they would demand I consummate the bond with marriage." Klaus took a breath and laughed.

"I am *so* glad you ran away and that I decided to run after you, dear Helena." She blinked her eyes and a little smile began to lift her lips. "If I had stayed behind the curtain with Rainia and her mother a moment longer they would have publicly called for confirmation of my seduction of her. Then I would have been forced to marry the girl. Even though she is not the woman I love."

28

Helena wiped her eyes, took a breath, looked up at him and asked "Is there a woman you *do* love, Klaus?" He looked down at her and pulled her to her feet.

"Yes, Helena. It is *you* that I love." He wrapped his arms around her and held her tightly. She shuddered and began to cry against his velvet jacket.

"Why so sad?" he asked, looking closely at her face. His experience with women up to now was entirely for physical relief. He had never known true love for a woman other than the unconditional love a son has for his mother. His mother had a happy life with few reasons for tears.

The love he felt for Helena was as different as air and water to his relationship with the only other woman in his life. Klaus's heart was pounding; he wanted Helena so very much. Women had been invisible to him. Never before had he felt emotions like those Helena evoked in him. Is love a kind of madness? He asked himself. Love had created a tender place in his heart for Helena – softening a heart which had been close to resembling a stone.

"Oh! I love you too, Klaus!" The stone inside him shattered as she cried, her tears soaking his shirt after admitting her love for him. His heart became the warm beating heart of a man beginning to know to love. He kissed the top of her head and held her until the tears subsided.

"I have ordered a bath drawn for you, my dear. It has been an eventful evening and hot water is the best medicine for this kind of hurt." Helena blew her nose and wiped her eyes on a silk handkerchief.

"Please don't leave me, Klaus, I couldn't bear it. I thought that I was dead in every way when I saw you with Rainia. That you loved *her* and not me - that without your protection the law would put me to death next week."

Klaus took her hand and led her into the marble bathroom where hot water steamed ready for bathing.

He took off his boots, jacket and shirt revealing his beautifully muscled body. Then he unfastened her dress and the corset underneath it.

"I remember the first day I met you, you fell asleep in my bath on the *Hieglund*." he said, smiling at her. Helena took several deep breaths as she relaxed and stepped out of her lingerie.

"Yes," she said. "My life wasn't worth much then and it isn't worth a lot now either. I think that the authorities are not going to believe that my grandfather was Atlantean. I want to go home to Greece, Klaus. I miss my mother and sisters and they will think I am dead when I do not return from my voyage."

Klaus held her hand as she stepped into the bath, watching the warm water as it rose gently up, touching every part of her luscious body just as he wished to touch her.

"You are my world, Helena," he said as he began to wash her with the sponge and scented soap. "I am deeply in love with you and believe me, love is all that matters. I don't care a jot about the politico's and their decisions for or against you. Somehow I will save you and you *will* be my wife." Tears fell from Helena's eyes and she shook her head.

"I cannot believe that will happen. I feel so afraid of those awful people, *your* people." She lay back in the bath, sobs racking her body. "They will never accept me. I am a horrid non-person kind of *animal* to them." Klaus began caringly to bathe her body, wiping her tears away with a wash cloth, using the sweetest scented soaps and oils to massage her hands, feet and shoulders.

She's right, he thought, I know she's right. They won't accept her; they have their heads buried in the mud of their beliefs. But I'll find a way for us to be married, *I will*. He set his jaw determinedly.

Gradually Helena relaxed under his touch. He handled her as firmly and calmly as if she were a frightened filly from his herd. He let the water drain from the bath, picked her up in his powerful arms and carried her to the wide plush bed where he laid her on a towel and gently dried her with another.

Helena reached up and put her arms around him, she pulled him down and kissed him hard, her mouth melding into his as their souls became one. He lay close beside her. Kisses were laid upon kisses. He stroked her soft full breasts and her nipples hardened, Helena rolled over and pulled his breeches off, revealing his eager manhood, firm and erect. Then she removed the rest of his clothes.

Helena moved up his torso, stroking him with her fingers and breasts. Repaying his tenderness with her passion. She kissed him fervently with her lips, allowing her hard nipples to play over his body with abandon. She inhaled his delicious intoxicating male scent and her femaleness responded ardently. Klaus sighed with delight as he relaxed under her touch and attentions. She felt entirely right for him. Now there was no foreignness between them at all.

Klaus realized that the laws against Uitlanders were a nonsense devised to keep the inventions of his people from other races. Could they not profit from selling and sharing these benefits? How closed minded and crazy the politico party was – to keep the joy of other humans away from Atlantea...

His attention was brought to the glorious vision of Helena leaning over him, her golden curls cascading damply from her head over his chest. Her kisses making his nipples respond, he slid his hand between her thighs and found a font of moisture which told him more about her feelings for him than any words could convey.

His fingers slid into her, he found her tight, virginal and then, unable to restrain her desire any longer, Helena mounted his aching manhood for the first time. She cried out, in pain and joy as she took all he had and made him hers. Tears fell from her eyes, he kissed them away and tears of completion flowed from him. All Klaus could be became Helena's as they communed physically, emotionally, spiritually, consummating their love.

Helena, though unschooled in the sensual arts of Dionysius, knew much of how to employ those arts from her life at Delphi. As priestess of Apollo she did not participate in the sexual orgies and dark drunken rites of the worshipers of Pan. But she had listened eagerly when the priestesses of the nature God shared details of the mysteries as they rested nearby, relaxing and gardening, birthing children of the God in the summer break before recommencing their festivals in the dark winter each year. All this knowledge Helena began to share with Klaus as the night went on.

For his part, Klaus discovered that sex with a harlot on the docks of Atlantis was an entirely different activity compared to becoming one with this glorious Greek woman. His body was transported to levels of delight and sensual pleasure which surely no other Atlantean man had ever experienced. When finally he released into Helena, they rocked back and forth crying out. The voices of angels could not be sweeter to the ears of the Gods as they took their humanity to a sacred level of love.

Remaining one with Klaus, Helena shook her hair back and gazed at him smiling. "I love you Klaus Meinbach." He saw that it was true and his smile lit the room.

"Please, will you be my wife, Helena of the Greeks?"

She smiled down at him "Yes, Klaus, I will be your wife. Will you be my husband, forever and ever?"

"Yes," he replied fervently "I will be your husband, forever and ever." He did not know one should never make promises when one is happiest.

They fell asleep, Helena lying upon his chest, their bodies still connected.

29

THEY ROSE AT DAWN AND WASHED TOGETHER, luxuriating in the glorious hot water of the bath. Dressed in white woolen robes they walked down the long drive hand in hand, to greet the dawn at the edge of the ocean. Klaus's yearling ponies galloped excitedly in the field beside them, stopping at the wooden rail fence beside the tram lines.

Klaus turned and looked at Helena. She smiled happily at him. The sun rose golden, gilding their faces and bodies in a glorious glow. He took her hands in his.

"As a token of my commitment to you I give you the traditional symbol we of Atlantis use. This was my mother's given to her by my father at their betrothal." He brought out a glittering silver bracelet and took up Helena's left hand. "With this token I take thee to be mine." he said, looking deeply into her eyes.

"I consent to be bonded to you by this betrothal bracelet," Helena said, tears of happiness in her eyes as she placed her hand over his. "I also claim the right to place my mark on you as a token of my deep love for you and our betrothal."

"You do?" he said, surprised.

"Yes I do." She said smiling up into his eyes. "When the right time comes, I will place a tattoo like this, on your wrist. It will bond us together, *forever*." She held out her left wrist. Upon it was an exquisite detailed tattoo of a lyre.

"Oh!" Klaus inspected it closely in the morning sunlight. "What is it a symbol of?"

"It is a symbol of the great God Apollo. All servants of the God receive this tattoo as a sacred mark." He bent his head and kissed the tattoo lovingly.

"I like the idea of being bonded to you forever, Helena," he said. "It means a lot to me." She removed one of the golden armbands in the shape of a python which twined around her upper arm.

"I give you this, in token of our bond made this day." Helena said, formally. Klaus took the armband and slid it up his left arm, loosening the curl of the soft metal so that it fitted his wrist. Then Klaus placed his right hand upon the bracelet on her left wrist, Helena placed her right hand upon the armband Klaus wore and they sealed their commitment with a long loving embrace. Then they turned and stood looking out at the bright horizon, the Atlantean islands blue in the distance. Hands entwined, hearts full of love, they returned to the Meinbach estate.

"Let me have the honor of preparing your food this morning dear Klaus," said Helena. Klaus nodded and kissed her lips.

So it was as his wife that Helena went into the house to organize the cooks and servants to prepare their breakfast, while Klaus checked the stables.

30

KLAUS HAD BARELY STEPPED BACK INSIDE HIS HOME when he heard the clatter of hooves approaching. Two riders eased their horses to a walk as they approached the house up the broad driveway. Not sure of their intentions he strapped on his pistols. They wore the orange and black livery of the Court of Genetic Purity. The older man dismounted and gave the reins to his companion.

"Captain Klaus Meinbach, of the Atlantean navy?" he asked walking towards Klaus.

"I am that person, sir," replied Klaus stiffly.

"I am to serve you these papers, sir. Requesting your presence at the Department of Genetic Purity five days hence. You are to bring the illegal Uitlander woman known as Helena to the court."

"Aye, you have my word she will be there under my protection," said Klaus "Now sir, what has she been charged with?"

"The woman has been charged with being an illegal immigrant of impure blood. Also that she is illegally co-habiting with a citizen of Atlantea, namely yourself." said the court official.

"What does the word co-habitation mean in a legal sense?" asked Klaus taking the papers, reading them quickly.

"It means living as man and wife and having carnal relations," said the court official. He watched Klaus begin to bristle.

"Tell your court official I am prepared to defend Helena of Delphi of the charge of being an illegal immigrant of impure blood," said Klaus coldly. "And you tell the cloth-eared scoundrel who implies that I have acted with impropriety towards the noble woman Helena that he shall answer to my sword or pistols if he does not remove that scurrilous co-habitation charge!" Klaus's anger rose as he re-read the charge sheet and he demanded,

"You make sure you tell Proctor Remulous what I have said. If I find out you have not conveyed my message verbatim as I have told it you, your head shall join his in the gutter! Do I make myself clear?" He rested his hands on the butts of his pistols, arms akimbo.

The man began to tremble, his lip quivered. "Of course captain. I shall intercede most vigorously on your behalf; the proctor may have been over zealous with his charges."

"He has been more than overzealous sir! He has impugned my integrity and that of the navy itself. So mount your horse and be off with you." shouted Klaus. The official mounted his horse hastily and the messengers trotted briskly down the drive towards the road.

Klaus sighed and smiled as his breathing calmed. He watched them go, once more pondering the events of Rainia's party. He now knew Ada Schmitt was not a friend of his and particularly not Helena's. He had no wish to be forced to marry a young girl whom he did not care for; nor could he imagine that Rainia cared one jot for himself. It was a comfort that Werner Schmitt would certainly stand in his corner like a good shipmate and comrade should. Klaus was still debating what to do first, the court summons gripped in his fist when Helena appeared beside him and touched his hand.

"What did those riders want, Klaus?"

"They brought the court papers to serve on me regarding your case at the Court of Genetic Purity, Helena." She frowned and pursed her lips. "I forbid you to worry about the issue. I will protect you from whatever harm they may try to inflict. I pledge my life on that promise." He looked deep into her eyes, then smiled. "Now let's have a good breakfast. We will go to the Naval Guild this morning. I need some legal counsel from an old friend."

"May I come with you?" Helena asked.

"Why, of course you may come along, but you won't be permitted in the Naval Guild building. No women are allowed in there. Regulations, I'm afraid, even the Grand Captain must abide by these rules."

"I will enjoy looking at everything in the harbor," said Helena. "I'd rather watch boats than be with navy men. I like watching the ships and fishing boats, I used to watch them in the harbor at Corinth for hours. Sailing fascinates me." They sat on opposite sides of an elegant small dining table. Klaus smiled at his wife, even after her near death experience she still wants to sail, he thought with admiration. They began to eat the eggs and bacon with hot cakes.

"I will have two marines assigned to escort you for your safety. The docks can be a rough and ready place, but no-one will interfere with anyone who is under naval protection."

I am not going to let legal buffoons spoil our special time, thought Klaus enjoying the warmth as the sun shone in through the paneled glass doors of the dining room. He reached out and touched Helena's betrothal bangle and made promises to himself.

She smiled at him and squeezed his hand.

31

TODAY'S TRAM WAS A LARGE OMNIBUS which seated fifty people. The passenger section was closed in with large picture glass windows. At the front was a driver and there were two stokers in the engine compartment at the rear. Helena watched all the driving and stoking operations of the tram with keen interest. What a contrast with the oxen carts of home, she thought; no swearing or cracking of whips required! It's a very different task driving these steam trams.

Just before noon Klaus and Helena stepped down from the green and gold tram onto the central dock of Atlantis. Helena took Klaus's arm. As they walked along the dock she noticed commoners doffing their hats or bowing slightly to Klaus and herself. She glowed; she felt as if she had married a king. Her confidence rose as they approached the ugly square building of the Naval Guild headquarters. In the entrance hall Klaus located two marines, tall young men in the usual dark naval uniforms.

"Greetings, what are your duties at this moment?" asked Klaus. The taller man saluted and stood at attention.

"Nothing pressing at present, captain. We are at your service."

"My companion is noblewoman Helena. You are commanded to escort her and keep her safe from all danger until she returns to this building."

"We would be honored, sir." The seamen clicked their heels and bowed slightly in Helena's direction. With the handsome young men walking on either side of her as she began her stroll Helena felt safe, ready to be adventurous. They were giving her admiring glances while signaling privately to each other. Helena smiled; surely today's lovely fashionable walking dress and corset must be the reason. She walked toward the lower dock where smaller vessels were moored. This low quay was nearly half a league long. It was broad and teemed with people selling all manner of things. Local vegetables and exotic fruits from foreign lands filled the displays in bounteous quantities. Some stalls cooked meals while customers waited. Then the meal was served to you while you sat in comfort upon a bench at an ornate carved table. There were cloths of many kinds, spices, oils and cobblers repairing footwear. The biggest market was the fish market located at the far end of the dock. Helena could easily find it with the aid of her nose.

As Helena strolled along looking with curiosity at the stalls, she passed dozens of small sailing craft moored to the dock. At the far end were two large ketches moored where the water was deeper.

Helena moved through the throng. She had a plan which she had not shared with Klaus. She hoped to find some fishermen and ask if they knew of any families who included green eyed and fair haired women in their ancestry. Her beautiful outfit and the two marines walking behind her guaranteed her a smooth but not unnoticed passage through the masses of stall-holders and their customers. The sellers were beckoning, calling out prices and discounts to attract buyers. Customers were shouting and bargaining with the stallholders to get the best price. Musicians, mummers and peddlers sang, danced and waved their wares at Helena.

I must look like a wealthy woman dressed the way I am, she thought, just the kind of woman who would want to spend money with them. Little do they know that I am a penniless stranger who will be in court to fight for my life at the end of the week.

The fish market was a warehouse with open sides; the cool airy building protected the fish from the sun. Although much of the fish was salted it still smelled strongly; but this did not de-ter Helena who went from stall to stall questioning all who would speak with her. She asked if they knew of families who had lost loved ones at sea. Men who had sailed out on a fishing or trading voyage and were never seen again. Most simply shrugged their shoulders and put up their hands. She suspected many heard her foreign accent and would not help.

She spent two fruitless hours asking questions. She stopped and bought a drink of fresh fruit juice. It hot in the sun, I'm tired and discouraged, thought Helena; surely Klaus will have finished his business by now? I must turn back, my plan is a failure. As she let her gaze wander to the horizon she noticed a young girl of about 11 years old. The girl was standing holding the rear mast of a fishing ketch, which was moving out from the wharf. The vessel's crew were typical Atlantean citizens; large men with dark hair and fair skin but this girl was different – she had long wavy blonde hair. Helena's hair.

Quickly Helena walked toward the edge of the dock and caught the girls' eye. She smiled at Helena and lifted a hand to wave goodbye as the boat eased away from the dock and the sails were unfurled. Two of the crewmen used long oars to maneuver the craft into the wind while pale blue sails were raised. Helena couldn't believe her eyes, the girl was a reflection of herself and her sisters.

"Stop! Please stop!" called Helena; she lifted her skirts and began to run. The tight corset restricted her breathing as she ran along the dock following the boat as best she could, panting, gasping as she dodged stalls and people.

Her bodyguards ran after her in a panic, wondering what had caused her to try to elude them. The sails filled and the sleek ketch began to heel over, revealing a painted eye looking forward.

"Stow the mooring ropes and tighten the sheets!" yelled the man at the tiller. The crew rushed about sheeting in the slack main sail. The fishing boat began to gain speed. The blond girl stood relaxed, looking back, smiling and waving at Helena, then she turned and looked towards the open sea.

"Curses!" gasped Helena as she stopped at the edge of the dock, looking despairingly at the ketch as it sailed swiftly out of the harbor. "The Gods have deserted me."

"What is the matter noble woman?" asked one of her escorts as he ran up behind her.

"That boat! Where is she going?" asked Helena urgently, pointing.

"Back to their village, madam. It is usual to sail to the southern end of Atlantea today; they will anchor up overnight in the sheltered bays near Reinhart. Then they will sail back to their home island at first light."

"You know this boat?" asked Helena, surprised.

"No madam. However, I know the boat is from the island of Perculous," said her bodyguard as the other young marine joined them panting from his run in the heat.

"The sails tell all, noble woman. Each island in Atlantea has a particular sail color for their boats; this is so the Navy can identify them at sea. The blue sails are from the island of Perculous nearly two days sailing from here. The island is one of many which are part of the Atlantean Empire."

"Thank you," said Helena, "this is very interesting. Now I must return to the Naval Guild. I have much to discuss with captain Meinbach."

As they walked back Helena chastised herself for her lack of faith. Indeed, Apollo was taking care of her. All she had to do was follow his lead.

32

KLAUS WATCHED AS HELENA WALKED BRISKLY towards the lower quay with her uniformed escorts in close attendance. He knew navy trained men would guard her with their lives. Satisfied, he went upstairs to find his old friend. Unfortunately captain Kurt Wagner had a previous engagement and Klaus was asked to wait. He chose to pace up and down the long marbled hallway outside Kurt's office instead of relaxing in the waiting atrium. At last the visiting captain left the office, shown out by Kurt. The three captains exchanged formal greetings as they passed, saluting and clicking heels.

Captain Wagner shook Klaus by the hand and slapped him on the shoulder.

"Great to see you Klaus, how can I help you old friend?"

"I need to defend these charges," said Klaus waving the papers at Kurt. "I have asked for the second charge to be withdrawn from the charge sheet." Kurt took the documents and sat in comfortable leather and brass chair behind a blue leather covered desk, to read them. His office featured shelves of beautiful scale model ships and unusual personal armaments of many kinds were racked on the walls above the shelves.

"Have they neither intelligence nor shame!" exclaimed Kurt after reading the court charge sheet. "That second charge is insulting. I hope you objected in the strongest terms Klaus? How dare the courts pry into a naval officer's personal affairs."

"Aye, I did. I threatened to remove the man's head," said Klaus "These petty bureaucrats who have only ever commanded an inkwell cannot resist taking liberties with naval guild members when they get a chance."

"Well, if they don't withdraw the charge of co-habitation they will hear from our Naval Guild in the strongest terms. As for the other charge - they *do* have a point. How will you present your case and what precedent will you use?" Kurt asked, looking up from the papers at Klaus.

"I will use the obvious; Helena has fair hair, green eyes and fair skin as white as my own. These are not Greek features at all." Klaus sat forward and rested his elbows on his knees. "She is prepared to give evidence that her grandfather – a man who had pale hair, white skin and blue eyes; was washed ashore near Corinth after surviving a shipwreck on the rocky coast. We have lost many fishing boats over the years so her explanation cannot be refuted. Plus I will give evidence of her high intelligence. She has learned to speak and read our language in a remarkably short time. No common Uitlander woman could do such a thing. It must come naturally to her." The pride in Klaus's voice was strong.

"The lawyers will make much of her other Greek ancestors – she can be at best one half to one quarter Atlantean. Hmm... Most - but not all - of our people are dark haired even though we match her eyes and skin," said Kurt frowning a little, steepling his fingers together as he thought.

"The way I understand it, Helena's Atlantean blood has over-powered the weak Grecian blood, otherwise she would have looked like her Greek ancestors and not her Atlantean grandfather. Indeed," said Klaus, "how can one tell how much of a human's blood is this or that? It is red in all of us."

Kurt could see that his friend was desperately in love with this woman and he sympathized with Klaus's anguish.

"Do you have a plan if you lose?" asked Kurt.

"Only to stand and fight until I die protecting her, or take her back to her homeland and leave her there. I will not stand by and see her killed, mark my words!" said Klaus.

Kurt sighed, he knew Klaus of old; but he had never known Klaus Meinbach in love.

"All I can do is wish you well, my friend. Please do not act rashly. Appeal the decision if it goes against her. The Naval Guild does not get involved in civil cases of this sort. While it affects you personally, this case does not affect the Navy – unless the CGP uncharacteristically decides we can allow Uitlanders to marry Atlanteans. If that happened the Navy would not have any patrol work to do. However, as you know, we stand by our captains - we are all brothers in the service. Don't count us out, Klaus." Kurt rose and walked around his desk.

"If you need help, ask me. If I can, I will. I think you would do well to get any possible evidence of her ancestry to strengthen her case. Perhaps reading the archive records will help? The navy archive keeps a record book listing the names of all of our ships and crew reported missing over the past six hundred years."

"Thank you old friend, I understand what you say. I will go to check out the archives at once." The two friends embraced and Klaus left the office with a heavy heart.

He was alone to fight the CGP. He shook himself and took a deep breath, he would not give up. He meant his vow of eternal wedded loyalty to Helena and if she was condemned to die, he would die himself in the effort to prevent her death.

Klaus stood on the street, the sun was shining; the noises, smells and people of the city he loved were all about him. Helena had not returned so he waited on a garden seat in the shade of a Paulonia tree. The tree dropped blue flowers down on the street around him. Eventually Helena rushed up, her escorts looked hot and tired after their walk and Klaus dismissed them with thanks. Once the marines were gone Helena talked busily about what she had discovered.

It was a kind of miracle. Klaus listened with a smile on his face as they embarked in another tram which took them to the Hall Of Records. The elegant curving Hall towered into the sky and was adjacent to the law courts where in five days Helena would be on trial.

The naval records were on the second floor and there were long shelves of books and great documents as tall as a man stored there. Dating back six hundred years to when the navy began to save all documents concerning the service. Klaus offered the clerk a week's salary if he could locate the record for anything relating to the island of Perculous.

By nightfall they found what they were looking for and Klaus slapped the old clerk on the back and paid him handsomely. They were in business to fight the CGP with some real evidence.

33

ADA SCHMITT PACED UP AND DOWN, her dainty ringed hands clenched into fists. Her big skirts rustled like storm winds in a forest. Rainia and Werner sat watching her with concerned looks on their faces.

"Mama, really, it does not matter if Klaus has no desire to take me as his wife. I do not want to be married to a man who does not care for me," said Rainia, her face twisted with concern, her voice shrill with anxiety.

"I know Klaus well, Mama," said Werner. "He is a dangerous man and he will kill anyone who stands in his way. I have seen him do it many times on the *Hieglund*. If he does not want Rainia, let us find another suitor; someone who will care for her and not be a danger to our family."

"He shan't do it! I won't allow him to get away with introducing that horrid Uitlander woman into our precious society!" exclaimed Ada.

"I admit I don't like the wench," said Werner. "She was a prisoner and about to be put to death on the ship. She was extremely rude and arrogant to the whole slave assessment committee. A woman has no right to be like that." He paused a moment, "I don't know what Klaus sees in her! It is ridiculous for him to want a total stranger when he could have any woman of marriageable status in the city."

A servant entered the room. "There is a messenger from the city. Shall I show him in?"

"Yes, I have been expecting him," said Ada. The messenger was ushered into the parlor and presented her with an envelope on a platter. Ada tore it open and read it quickly. Still reading she walked to a small desk and from a drawer took out a leather purse.

"Here, take this for your trouble." She flicked a coin in the air which the messenger quickly snatched. "There is no message, you are dismissed," she snapped. Ada waited until he had gone.

"Werner, remind me to send a generous gift to your friend in the Department of Genetic Purity. This is the information I have been waiting for. It is a list of the judges chosen to hear the case against the Uitlander next week." Ada frowned, her eyes flashing like a viper. *You will* rue *the day you crossed swords with* me, *Klaus Meinbach!* She thought.

"But what if Helena really *is* descended from an Atlantean trader? She does look like us, Mamma. Her golden hair is different from most of us but some of our people *do* have that kind of pale hair, I've seen it." Rainia said, trying to placate her mother.

"Rubbish! What would a chit of a girl like you know?" Ada said. "Now be silent! I am making a plan."

Werner passed a look to his sister which said 'Mama has a bee in her bonnet now. We cannot deflect her from this path, no matter how foolhardy it may be.' Rainia rolled her eyes and sat primly, back straight, her hands in her lap, her big skirts spread out around her as a noblewoman's skirt should be.

Ada looked again at the list she had received.

"Mrs Farzang, hmmm - I think I can deal with her quite well..." she mused, smiling. "I believe I saw her at the recent Zimmer Art Exhibition. I've heard she is a fan of our greatest painter. I shall ask her if she wishes to view my private collection. Then there's old Sherman Helmut, I shall take him in hand myself. The other fellow - Artur Schwartz, he's more of a liberal," she frowned. "A tall, honorable, strict kind of man, married to a beautiful young wife if I recall rightly... hmmm no chance of wielding any influence there... I'll have to work on the other two."

Ada sat at her writing desk. She wrote on two personalized gold-edged cards, put them in envelopes and turned to her children.

"Now you two, you are going to do what you are told. Our future depends upon your obedience. Werner, here is your task." she gave him instructions regarding the destination of the two cards. Werner ran out the door and caught a tram immediately.

"Rainia," said her mother, "Make preparations for a formal afternoon tea for one caller this afternoon. Make sure the Zimmer paintings are hung in the parlor where we will receive our guest."

Mrs Karla Farzang - Judge at the CGP was surprised when Werner Schmitt arrived at her home with an invitation to afternoon tea that afternoon from his mother. Although she was a judge she was in a very different echelon of society from the Schmitt family and had never dreamed of qualifying for invitations from Ada. Werner stood in front of her, almost at attention.

Karla stood, her slim frame bringing her up taller than the young man.

"It is a great compliment your mother does me," she said. "I'm a *devoted* follower of the artist Zimmer, I know all his works. Indeed, is it not true that your family own some of his exquisite art works?"

"Indeed we do, madam," said Werner.

"Mr Zimmer's work is something I love. Because I am a judge I do not have the resources of a wealthy family like yours behind me. Yet, it has always been my dream to have a Zimmer painting on my wall." Werner smiled stiffly, wondering what she was going on about. He had always taken their art collection for granted. An investment was what his father had said when he brought the paintings home. Then his father had treated them as mere wall decorations – expensive wallpaper.

Mrs Farzang walked up and down, her blue gown swishing over the cool stone floor of her parlor. She clasped her hands, tucking them under her chin, then she smiled radiantly at Werner.

"I am grateful for your mother's invitation. I can make do without owning one of Zimmer's paintings if I get to view some now and then." She sat down and wrote a reply.

"Please take this to your mother." she said, giving the note to Werner. He left in a hurry; thinking only of his next call, to deliver the other card.

Judge Sherman Helmut was surprised to receive an invitation from Ada Schmitt to meet her for dinner at the most luxurious country club in Atlantis that evening. He had just finished reading his instructions from the CGP ordering him to preside over the trial of an Uitlander woman whom the dangerous, heroic and wealthy Klaus Meinbach was championing. Now with a pending court case and an invitation, he found life intensely more interesting than it had been for some time.

He wrote a note accepting her invitation with pleasure. He recalled she was a buxom woman, who had been beautiful in her youth and, as a matron, could easily be seen as desirable now. As beautiful as she is, I am nothing much to look at, he thought, as he contemplated himself in the mirror. Rotund, rather short and balding, his once luxuriant black hair now thinning; Sherman could not think of a reason why Ada Schmitt should unexpectedly show an interest in him.

Since his wife died he had been lonely but accepted his career as occasional judge and working part time for the CGP, policing closely the genetic purity of the Atlantean race.

Now he had an invitation to a private country club - the Nepenthe; a club which he could only dream of joining. One had to be invited and he did not know any members - until now. He preened and decided to wear his best suit. Or should he wear his most elegant sporting outfit? Oh! Decisions, decisions! He hadn't had to make a real decision for years!

"I had no idea you loved Zimmer paintings so passionately," said Ada, as she stood before her three priceless Zimmer paintings with Mrs Farzang who was in raptures.

"Oh my, oh they are so, so lovely - the brushwork..." unable to continue she waved her hands at the canvas. "The depth of color in the corners, see how he has that green fading into white just there? Oh it is simply divine. Exquisite." Turning to Ada she gushed,

"Thank you so very much for letting me see their beauty."

"It is a pleasure," said Ada smoothly. "Which one do you like the best?"

"Oh, the skyscape at dusk," Karla gasped. "The colors placed together are incredible."

"Goodness me," Ada said. "I did not know there were other people like my dear departed husband, who loved these paintings so much. I don't really appreciate them myself. Dear Trevon liked to spend his inheritance on frivolous things like paintings." She moved away from her guest towards the parlor where tea was laid.

"Do come this way, Mrs Farzang, Rainia has tea for us."

They sat and Ada turned the conversation to the latest news.

"I was awfully shocked to hear that captain Meinbach has a Greek Uitlander woman living with him."

"Does he really?" asked Karla, "I wonder why he has done that? A man with his background, he is so brave and handsome, he could have any woman he wanted, surely?" Ada listened to this with interest. Was it likely that Judge Farzang honestly did not know the gossip about Klaus? Her shrewd mind explored all the options, but came up with nothing.

"I hear that he has applied to the CGP to have her declared an Atlantean!" said Ada, taking a macaroon from the glistening silver dish in front of her and offering some to Karla.

"Thank you. I find it quite astonishing that a member of the Meinbach family; one of our oldest and most respected, should wish to do this," said Karla, "However, we have heard several cases like this, particularly to do with women who have been captured and used as concubines by our brave naval officers. The poor deluded men get taken in by these wenches and then want to marry them." She munched her macaroon with obvious enjoyment.

"So what happens then?" asked Ada.

"Oh, most often we allow the women to stay in the household, where they are wanted." Ada was shocked.

"How can you allow that to happen? Surely it is against the law?" she exclaimed.

"The woman remains a slave, they are a necessary evil. Our wonderful nation state needs slaves to keep it functioning. From what you say it seems captain Meinbach wants to marry this woman legally once she is made a citizen. We could never allow that. Every generation has a responsibility to keep our blood pure."

"I do so agree with you." said Ada, relieved. "We need more of our brave naval men marrying beautiful noblewomen like my Rainia," she smiled at her daughter, who looked modestly down at her hands.

"Of course, if captain Meinbach proves his case – it could be that this woman *is* of Atlantean descent. Then we would approve her citizenship." continued Mrs Farzang. "Do you know what she looks like?"

"He brought the woman to my home. She certainly looks like an Atlantean, but she has dreadful uncommon pale hair," said Ada, a pang of jealousy stabbing through her.

The woman was living with Klaus. It should be me! I'm not so old – I could be mistress of the Meinbach manor – No! I *ought* to be! She remembered how handsome Klaus was as he danced with Rainia. It should have been *me* dancing with him, she thought. He would not have escaped from *me*. Her heart quickened as she imagined his arms holding her tight, warm breath tickling her neck. She could almost taste his first sensuous kiss on her lips. She was jolted from her thoughts by Mrs Farzang saying,

"Blonde hair? Well that is unheard of in a Greek woman; they are all swarthy, dirty-looking creatures. That is very interesting, perhaps Meinbach has a case after all?"

"Well, never mind!" exclaimed Ada, "I'm sure the court will do the right thing. Perhaps you would like to view the paintings again, when you have finished your tea, of course?"

34

ADA TOOK A BATH, THEN HER HAIRDRESSER and makeup artist completed a superb makeover. Donning her most flirtatious gown she took her private steam tram to Club Nepenthe. Sherman Helmut arrived when she said he should. By this time all her arrangements were in place. Ada waved a bejeweled hand to the door keeper indicating he was to show Helmut in. Greeting him with enthusiasm she sat him down in a private dining room with a view over the sunny manicured scented gardens. Sherman looked around at the luxurious surroundings with undisguised awe. Everything was furnished in exotic timbers, ornamented with gold and silver inlays and scenes from history. The gaming lawns stretched beyond, he could see some club members playing at their special games.

"Thank you for your invitation Mrs Schmitt," he began warmly. "I don't know to what I owe this honor but it is indeed a treat to be invited to a delightful location like this with a lovely lady like yourself for company." Ada smiled dazzlingly at him.

"Why Judge Helmut," she cooed, a welcoming smile on her full crimson lips. "I have been thinking about you. I met you maybe five years ago, at a Politico rally I think. My dear husband was alive then; in fact I think your lovely wife was too, was she not?"

"Uh - well yes, I think I remember that." Sherman stammered, recalling that she had walked past him, largely ignoring him while engaged in chatting to a woman friend. It was her husband who had spoken to Sherman and his wife. "It was not long after that my wife died," he said, his lips curving into a downward bow.

"Yes, that is so very sad," Ada smiled at him again. "My darling Trevon also tragically passed away, taken in the prime of his life." Rapidly tears filled her eyes.

"I am so sorry to hear of your tragic loss, it must have been hard for you," he said tears of sympathy dewing his eyelashes.

"Thank you, that is so kind of you Sherman, you don't mind me calling you Sherman, do you?"

"Of course not, I would be honored. May I call you Ada?" She smiled through her tears and dabbed at her eyes.

"Oh yes! It has been such a long time since I have talked to a noble gentleman like you. I have been so lonely since dear Trevon passed away."

"Yes, I miss the company of a woman, but at my age one considers he is over matters of the heart."

"Oh, it is *never* too late for love, Sherman. Sometimes I feel it is time to move on, my children are grown up and I do not relish the thought of being a widow forever." Ada fluttered her lashes and smiled at him. "Would you like some refreshment, Sherman?"

"Well - yes," he said cautiously. "I don't drink much as a rule. Strong wine goes straight to my head."

"I know just the beverage for you," Ada said warmly and rose to call the waiter. She whispered an order to him. The waiter reappeared almost immediately with two glass goblets and a decanter of golden liquid which he placed on the small table between them.

Goodness, that was quick; the man must have had the order close to hand, thought Sherman. Raising his glass, he clinked it gently against Ada's proffered goblet.

"The Empire," he intoned in the traditional toast and took a cautious swallow. He looked at the glass in amazement, the wine was delicious. He had never tasted anything so delectable before. He took another sip, he was not mistaken. Where do they grow the grapes that produce wine like this? I shall savor every drop of this ambrosia, he thought, his mouth watering for the next mouthful.

"This is absolutely delicious," he said, holding up his glass. "Where is it grown?" To his surprise Ada gasped and began to fidget. Her chest was heaving in quick pants, her hands fluttered at her throat. Then she pressed her hands to her breast which was tightly restrained by a fashionable silk whale-boned corset.

"Are you quite well Ada? This wine is too strong for you perhaps?" he inquired leaning towards her.

"Excuse me Sherman, but these new whale bone corsets can be *so* uncomfortable. I wonder if I could ask a favor of you?"

"Why of course Mrs Schmitt, I mean Ada. How can I help?" Ada stood and turned her back to him.

"I need to take this corset off. Please can you loosen the cords at the back?" Sherman gasped internally. Good gracious, what a request from a noble woman! But how can I refuse her? His hands trembling, he unlaced her corset clumsily. She waited patiently as he fumbled. Finally it was undone.

"Ah! That feels so much better. Now lift it over my head." Ada turned and faced Helmut with a lovely smile on her face. He felt a stirring in his loins, something simultaneously alarming and pleasant. He lifted the corset over her head, careful not to muss her lovely hair. Ada took the garment from him and quickly dropped it behind her chair. Sherman resisted a strong urge to stroke her neck, which was soft, creamy and inviting to his starved gaze. Her elegant gown revealed a lovely figure which hardly required a corset at all. His breathing became rapid; he had no corset to hide his discomfort. The temptress sat down, and took a deep breath to relax.

"Do drink your wine, Sherman. I have booked us a private room for the whole evening, where we can *completely* relax." She smiled and lifted her glass to him before taking a generous mouthful herself. He sat down and quaffed the rest of his wine in a nervous swallow. The wine became a pleasant blaze in his stomach. He looked at Ada; she gazed back at him, a beguiling smile playing over her soft lips. She leaned forward and refilled his glass to the brim.

"Don't you think this wine is wonderful? It is grown in foreign parts – I have a friend who is an official trader who buys it abroad especially for me. Please feel free to imbibe," she smiled and looked him in the eye again. "This wine is very exclusive - but I think we can do justice to it."

As she moved forward to fill her glass Helmut's eyes swiveled to her breasts. He could swear her bust had somehow grown sensuously fuller since she was released from the tight constraints of her corset.

I must refrain from drinking this wine too quickly, thought Sherman. If I am to believe what is happening, Ada finds me attractive. She is a caring noblewoman, who is alone in the best years of her life, just as I am. We have a great deal in common, now I consider the matter.

"Is - is there anything I can do for you Ada?" he asked softly.

"Maybe there is Sherman. I'd really like to get to know you better, a lot better." Ada took one of his hands in both of hers and squeezed gently. Then her hand strayed to his cheek and, as if it were the most natural movement in the world, she kissed him gently on the lips.

Oh! He felt shock, of a delicious sort. She wants me! What shall I do? I hope I don't have a heart attack! I can feel my chest pounding so hard. Before he knew what was happening Ada had placed her ample behind on his lap and was kissing his face and lips. Her mouth was soft yet demanding a response.

"Oh, Sherman I have wanted to get to know you more closely for some time. I hope my dear departed husband will forgive me for my carnal thoughts."

"I am sure he will. The human heart is not meant to live on memories alone. I too, have wondered if it is time to let go of my loyalty to my dear departed wife."

Sherman took this opportunity to run his hands over the fullness of her breasts and across the soft silk of her deep green dress to her hips and other places no longer protected by her corset. He began to get very excited, lusting for her, realizing gradually that tonight it was likely he could have this glorious noblewoman for his own. His fingers were a conduit of intoxicating sensations which ran through his body accompanied by that amazing wine. Ada shuddered and closed her eyes.

"Oh, Sherman you are so masterful, I do like a man who knows how to take charge sometimes."

They dined, hands trembling, eyes meeting and smiling; making small talk as a prelude to what they knew was to come.

At last Ada stood. "Come with me, Shermie." She smiled with her full rosy lips and he followed like an obedient beagle. Sited in a distant wing of the club the suite was quiet, private and secure.

The perfect place for an affair, thought Sherman as, dazed with desire, he wandered through the room his bare feet caressed by soft rugs.

Through one door was a bathing room outfitted with a steaming spa bath. The bed room boasted a huge ornate four poster bed hung about with deep red velvet curtains trimmed with matching red and gold satin bows. Outside was an immaculately tended private garden, two chairs and a low table with a glowing brass lamp placed in the center shedding a soft golden radiance.

A slave brought a tray of sweets, two more bottles of wine and fresh glasses. Ada adjusted the lighting and switched on musical entertainment from the audi; soft romantic music filled the room. The fragrance of sweet flowers wafted through the rooms. The suite was an alluring boudoir in which Ada was the jewel.

I believe I am in a dream, I will wake up any moment now and find myself at home lying in bed, Sherman thought. His heart was pounding as if he had run a lap of the country club circuit. I hope I am truly up to this experience, he worried. It's been a long time since 'little sherm' has had a workout.

Ada sat on the bed and patted the quilted cover.

"Come on handsome, I haven't had a man in a long time. I hope you are up to pleasuring me." Sherman smiled nervously; sitting awkwardly on the bed he took her hands in his.

"Thank you, Ada, thank you for this wonderful evening," he mumbled, but his thanks were muffled by kisses from Ada. After kissing, fondling and tumbling on the bed Ada insisted that they get into the hot spa together.

Sherman discovered that while his body had deteriorated into a rotund mass, Ada's had not followed suit. Removing her dress revealed a beautiful voluptuous woman, who kissed him passionately and pressed her lovely body ardently against his.

"Ooh Sherman," Ada cooed, her breath smelling of wine, "You are going to be my stud tonight! I am longing to have you sleep all night beside me." Their kisses were long, slow and sensual as their bodies met beside the spa in a passionate embrace. Watching Ada slip into the steaming water, Sherman thought, I'm incredibly lucky, maybe I was wrong? Am I really a handsome fellow? She seems to find me desirable. Perhaps my looks have not declined as much as I thought?

"Dearest Ada," he murmured into her mouth between kisses, as their bodies fitted together deliciously in the warm water. His unpracticed hands found her nipples; her hands roamed his body and aroused him painfully.

Ada was unaware that this evening would raise Sherman's score of personal sexual experiences with women to double his previous total.

Sherman did not know that Ada was imagining his soft flabby arms and tubby stomach were actually the strong muscular arms and taut stomach of a certain handsome naval captain.

35

KLAUS AND HELENA AROSE EARLY THE NEXT MORNING to help the crew of the Meinbach II store provisions and water for their voyage to Perculous Island. The small steam cruiser was the only family boat after the tragic accident which had killed Klaus's parents. She had a deep forefoot with a moderate beam and was large enough to have her own boiler amidships; the coal bunker was slightly further aft. The saloon, galley and wheelhouse were combined as one. The master cabin was complete with an opulent bathroom. Water was stored in large iron tanks in the bilge under the saloon. Crew quarters were forward under the chain locker in the bow. The two crewmen, both stokers, loaded sacks of coal into the Meinbach II through hatches on the rear deck.

With a full head of steam the 70 ton vessel could make three times the speed of a fast sailing yacht. Beginning with a full load of coal she had a range of 600 miles traveling at full speed or 1500 miles if cruising at a more moderate speed. She was originally a gunboat; purchased and converted into a pleasure cruiser by Klaus's father. She had a short mast and could sail if needed but was slow in the water under sail.

The crew kept her in pristine condition; constantly painting her black iron hull and green fittings. They meticulously cleaned and polished the bright brass work until she shone. Her steam propulsion system and boiler were kept fully maintained so she was ready for a voyage at any time.

They packed the brass and quartz ice cooler with stores and made sure the coal fired ovens own tiny bunker was full.

Klaus loaded three long barreled hunting rifles, packed spare powder and ammunition, his cutlass and pistols. Occasionally a pirate ship would slip undetected into Atlantean waters and he wasn't about to take any chances.

They cast off while the sun was still low on the horizon. It was a beautiful day and Helena sat in a comfortable chair on the foredeck with a cup of tea, enjoying the view as they slowly left the bay where the Meinbach II was moored.

Klaus told Helena that the island of Perculous was approximately 200 miles to the east, and it would take most of the day to get there if the sea remained calm. Klaus ordered the crewmen to be on alternating hour stoking shifts to keep the boiler at optimum heat. Soon the little ship was leaving a long foaming wake behind her.

Once they were out in the open ocean, the wind grew stronger and a moderate swell began to move the ship around. Helena sat next to Klaus as he stood in the wheelhouse at the helm. The Mediterranean was in a friendly state, the moderate sea swells inviting the small ship to dance and dance she did. The sharp, deep bow dipped through the sparkling blue water; dolphins came to play gracefully in the pressure waves created by the passage of the bow. Fresh air flowed through the open hatchways creating a soft breeze which wafted through the ship.

As the passage continued they had chilled wine, fruit, fresh bread and cheese which Helena shared with the two stokers who smiled and doffed their woolen sea hats. The island was sighted in the late afternoon. Klaus opened the steam valves to blow off excess pressure, while the stokers stood down as the throttles were eased. The sleek ship entered the small fishing harbor of Perculous.

Gulls wheeled above the few fishing boats left in the harbor for repairs. Most of the fishing fleet were working further east, their blue sails barely discernible on the horizon. Klaus eased the Meinbach II alongside the large jetty in the center of the sheltered harbor. Village children appeared in droves and two big boys took the bow and stern ropes thrown by the crew and tied them off to bollards on the jetty.

Klaus and Helena readied themselves for a walk and climbed the steep weed encrusted steps up the jetty. A throng of chattering children chorused hello and followed Klaus and Helena as they walked towards the mayor's residence which was set upon a low hill overlooking the harbor.

The village consisted of bright white and blue-washed stone houses with orange terracotta tile roofs. Most homes had carefully attended vegetable and flower gardens. There were fishing nets drying, draped over frames in the sun. Smells of the sea and fish added to the bouquet of sweet perfume from the wild flowers which bloomed in the meadows around the village.

Chickens and geese scattered, honking and cackling as they tried to avoid the excited crowd.

The path through the village was really a track paved with rough broken stones from the seashore. Helena wished she had worn boots instead of sandals. Today she wore a scarf covering her head and a simple dress in keeping with the locals' modest attire. She did not want to wear expensive clothes from Atlantis, and seem like an arrogant noble woman.

Klaus looked at home in his seaman's jacket, peaked cap, tall sea boots with a hunting rifle over his shoulder. The Mayor, a stout grey haired man, limped toward them leaning on a cane.

"Welcome to our humble village, I am Mayor Druckman," he said shaking Klaus's hand with an iron grip. "To what do we owe the pleasure of your visit, captain Meinbach?"

"You are correct, I am Klaus Meinbach. But I do not know *you* sir. How do you know my name? Is it because of the name on the bow of my ship?"

"No, indeed," Mayor Druckman said. "I knew your parents well. Several times they visited our humble village in the Meinbach II. My condolences to you sir, I heard of the unfortunate accident, which took them from us." He bowed his head.

"Thank you," said Klaus stiffly. He never knew how to respond adequately when his parent's death was mentioned. He took a deep breath.

"We are here regarding a personal matter. We seek the relatives of men lost at sea from this island."

"Yes," said Helena eagerly, "I seek my lost family here on Perculous." Her face was animated, bright and rosy.

"Come in, you are most welcome." Mayor Druckman called, opening the door of his home and beckoning his guests inside.

"We will talk about the reason you are here in private." His invitation was not extended to the village children and the door was closed firmly on their disappointed faces.

The Mayor's friendly red cheeked wife Marie served them village wines, fresh breads and cold roast chicken served with grape leaves, oranges and melons.

Klaus explained to the Druckman's that he sought any remaining members of the Diocles family. Mayor Druckman sent messengers out into the village inviting the elders to a meeting. While they were eating, a stream of village elders arrived. They gathered in groups and looked at the strangers; maybe they would speak to the mayor's guests if they could surmount their shyness. The small garden and atrium were overwhelmed by guests sitting and standing about. Some were talking amongst themselves, and some were looking at Helena curiously. Helena smiled at these people, and was excited to see that amongst the crowd there were some who bore a strong resemblance to her mother and grandfather.

I feel so close to the solution of this puzzle, she thought. Surely, if I find my long lost family here, the Atlantean authorities will allow me to become a citizen and then I can marry Klaus publicly! She sighed happily, as a wonderful vision of a happy life at his estate with many children, beloved horses, and sailing the ocean passed before her inner eye.

Klaus was eager to discuss with the mayor and the elders the reason for his visit, but a famous sea captain like Klaus Meinbach did not visit this village very often so he had to endure many speeches of thanks and toasts from the Mayor and elders. Finally, after the tenth toast to their health Klaus stood up.

"Thank you, thank you." He bowed in the direction of his host and again to the elders. "Your hospitality and generosity are greatly appreciated by Helena and myself; however we are on a serious mission. We seek members of the Diocles family. According to naval records a fishing boat never returned to this harbor in March of the year 752. This was a full 60 years ago. Does anyone remember this?"

Everyone began talking at once. There was a lot of laughter and a great deal of pointing, arm waving and shouting. Slowly a bent old woman, leaning on a stick shuffled forward and stood beside Mayor Druckman. Klaus held up his arms until silence fell. He gestured to her to begin.

"I am Euthalia Diocles." she said. "I lost my father, my brother and a cousin a long time ago. My mother told me of a great storm which blew with an unbelievable force for ten days and nights. Our fishing fleet were scattered to all corners of the ocean. Alas my father and his crew were never heard of again." A sob came from Euthalia's throat and her hands shook as she held her walking stick.

Helena stood, walked forward and gently took the old woman's gnarled, trembling hands in her own and gave them a gentle squeeze, then untied her headscarf and let it drop. Her long fair hair cascaded down over her shoulders. Euthalia put both hands to her mouth and cried out in shock.

"By all the Gods of the sea and land!" she exclaimed. "It is my daughter Eunice herself or her twin sister!" She stepped forward and touched Helena gently on the cheek. "Eunice has a daughter Delmania, who looks like you must have as a child. It's as if the Gods have restored our family – bringing you back from the ocean." Tears began to stream down her face and matching tears appeared in Helena's eyes.

"Who was it my child? Who lived to be your father? Or was it your grandfather?" Euthalia asked.

"My grandfather was washed ashore from a ship wreck upon the coast near to Corinth. He married my grandmother Athena, and they had two children, my mother Thelma and my aunt Agatha. Both of them look a lot like you, Euthalia."

"So my father Clive Diocles was your grandfather!" gasped Euthalia peering shortsightedly up into Helena's face.

"Yes! That was his name, Clive Diocles! By Apollo, this is so amazing!" Helena was quite overcome. Klaus gestured and chairs were brought for the two women who sat together, holding hands, tears flowing down their faces.

"You must take Helena to meet Eunice and Delmania," said Euthalia to two women who had come up and stood beside her, looking at Helena.

They took Helena by the hand and led her through the village to a small cottage surrounded by a large garden. There she found a woman a little older than herself, and the young girl she had seen on the fishing boat leaving the docks of Atlantis. Both of these women looked like Helena's sisters, with their long blonde hair, beautiful green eyes and fair skin. Many tears were shed and Helena was invited to spend the next two days with her cousins.

The fishing fleet returned in the evening and that night the village staged a celebration party for everyone. Helena and Klaus were the guests of honor and feasted on flatbread, fresh fish, fruit cake and wine, which was drunk in copious quantities. It was after midnight when the rather befuddled couple staggered back to the jetty and awoke the crew as they made hard work of clambering aboard, laughing and whispering loudly.

Helena spent the next two days finding out about her family. She visited the little cottage, cooked and gardened with Eunice.

"I still find it hard to believe that I have found my family on this island," said Helena as she tugged out strong grasses which were invading the herb garden.

"You *are* my family!" said Eunice, sitting back on her heels.

"We look *so* like each other, we could be sisters. I always wanted a sister, Helena. Would you be my sister? Please?" She put her hand out towards Helena who clasped the proffered hand.

"Oh, yes! I have two sisters but I do not know if I will ever see them again so I would love to be your sister Eunice."

"Where are your sisters?" asked Eunice.

Helena sighed "Corina and Tianike are my sisters, but they are older than me. I fear since I have not returned from my voyage that my family will be told I am most likely dead, like most of my shipmates are. My mother was so afraid when I went on this voyage that I would never return." She bowed her head sadly. "Mothers are so often right about these things."

"Tell me about them," said Eunice who put her arms around Helena to try to comfort her.

"My mother is Thelma of Corinth and my father Drouiad was a fisherman and before that a veteran of the wars between Athens and Sparta. I remember he had many scars on his arms and a long groove on his face where he had been slashed by a sword." She paused for a moment.

"Mine is not the first tragedy for our family. Father went out fishing one winter's morning, a freezing storm from the North blew up and we never saw him again." Eunice held Helena tightly.

"My father Gerontias also died out fishing. I really miss him," said Eunice very softly.

"Oh, I am so selfish," said Helena, "I did not think to ask why there were no men in your family. What about Delmania, is she your daughter?"

"Yes, she is my daughter. Her father is a trader on a ship which travels to the far lands of the world. We do not see him often because he is away sometimes for years at a time."

"You must be lonely," said Helena.

"I have my family," said Eunice. "My husband prefers to travel and we are dull compared to the strange and interesting places he has been. I wish now that I had married a man who wanted to stay closer to home. It would be nice to have a companion and a father to help bring up Delmania."

"I hope Klaus and I will never be parted," said Helena sincerely, "Meeting you, Eunice, your mother and Delmania has shown me that I have a real chance to be a citizen of Atlantea. I am not permitted to go home to Greece, Klaus says, therefore I must stay in Atlantis or die. I feel afraid. In two days they will hear my case in court." Her shoulders trembled under Eunice's embrace.

"I do not know if the court will allow you to stay and marry Klaus," said Eunice. "There are many in our nation who regard outsiders as slaves and animals. They have helped create the laws which prevent citizens from marrying into bad blood." Helena trembled again as she heard these words. She sent a silent prayer to Apollo.

"We look so alike, dear sister," said Eunice, "I could come to the court and show them that I am an Atlantean citizen and that you and I look like true sisters in every way. I have my ID tablet in my reticule."

"Oh!" said Helena looking more cheerful, "Would you come? *Please* come and be with me through the court case." She clasped her hands together and looked beseechingly at Eunice. "It would be wonderful to spend more time with you."

"You are my sister. Of course I will come with you and do whatever I can!" said Eunice.

After an emotional farewell from the Diocles family and the entire village; Helena, Eunice, Delmania and Klaus made the voyage back to Atlantis at half speed; the stokers had an easy time keeping the furnace fed.

That evening Klaus and Helena climbed up the narrow stairs to the roof of the mansion where his father Albrecht had built an open lookout tower. The tower had unbroken views of the ocean, the great mountain and the night sky. They lay on a blanket drinking wine together; taking turns at observing the night sky through the telescope.

"I can't believe I am actually Atlantean." Helena laughed.

"Why is that?" asked Klaus looking at her with raised brows.

"When you first questioned me aboard your ship, I did not truly believe I was of your race – I – I made a bold guess because I wanted to live. Mother talked about my grandfather having unusually fair skin and blue eyes – the marks of your race, but she never said it was because he was a ship-wrecked foreigner. In fact, apart from telling me he was shipwrecked as a fisherman she did not tell me much about his youth. He died when I was young so I do not remember him."

"So - you tricked me?" said Klaus turning to look directly at her. He thought she had never looked more beautiful. The soft light of the electric lamps set around the balcony platform glowed from her hair with a radiance to match the gold of the rising moon.

"I had no idea Atlantea existed, even when you captured me I did not know you were an Atlantean ship. I suppose my grandfather guarded the secret of his birth, just as you say all citizens are trained to do. I never realized I was truly of your blood until I saw Delmania and then met Eunice and her mother. Oh, I got teased about the way I looked as a girl. I was the only one with pale hair amongst all the dark curls, but we Greeks are not so consumed by racial purity. We *like* peoples from other lands." She said this in such innocent delightful tones that Klaus laughed.

"I confess, Helena, I have had a change of heart concerning the rigid attitude I had towards our laws regarding human bloodlines. Meeting you has changed my thoughts a lot regarding the value of other peoples."

"I'm glad of that, my love." Helena placed her soft arm around his neck and moved her face close to his. "I can understand your culture not wanting to share the advanced technology you have. We Greeks do not share all our secrets with the Persians. But we are all human, Klaus. I will bear you a child someday to show you that our humanity is one."

Sealing this promise the two lovers kissed many times, as unseen above them a series of fiery meteors blazed across the star laden sky.

It was a perfect end to a perfect week and Klaus kept any doubts about Helena's chances in court the next day to himself.

36

THE MORNING OF HELENA'S TRIAL DAWNED GREY AND OVERCAST. The trial was convened in one of the main court rooms on the ground floor of the Courts of Justice tower. The court hearings of the Department of Genetic Purity were open to the public for a modest price. There was so much public interest in this trial involving a popular navy captain and a Greek priestess of Apollo that the court changed the entry fee to an immodest one. This ensured that the audience would consist entirely of the elite of Atlantean society.

The court room was full of chatter and an air of excitement as the public waited impatiently for the court proceedings to commence. Dozens of society ladies twittering like exotic birds jostled for the right to sit in the best seats. The color and splendor of the clothing and accessories of the noblemen and women were in stark contrast to the somber timbers which lined the walls and the ceilings of the chamber.

Ada Schmitt was seated with her friends in the front row in full view of the judging panel. Her low cut dress showed off her bosom causing many to titter and pass comment on her daring to wear such a revealing costume, more suited for the evening than a public forum like a court room. A golden locket trembled on her cleavage, a gift from her amorous suitor who had yet to enter the court.

A man in dark clothes settled himself quietly at the end of the front row of the upper tier where he had a good view of the proceedings. He sat with collar turned up and hat pulled down over his forehead. On his knee rested a large notebook and brass fountain pen. A monocle-like view-scope dangled from his fob pocket, for use when he wanted to see details.

Helena wore a simple pink dress under a doe brown colored corset with her silver betrothal bracelet. A scarf covered her hair hiding much of her face from view. She sat beside Klaus who was attired in the magnificent formal dress uniform of a naval captain, minus his sword and pistols, since all weapons were banned in the courtroom.

Abruptly there was a loud ringing sound of a stave striking the flagstones of the court, a booming voice commanded.

"All stand and pay homage to the court; the judges are now in attendance."

Three judges wearing formal silver edged black robes and red velvet caps entered from behind the raised dais. Court scribes followed in solemn procession. Officers of the court armed with wooden staves took positions blocking all exits to the hearing chamber.

The three judges bowed to the nobles before taking their seats behind the highly polished judgment bench. The nobles bowed formally in return and sat down.

Artur Schwartz, the most senior judge, struck his gavel on an electrically controlled bronze pad. The sound amplified and reverberated around the room. The expectant crowd immediately became silent.

"This case will be heard in silence." announced Schwartz.

"Presiding over this case are myself Judge Schwartz; to my right is Judge Farzang and on my left is Judge Helmut." Each judge nodded as their name was mentioned. The man in the hat thought that Schwartz was every bit the upright solid support of the establishment that he should be, tall and imposing, while Judge Farzang was a remarkably pretty woman if a trifle tall. By comparison to the other judges Helmut seemed a tired, rather overweight, stocky fellow.

"The proctor of the court shall read out the charges," continued Judge Schwartz

The proctor, seated at a desk below the dais, approached the bench where he whispered to Judge Schwartz. Before returning to his seat the proctor shot a nervous look towards the accused Helena of Delphi and her counsel, Klaus Meinbach.

The crowd began to talk in whispers and as the noise level rose, Judge Schwartz struck the gavel again.

"Quiet!" he bellowed "I understand one of the charges has been withdrawn. So the proctor shall read the amended charge sheet." The proctor read out the remaining charge.

"On the 9th Day of New Summer in the year 812 of the Atlantean Republic, Helena of Delphi, a priestess of Apollo entered the port of Atlantis. Being an illegal immigrant the accused is therefore subject to the Genetic Purity Act of 505. This is an offense punishable by death and, or the offender is to be made a slave of the state."

"How does the accused plead?" said Judge Schwartz. Klaus patted Helena on the hand. Standing he addressed the court.

"The noble woman Helena pleads not guilty your honor." Judge Helmut cleared his throat.

"The accused is not considered a noble woman and shall be addressed as 'the accused'. Let us not lose sight of the fact she has Uitlander status and we shall not pay her false homage."

"In this court you may address her as you will sir, but she has a name and it is Helena." Klaus replied, "You sir, may be seated up on high; but when you walk amongst your fellow citizens you are, if I am not mistaken, a man of almost no stature at all."

The courtroom exploded into laughter and Judge Schwartz' gavel pounded the amplifying pad causing many to hold their ears.

"Quiet! I warn you, captain Meinbach, you must not make personal aspersions against judges of this court sir! Now you will apologize to Judge Helmut," ordered Judge Schwartz.

"I shall sir and gladly so; but I wish to be met halfway and request the court refer to Helena of Delphi by her given name," said Klaus.

"We shall name the accused Helena when appropriate to accommodate your request captain Meinbach. But if you are to start an argument at every question this trial will last a lifetime. I won't have it, sir."

"Very well, but I expect this court to hear and treat all facts as they find them and not make statements which indicate a bias." replied Klaus looking at Helmut with a withering stare.

"And so do I, captain Meinbach," replied Schwartz, "Now the prosecution shall state its case."

The prosecutor, a thin man whose polished beak of a nose suggested a love of strong liquor, adjusted his spectacles.

"Judges of the court of Atlantea; the case is simple. The woman Helena was born in Greece. She is neither of our blood, nor our ancestry. She was taken prisoner by captain Meinbach and brought to Atlantis to have her status examined. The accused Helena of Delphi has no birth certificate and no relatives in Atlantea. I cannot understand why the good captain has taken her under his wing. She is a low blood Uitlander. I suspect she is also a witch and has cast a spell on the brave captain."

Klaus jumped to his feet and slammed the palm of his hand onto the table.

"You crass swine! You cross-eyed, sea toad! I shall meet you outside for satisfaction immediately!" he yelled.

More pounding of the gavel was needed to restore order. The buzz in the gallery showed the crowd were thoroughly enjoying the entertainment.

"Captain Meinbach!" shouted Schwartz, "You must not act this way towards the prosecutor. You are entitled to disagree, but you cannot threaten to shoot the man sir! He is an employee of the state and has the protection of the Empire."

"I shall withdraw my remark about the accused, Helena, having cast a spell upon the captain, noble judges," said the prosecutor insincerely, playing the proceedings as an actor to an audience. "I now call as the first witness, Proctor Wendt who oversees the birth records."

"Very well call the witness," said Schwartz.

Wendt was called and gave a longwinded explanation about the documentation showing no trace of Helena of Delphi in the records.

"Your witness captain," said the prosecutor.

"I have no need to speak to this man, sir, as I do not deny Helena was not born in Atlantea. However I shall prove she carries Atlantean blood in her veins when I am allowed to call my witnesses."

The prosecutor called more witnesses: minor port officials who observed Helena walking ashore without authorization. Another state witness gave an explanation which lasted for more than an hour regarding the urgent necessity for the Atlantean Republic to keep their genetic breeding pure.

Listening to these officials, Klaus understood for the first time how much of the laws which he unquestioningly obeyed, were based upon speculative science and prejudice combined with legalese. Many in the crowd were yawning by the end of this dissertation. Captain Meinbach's outbursts were far more interesting. Finally the prosecutor walked to stand beside Helena.

"I wish to show you proof of this woman's connection with the Greek nation. The goddesses of Apollo when they are anointed have a small tattoo of a lyre or a Greek harp. I ask the accused to show the inside of her left wrist to the court." Helena stood proudly and turned her left wrist towards the judges. They noted a small blue tattoo of a lyre on the inside of her forearm. The prosecutor bowed to the judges.

"That is the case for the prosecution; it is simple and clear that this woman has no claim to any Atlantean bloodline. I cannot think of any plausible reason for her to claim otherwise. However the good captain has indicated he has some sort of defense, but for my part, the case for the prosecution is closed." Judge Schwartz cleared his throat.

"I am going to order a short adjournment to allow time for the defense to prepare. I am interested in what captain Meinbach has to say. Everyone shall reassemble in two hours for the start of the defense. The court is in adjournment." The three judges stood as one and filed out of the courtroom.

37

ADA MOVED OUT OF THE COURTROOM along with the rest of the throng but she waited until most had left the foyer before re-entering the courtroom where she approached one of the orderlies.

"I wish to see Judge Helmut on important business. My name is Ada Schmitt. Please give him my card. I will wait here for a reply." The orderly bowed obsequiously,

"Certainly noble woman if you will wait, I shall bring a reply immediately."

Ada amused herself strolling about, looking at some of the artwork which hung in the courtroom. She barely noticed a

man, wearing a hat and coat, who was also looking at the art-
works.

The orderly returned and ushered Ada through a side door
which led to the judge's private rooms. Unseen by Ada, the
man in the hat quietly spoke to the orderly and followed Ada
through the door. He stood silently watching as Ada was admitted to Judge Helmut's rooms.

Helmut stood as Ada entered; her face broke into the bewitching smile which completely disarmed him every time he
saw her. He bowed and kissed her proffered hand.

"My love," he said in a low voice, "We must be careful. The
law must be seen to be impartial."

"Oh, Sherman! Stop fussing so, you are a judge and she is a
common Uitlander. It is certain that she will hang with all the
other petty criminals within the week. She is of no consequence
and I intend to give the matter no more thought. It is *you* I
have come to see my love. I long for your touch. Kiss me, my
darling Sherman."

Helmut tilted his head and Ada bent to kiss him on the lips.
When they parted she moaned,

"My darling, you mean so much to me, as soon as you are
free this evening we shall go to my spa. We can stay the night
together in bliss." she smiled again.

He was flustered, he was about to melt into his shoes, yet he
had other paramount responsibilities.

"Tonight, uh – well, we judges must debate the case my
love. I'm very sorry but it may take hours, my sweet lady," said
Sherman brushing her breasts with his hands. She held his
hands to her and whispered,

"Don't debate too long my love. I want to spend the whole
night with you. Now I will go and leave you to your duty, my
darling."

Ada blew him a kiss as she opened the door and stepped out into the corridor. As she swept down the long wood paneled corridor, a satisfied smirk on her painted lips, the man in the hat left Judge Farzang's chambers.

He watched Ada settling her corset and straightening her hair while she waited for an orderly to open the door into the courtroom. He remained in the corridor hidden behind an archway until she had gone.

After a few moments he followed her.

38

DURING THE ADJOURNMENT Eunice and her daughter Delmania arrived outside the court room in a steam tram. They wore veils covering their hair, obscuring their faces and waited outside in the witness waiting room until they were called.

After the court reconvened Klaus took the stand.

"I am captain of the *Hieglund*, and while out patrolling our waters searching for invading Uitlander craft, we came upon a foundering Greek merchant ship. We rescued those of the crew that were useful to us as slaves. As a part of this process each captive is interviewed by a special panel formed by the political officers and myself, the captain.

"A young woman was captured and we interviewed her. Unlike other Greek women I have seen who have dark skins, brown eyes and black hair; this woman had long golden hair, green eyes and a very fair skin. Indeed she looked like an Atlantean noble woman and when she spoke to us she demanded to know what we were doing and why. She questioned our interview process – which often makes use of torture. Then she demanded that we cast her back into the ocean where she would certainly have drowned in the foundering of her own ship, had we not rescued her.

"As is my right, I may choose any of the captives to interview myself, and make use of in whatever way I wish. I decided that I wanted to investigate this woman and her background because she seemed too much like one of our own for our crew to take responsibility in killing or enslaving her. When I spoke to Helena, she told me that her grandfather was a foreigner, perhaps an Atlantean. I decided to bring her back to port so that this court could decide her future.

"While in my custody I have allowed Helena to learn our language, which she has achieved with marvelous ability, certainly she has far more intelligence and aptitude for our language than any Greek slave. Helena has mastered many of our technological items; she can also ride and dance well. Although she is perhaps only one quarter Atlantean blood I believe she deserves noble status. It is my opinion Helena will be an asset to our society as she has much to offer us."

His chair scraped across the wooden floor as the prosecutor stood. Rubbing his nose in contemplation, he waited a moment before speaking.

"Captain Meinbach, what are your qualifications regarding genetic purity?"

"I have a naval captain's training and I have judged hundreds of Uitlanders before putting them to slavery or death. This is one of my responsibilities as a naval captain."

"However your testimony regarding Helena of Delphi' bloodline is more speculation than fact, is it not?" insinuated the prosecutor.

"It is the truth. In fact I am convinced of her lineage, and today I will prove it. I am a man of the sea, I have seen savages and plenty of them; and I know noble Atlantean blood when I see it. As we all know, there is no comparison. Your experts are book dwellers who spend their time in dusty hallways. I wager none of them have seen a real Uitlander savage close up." The audience murmured with approval and there were a few voices laughing here and there as the prosecutor looked uncomfortable and primly pursed his lips.

"Their qualifications are not in question, captain, it is the factual basis of your opinions, and in the science of genetics your cupboard is bare, is it not?"

"Are you accusing me of being an empty vessel? An addleheaded moron?" demanded Klaus.

"Your words, not mine, captain," said the prosecutor retreating.

"I do not like your tone, sir!" said Klaus. "You seek to undermine me and my experience as a naval captain with your words. But I see you for what you are – an assassin who hides in the unproven theories of books. By using devious words; your intention is to plunge a knife in my back!" Klaus folded his arms. "I hold fast to what I believe and I care not whether you respect my experience."

"Gentlemen, Gentlemen." interjected Judge Schwartz, "We have heard captain Meinbach and concur he is sincere in his beliefs. If you have no further questions; it is time to take your seat sir." The look Schwartz gave the prosecutor left no doubt as to his next course of action.

"Of course sir, I have no further questions," said the prosecutor hurriedly. Klaus rose, bowed to the judges and returned to his seat.

"Captain Meinbach, you may call your witnesses," said Judge Schwartz.

"I call Eunice and Delmania Diocles," said Klaus. Mother and daughter entered the courtroom and walked hand and hand to the witness box where they calmly turned to face the room full of curious strangers.

"Captain Meinbach is there any reason these women have their faces covered?" asked Judge Farzang.

"Yes there is. All will be revealed at the appropriate time," said Klaus moving to stand before the Diocles family.

"You are Eunice Diocles and this is your daughter Delmania?" Klaus asked.

"Yes and we are from the island of Perculous in the Empire of Atlantea." she replied.

"Does your family have long association with the island?" asked Klaus.

"Yes sir, for more than 600 years and we have records and certificates which prove our family have lived in the Empire since the beginning of recorded time," said Eunice. Klaus went to his desk. He smiled at Helena, picked up a sheaf of papers, turned and faced the judge's bench.

"I have here records of the Diocles family and it shows hundreds of years of their association with the island of Perculous." Judge Farzang moved restlessly and spoke.

"This is all very interesting, captain, but what have the esteemed and ancient Diocles family got to do with this case?" Helmut nodded.

"I am coming to my point, if you give me a small measure of your patience, madam," said Klaus. He held up another piece of paper. "In the year 752 the records show a fishing vessel with three men on board went missing in a storm. The missing men were Clive Diocles, his son and a nephew; they were lost at sea, presumed drowned."

"Who was that man, Eunice?" asked Klaus.

"He was my grandfather, captain."

"Thank you." Klaus went to Helena and extended his hand. She rose and gracefully took his hand in hers. Klaus escorted Helena into a position beside Eunice. The onlookers in the gallery muttered to each other.

"Helena of Delphi what is the name of your mother's father?" Klaus asked Helena in loud tones.

"His name was Clive Diocles, captain Meinbach," said Helena clearly.

"Clive Diocles did not drown but was washed up alive on the shores of Corinth, in the nation of Greece, announced Klaus, "He married into a Greek family and had a daughter with fair hair, green eyes and fair skin. This woman's daughter is Helena of Delphi." A gasp came from the front.

"No!" shouted Ada Schmitt.

"Yes!" crowed Klaus, "ladies, please remove your veils." Helena, Eunice and Delmania took off their veils.

The crowd leaned forward as one and all gasped in astonishment as revealed were two beautiful blonde women who looked like identical twins and certainly must be sisters; and a girl who was a younger version of them. Indeed all three women were a vision of loveliness, the golden tresses of their hair flowing down almost to their waists.

"Please turn to face the bench and show our honorable judges the plain evidence of their own eyes," said Klaus. "What more evidence do you need? Is it necessary to go to your chambers and deliberate upon your decision? Because it is certain you have only one decision available; it is proven Helena of Delphi is truly of Atlantean blood. She is the granddaughter of an Atlantean fisherman, returned to the bosom of her family on Perculous Island. Honorable judges – I believe you have no choice but to render a verdict of citizenship proven." The audience was amazed and a loud buzz of conversation filled the room.

The judges looked astonished at the three identical women standing side by side before them. Judge Schwartz eventually brought the court to order, rapping his gavel until everyone's ears rang.

"What do you propose will happen if we permit Helena of Delphi to become Helena of Perculous?" asked Judge Schwartz.

"Your decision will allow captain Klaus Meinbach to take Helena of Perculous as his lawful wedded wife!" proclaimed Klaus triumphantly.

At this the entire crowd roared their approval and stamped their feet. Even the man wearing a hat in the upper gallery quietly applauded.

All except for Ada Schmitt who sat scowling in her seat; then she looked hard at Judge Farzang until she caught her eye and it seemed an understanding passed between them. Then she looked at Judge Helmut and her gaze softened as she toyed with the locket at her throat in a meaningful way. He noticed her look and seemed unsettled. His cheeks flushed and he bit his lip.

Judge Schwartz again pounded his gavel on the bronze amplifier until peace was restored.

"Well done captain Meinbach. Now we will retire and return with our decision later in the day. Until such time Helena of Delphi shall remain in the captain's care."

"All stand," cried a court official as the gowned figures of the judges bowed and walked from the courtroom.

Many of the nobles shook Klaus's hand, or patted him on the shoulder congratulating him on his case and his impending nuptials. They were convinced the captain had scored a certain victory and that it would merely be a matter of time before their wedding invitations arrived.

The prosecutor also held out his hand and offered congratulations.

"Well played, captain Meinbach. I am not often vanquished in these matters but I was not prepared for such a well-documented approach in a case like this. I wish you every happiness with your bride to be, sir." Then he turned and walked away leaving Klaus wondering if he was really sincere or perhaps the man was afraid he had made an enemy and was trying appeasement as a last resort.

Night was falling as Klaus, Helena and Eunice waited outside with a noisy group of supporters for the verdict. One of Klaus's servants brought them a meal and Delmania was taken home to bed. The judges seemed to be taking a long time to come to their decision. As the evening drew on people drifted away in pairs until only Klaus, Helena, and Eunice remained waiting in the foyer of the court.

A man wearing a hat and dark coat greeted Klaus, clapping him on the shoulder.

"I fear there is treachery afoot behind the scenes, my friend. I have a feeling that the verdict will not be as we would wish." Klaus raised his eyebrows and then frowned and tightened his lips into a line.

"What do you think we should do?"

"I think we need one more strategy, in case this goes awry. Something simple they will not expect," said his friend, looking around to see if they could be overheard. The men stepped away and spoke for a time in quiet tones. They shook hands and the man in the hat walked away into the dusk. Klaus hurried to Helena and Eunice.

"I have grave news, my friend has been investigating behind the scenes and he has warned me there may be a miscarriage of justice and we need to take steps to avoid a tragedy."

Helena looked frightened, Eunice covered her mouth, her eyes were large with concern.

"What can we do?" asked Helena.

"I have a plan which will require both of you, to carry it out. What you need to do will require risk and trust in my friend," said Klaus.

"I will do anything to help Helena, whom I truly believe is my long lost sister," said Eunice in a low but determined voice.

"Come then," said Klaus leading them into the darkness between two great pillars. After a time they returned to the foyer of the court. Finally a clerk appeared in the doorway of the court room.

"The verdict is in captain, you are required to attend the court with the accused."

Helena adjusted her veil, Klaus took her by the hand and they entered the courtroom. The lighting was subdued, it seemed foreboding. Several court officials and guards stood behind Klaus, Helena and Eunice as the judges returned to the dais.

Judge Schwartz looked at Judge Farzang, then at Helmut. He did not seem at ease.

"Are you firm on your decisions?" he asked them. Each of them nodded without looking at Klaus or Helena. The judges seemed tense and tired.

"By a margin of two to one this court finds the accused guilty as charged. Helena of Delphi is an Uitlander and unwelcome on Atlantean soil. She is to be incarcerated in the dungeons of this court immediately," announced Judge Schwartz. Helena and Eunice gasped and began to weep into their veils.

"What!" Thundered Klaus. "I smell treachery. I will appeal this decision at once."

"You have the right, captain." confirmed Judge Schwartz. "We shall bring Helena of Delphi before this court in five days and if your appeal is successful she will be released. If not she will be hanged on that day."

"I have one request!" said Klaus. "Please allow me to visit with Helena for an hour this night to support her in her grieving."

"Very well, captain, but I warn you this woman is now in the custody of the state and you will respect the officers of the court and its rules."

"Very well, you have my word," said Klaus. He watched as two jailers led Helena away through a door from the foyer of the court and down stone steps into the dungeons below the court room. Klaus and Eunice followed.

Klaus sat with Helena and they talked quietly. He held her hand and tried to comfort her tears. When the hour was up, the head jailer beckoned to Klaus. He kissed Helena on the cheek in a reluctant farewell. As the door clanged shut Klaus whispered in the jailer's ear.

"I see by your tattoo you are an ex navy man."

"Aye sir, twenty years before the funnel," said the former sailor saluting the captain.

"Here are two gold coins. They are yours if you promise that Helena's food will be of the highest standard. But more importantly, I want your word that she shall be fairly treated. A further two of these shall be yours in due time should you be true to your word."

"Aye, you have my oath on that, captain! For the next five days she shall be fed by me personally. I will watch out for her, sir, do not worry."

"The Navy Guild will remember your kindness," said Klaus. "Come Eunice." Placing his companion's hand on his arm, he walked back up the steps to freedom.

As he stood and looked up at the moonlit sky above his home city of Atlantis, Klaus considered how differently he now viewed his life as a ship's captain. No longer did he have respect and reverence for the laws of his Empire. His eyes had been opened to a most unpleasant reality. Not only were the laws unfair and wrong; but the justice system, when faced with true and honest facts could still bring down an entirely unjust decision and kill innocent human beings. He took a deep breath.

"We will leave this godforsaken den of snakes, Eunice. I shall return you to Perculous Island this night in my own ship. This city is tainted by the foul smell of injustice."

As they were swallowed up by the night, an orderly ran to Judge Helmut's room to tell him the coast was clear, Meinbach had gone and it was now safe to leave. Trembling he made his way to the arms of his paramour. Ada greeted him with every sign of affection. Sherman tried to believe that the physical satisfaction he was receiving would ease his guilty conscience. Only Ada's skillful touch temporarily relieved his impotence.

Afterwards as he lay staring at the ceiling, a vision of that beautiful young woman hanging dead from a rope around her neck kept him awake. He could not understand why Ada should want Helena dead and the responsibility of the day's decision weighed heavily upon him.

39

ON THE FIRST MORNING OF HER INCARCERATION the warden received a letter on official naval stationary requesting that the prisoner have a guard outside her cell all day and that no visitors except those specifically from the navy should be permitted to visit or speak to her.

Every day captain Kurt Wagner visited the prisoner. He brought her treats and read to her from several books. Why an Uitlander woman, sentenced to death should receive such attentions from the naval authorities, was beyond the warden's comprehension. But the silver coin he received after each visit convinced him not to pry further.

The day before the prisoner's scheduled execution a servant in the livery of the Schmitt family delivered a letter addressed to the warden. He found a note and a gold coin inside the envelope. He unfolded the letter and read: 'Herr Honorable Warden: Greetings good sir, my name is Noble Woman Ada Schmitt. As a compassionate woman I wish to be allowed to give comfort and solace to the condemned woman named Helena of Delphi who is in your care. Please grant me this one request dear sir, and allow me to visit her today. Please find remuneration for your kindness enclosed.' It was signed *A. Schmitt* in an elegant scrawl. The warden pocketed the coin, thinking that surely this visit could be a kindness to the condemned prisoner and could do no harm, despite what the Navy might think.

"Tell your mistress she may visit the prisoner for a few minutes; however she must remain outside the cell. My men will stand at a discreet distance so they may have privacy," he said to the servant, who bowed and went to fetch his mistress.

Ada swept down the steps causing the prisoners gawp in silence since she was wearing a spectacular dress more suited to a ballroom than a prison. The warden beckoned to the prisoner to approach the bars and speak to her visitor, he then withdrew. The prisoner, her face almost completely covered by her shawl, advanced to the door of her cell.

"Not so high and mighty now!" hissed Ada scornfully. "Your brave captain has deserted you has he not? I know he has not visited you these past four days. No doubt he is ashamed of consorting with the likes of you." The condemned woman opened her shawl enough so Ada could see her smile.

"You smile woman, like you have secrets!" said Ada venomously. "But your secrets will be of no use to you when they hang you from the prison gates tomorrow. Hah! I will watch your twitching body with pleasure. You are nothing more than a sub-human despite your opinion of yourself. A filthy animal in human form."

Ada was enjoying herself. She stopped when the prisoner crooked her fingers and gestured for Ada to come closer.

"Listen, you painted old *whore*." she said loudly, her words in perfect Atlantean carried to all the cells. "You may be rich but you have a demeanor far lower and more disgraceful than any of the common *sluts* who ply their trade at the docks. One day captain Meinbach will return. When that happens I hope he removes your ugly head from your equally repulsive shoulders."

The prisoner turned on her heel and walked to the far corner of her cell where she faced the wall.

Ada, dismissed and speechless, put a jeweled hand to her cheek which was rapidly turning red. The other prisoners were delighted by the scene and Ada received a series of rude catcalls and suggestive remarks from them. She stormed out, her face a smoldering mask of hatred.

The warden stepped forward to speak to her, but Ada's angry face stopped him in mid stride. He let her go and hoped for more prisoners like this Helena. She had been his most lucrative charge in all his many years as jailer.

40

KURT WAGNER WAS USHERED INTO Judge Schwartz's chambers.

"To what do I owe this honor, captain Wagner?" said Schwartz, smiling, extending a hand and pointing to a chair opposite his desk.

"It is official naval business, sir," said Kurt, shaking the judge's proffered hand. "I have a warrant for the arrest of captain Klaus Meinbach to lodge with the court."

"Captain Meinbach? Surely you are mistaken, this court has no charges outstanding for him," said Schwartz, his eyebrows raised in surprise.

"It is purely a naval matter sir, I assure you. Meinbach penned a letter of resignation from the Navy on the evening of the loss of the case re Helena of Delphi; citing loss of confidence in the laws of the Empire. He has since disappeared. The Grand captain wishes him to be arrested in order to explain the reasons why he has taken such a rebellious course of action."

"I see, captain. So how can I help?" asked Schwartz, steepling his fingers together. "I'm sure if the naval authorities cannot find captain Meinbach then my men will be of little use."

"The warrant for captain Meinbach is purely a formality, judge, I assure you. I also have a warrant for Helena of Delphi. My orders are that she is to be held in naval custody. She is a material witness in this matter," said Wagner, handing the judge the sworn warrant.

"But - but she is to be hanged tomorrow. If her protector captain Meinbach has indeed gone missing, then her fate is sealed. Her appeal will fail immediately," said Schwartz, more than a little flustered by this turn of events.

"The law must be obeyed, captain Wagner. All I can offer you is an opportunity to speak to her."

"Tell me Judge Schwartz, have you ever met the Grand Captain of the Atlantean Navy?" asked captain Wagner, getting up from his seat and strolling to the window.

"No I have not, very few of my officials have met the Grand Captain, he seems a reclusive sort of man,"

"I must remind you in the strongest terms that this warrant is signed by the Grand Captain himself. My instructions were particularly explicit. He said, 'You shall post the warrant for captain Meinbach and take the prisoner known as Helena of Delphi into Naval custody. Do not return empty handed. If necessary you may use a squad of marines to enforce my orders.'

That is a direct quote," said Wagner, "So I ask you again, will you release this woman to me?"

"Oh – ah! I'm sure I can order a stay of execution for you, captain Wagner. I had no idea this woman would be such a matter of importance to the Grand Captain," said the judge hurriedly, picking up his fountain pen and lifting a piece of official stationery from a slot in his desk.

"Should I draw up the papers to postpone the execution for two weeks from today?" he looked up, pen poised.

"Write 'for a period yet to be determined by the Naval authorities' " said Wagner firmly, looking out the window.

"Oh – why of course. The woman is of no importance in the larger scheme of things," said Schwartz. He wrote rapidly on the sheet of paper and offered it to Wagner. "You may collect her immediately captain, I shall get the paper work done in good time."

"I am obliged to you sir, and wish you a good day." Wagner clicked his heels together sharply, turned and left the office.

Judge Schwartz poured himself a stiff drink from the flask he kept in his top drawer. He went to the window and gazed out. Below in the courtyard, he saw a company of marines with bayonets fixed standing in three lines. An officer in dress uniform was standing with sword drawn in front of them. The judge sat down heavily in his elegant brass and oak chair and mopped his brow with a handkerchief. His hands trembled around the beaker of liquor.

What is it with this woman and the Navy? Why did the other two judges refuse to acknowledge her heritage and admit her to our society? He wondered, feeling out of his depth yet again. I wish I'd never set eyes on Helena of wherever she was, he declared hurriedly filling out the documents to hand her over to the naval authorities. Good riddance, now perhaps I can sleep easy tonight.

41

WERNER SCHMITT WAS NOT A HAPPY MAN as he stood in the portico of his home and contemplated the news which he had to give his mother. Early that morning he had been dispatched to view the execution of Helena Delphi and then to report back to Ada on the proceedings. He knew his mother had a headache and the news he had would not assist his mother's recovery. He took a deep breath and stepped inside the door.

"What? What! I don't understand what you are telling me!" Ada was white and her hands were gripped into tight fists as if she wanted to punch her son.

"There was no hanging, mother. I was told that the woman had been taken from the cells last night by armed marines and she has not been seen again."

"How could that be?" Ada frowned and bit her lip. Her face was flushed and blotchy.

"I tried asking for more information but none of the court warders could tell me anything. One of them was rather rude, when he mentioned you, mother."

"What did he say?" Ada flushed deeply red. Werner coughed and chided himself for mentioning the incident.

"He said you had visited the prisoner and that you came off rather second-best. He was laughing about it."

"The ungrateful wretch! After all the money I paid him too!"

"I did not know of your visit to the prisoner, mother so I could not defend you. But he did tell me that the navy took custody of the Greek woman."

"You are still slated to serve on the *Hieglund* as Political Officer. Go to the navy building immediately and find out what happened to that woman," Ada commanded, pacing up and down her parlor. "I will *not* have her escape death. The court has condemned her and I shall make sure the sentence is carried out."

Later that day Werner returned from the port.

"I have much news, mother," he said, standing again in the parlor watching his mother pacing back and forth. A caged tiger would have given a similar energy to the room.

"Out with it, son. I cannot wait to make sure that wretched woman dies a miserable death as befits Greek animals like her."

"I was told by a marine who was on guard at the door that he had accompanied the woman from the cells to the naval prison. He was dismissed from duty, but later that night saw a woman he swears was the prisoner being escorted by two ratings and a captain to a small boat at the lower quay."

"We have traitors in our midst!" declared Ada loudly, "I knew it! We must crush the power of the navy and increase the power of the Politico Party or these foreigners will bury our proud Empire in their filth."

Werner listened with his head bowed, a tight smile played over his face. He had a feeling that his destiny was changing forever.

"Did you find out where they took her?" Ada demanded.

"No mother, but I strongly suspect she was taken to Klaus Meinbach. I was told that Meinbach has resigned from the navy and that he has disappeared. Right after the end of the court hearing, in fact." Ada gasped and held her breath. Werner had never seen his mother so agitated.

"He is mad! His mental affliction is worse than I feared. We shall hunt them down, Werner. I shall not rest until Klaus Meinbach and his whore are found and destroyed forever."

She took a deep breath and thought for a moment.

"I shall begin today." She sat at her writing table and picked up her pen. Then she swung around and looked hard at her son.

"Do as I say, dear son, and you shall go very far indeed in Atlantean politics."

"Yes mother, thank you mother." he said, and sat down, awaiting her next order.

42

THE MEDITERRANEAN SEA WAS CALM, with a gentle breeze, scarcely a cloud marred the blue sky but captain Ainyu Daungha was worried. He was a proud Persian sailor and warrior, but he was far away from home and in waters which were unfamiliar to him. They had not seen land for days; food and water were running dangerously low. It was mid-morning and the heat of the day was taking a heavy toll on his men. The wounded were many and the hot days and lack of water had caused some to die already.

His crew had won a bloody fight with the Phocaeans from Massalia four days before. Captain Ainyu remembered the battle clearly. The lookout cried 'ship ahoy' and there it was, a rich prize for the Persian privateer; a Greek trading bireme like a fat bird sitting in the water ready to be taken. That was his first mistake and almost his last.

The privateer closed rapidly for the kill, his soldiers on board readied their javelins and arrows. Their orders were to board the prize, slay all the commanding crew, but preserve the rowers, who were useful to propel the ship and usually were slaves chained to their positions on the rowing decks so they could not escape a battle.

Rapidly the prize began to turn, closing with them faster than he had anticipated and to his shock Ainyu's own ship was rammed amidships by the Greeks. The Persian privateer's oars and hull were smashed to matchwood by the bow of the Phocaean ship which he belatedly discovered was well armed with a huge bronze ram fitted below the water line at the bow. The Persian's ship began to sink and it was vital that they board and capture the other vessel.

The Greeks began to row astern in order to pull their ram from his shattered hull. Naturally they planned to let the pirates sink and pick off any swimming survivors in the sea at their leisure. Before they could complete this tactic Ainyu commanded his men to board the Greek ship over their bow which was still embedded in his stricken ship.

They swarmed aboard the trader as his archers fired arrows into the Greeks. A long bloody battle to the death ensued. In the end it was the sheer ferocity of his own crew striving to survive which won the day for Ainyu. They killed most of the crew of the Phocaean ship and those who tried to survive the mayhem on deck jumped to their deaths in the unforgiving sea.

Victory was tainted with sadness as his crew suffered many casualties. Now there were barely enough men to man the ship as the Greek rowers were freemen who fought with the crew and perished in the battle. When they lifted the cover boards over the hold they found the cargo was hundreds of beautiful green and gold triangular copper ingots. Their mood changed to one of joy.

A sacrifice of a young goat was made in the name of Hashang, Ainyu's God of fire. Still in the God's favor the captain and crew then discovered the Phocaean vessel was faster and more seaworthy than their Persian designed vessel. All that was needed was a favorable wind to sail to their home port of Halicarnassus. On the way they must find land or a friendly port to resupply the ship which had little water or food on board.

Captain Ainyu stood on the high poop deck next to the rail, gazing out over the bright horizon. He would never admit it but he was utterly lost.

Asuk the first mate stood at the tiller, he was an impressive figure. His muscular bronzed chest was bare, a white turban on his head and he had a cutlass thrust through a wide leather belt. The muscles of his upper body rippled each time he moved the tiller. Yet he had little to do as the sail hung limp from the spars, the light breeze only occasionally flapped them. Another man stood beside Asuk, both of his arms were bandaged yet he was ready to take the helm if necessary.

All the crew had shipped their oars at Ainyu's orders. Most were below sleeping or resting away from the heat of the sun. The huge square sail billowed full again as the wind came, for a moment the ship began to make way, then the breeze died, the sail fell slack and slowly the ship came to rest. A lookout stood on a small platform atop the main spar peering into the distance. Ainyu sighed, and looked up; he mumbled a short prayer to his God and began to pace up and down the deck. Despite a thorough scrubbing the deck was stained with blood and reeked of death in the hot sun.

"Sail a port!" came a loud call from the lookout. Ainyu looked up to where the crewman was standing and followed the direction of his outstretched arm with his eyes. There it was, a pinprick of triangular blue cloth, bobbing up and down on the horizon. They were not making much progress in the light airs, they had all sail aloft. The captain watched for a while. The small sailing craft appeared to be on a parallel course to port and very slightly ahead. It wasn't much of a prize to hunt but certainly they would have some food and water aboard. If they could capture it, this would mean survival for another day or two. The wind would be of little assistance for Ainyu and his crew to catch this prey, but the pirates had oars and the light airs would not save the faster smaller craft from capture.

"Sound the drums! Call to oars!" roared Ainyu, sending a prayer of thanks to his God. The bandaged crewman picked up a bronze hammer and beat a crude cowhide drum that was at his feet.

Men appeared from everywhere in various states of undress. Six men picked up their quivers and bows ready to attack their prey, the rest manned the oars. There was a loud clattering as all the oars were positioned, ready for the order to ship them outboard.

"Ship oars!" yelled Ainyu and the rows of oars dipped into the water and pulled; the privateer began to surge forward.

"Closing speed," ordered Ainyu to the drummer who beat his drum at the pace required for closing. The men bent with a will to their work. Asuk moved the two connected steering oars so the ship turned to port until it was on an intersecting path with the quarry.

Once they closed some of the rowers would be released for fighting. The archers were donning their leather jerkins and wrist bands. The fire pot to ignite the burning arrows was prepared.

43

HELENA WAS AS HAPPY AS A WOMAN FLEEING FOR HER LIFE COULD BE. She was taking her turn on watch at the tiller so Klaus could sleep. She relished the chance to help him with their voyage home to Corinth.

I can't believe that we have had fair winds for four whole days, she thought. I hope those accursed Atlantean navy ships fail to find us. Klaus has managed to evade them so far because he knows the usual routes and the timing of their navy patrols.

Helena looked down the companionway and gazed at Klaus, stretched out asleep on the simple bunk next to the galley stove. Wonderful Klaus, he manned the tiller all night while I slept, she thought.

The day was hot, the sun shone brightly and reflected off the sea, small waves lapped at the sides of the boat, the wind had almost died and so her task was a simple one. Her small hands gripped the rough wooden tiller with purpose as she tried to keep the boat headed towards the east. Oh I am so thirsty, but I can't leave the tiller right now to get a drink. There is a little wind and we are making some way. She peered forward at the hazy horizon, longing to be further away from the Atlantean Empire.

I wonder how captain Kurt is managing the court? It was so wonderful that Eunice, my dear sister, agreed to take my place in the dock for sentencing. Helena shuddered and felt guilty. I hope Kurt has kept his promise and released her before they hang her. I so hope that nothing happens to her as a consequence of us switching places. If she were put in prison or enslaved or – executed – she shuddered, I could never forgive myself.

I have never seen anyone as angry as Klaus was that night; he said that he was disgusted and disillusioned with Atlantean law. What a travesty that a citizen like Ada Schmitt could rig the court against all logic and proof. We underestimated that dreadful woman and how far she was prepared to go in order to make sure I died. Helena winced and a chill passed over her stomach as she thought of the look on Ada's face at the end of the court case. Ada had smiled, her lips tight, her eyes roaming between one judge and another searching their faces. That little man, Helmut, I'm certain he blushed. I'm sure she had the verdict arranged, no matter what evidence we put forward, we were going to lose. That is why her attitude was so different from the other onlookers at the court. She will stop at nothing to get Klaus for her daughter – or herself. Helena's chest panted in tiny gasps, lost in anxiety. Then she gathered her strength, refocused on the sails, the sunny ocean around her and took a deep breath to calm herself.

Klaus really loves me, I know that now. He has abandoned all his inheritance; his house and land, his horses and boats; his powerful standing in the navy to leave Atlantis and take me away from their killer laws. I love him so very much.

The deck tilted a little and the tiller pulled on her hands, a lift of wind had moved over the boat and she began to make way. What a wonderful boat the *Delphine* is, thought Helena, pulling the tiller in. It was so kind of Kurt to find her for us to escape in. He made sure the *Delphine* was stocked with lots of water, excellent salted fish, and the other foods we need like oil, grapes, oranges, an amphora of wine, hard cheese and a basket of ship's biscuit. These navy captains know how to provision ships.

Klaus's head appeared in the companionway. His face was tanned golden by the sun, his blue eyes by contrast seemed a much deeper blue and he was more handsome than before. He wore the smile of a man much in love as he looked at her and then checked the boat. His smile vanished. He jumped up the companionway ladder and stood beside the tiller looking out to starboard.

"How long have *they* been following us?" he asked, picking up his telescope and adjusting the focus.

"Who?" said Helena turning her head. "By Apollo! Where did they come from?" Now she saw a huge sailing ship on the horizon. It was too far off to tell how it was headed but it was pointed in the same direction they were going.

"You must keep a lookout to *all* points of the compass, not just ahead of us," said Klaus. "But no matter, they are still a way off."

"Will they want to catch us?" asked Helena raising her eyebrows, narrowing her eyes and looking hard at the ship.

"If this wind does not pick up I would say they will reach us in about two hours." Klaus looked through the telescope again.

"She looks like a Greek bireme, a trading vessel most likely. It's unusual to see a bireme rowing so fast this far out in the ocean. Usually on ocean trips they will use the sail and rest the rowers. They may mean us no harm, but we will take no chances."

"What if she tries to take us?" asked Helena, feeling afraid. There was so little wind that the *Delphine* was scarcely answering the helm. Helena knew that without oars and with the wind so light they had no chance of escaping from the muscle power of a bireme by outrunning them.

"Then we fight." Klaus had a very stern look on his face. "An Atlantean captain does not surrender *ever* under *any* circumstances."

"Then we shall die together," said Helena proudly. "I will need a dagger to take my own life if we do not prevail."

Klaus smiled and squatted beside her, looking into her eyes. His big hand brushed her cheek lightly.

"You will not need a dagger, if it comes to a fight, dear Helena; it is *I* who will prevail. Now, we have plenty of time." Helena kissed his fingers, then leaned her cheek against his and sighed. She felt so safe when her husband spoke like this. Klaus adjusted the tiller so the boat came about making best use of the light airs to propel them away from the bireme.

"Hold this course while I make preparations to defend us." Klaus went below and reappeared with his three long barrelled muskets, ammunition, his pistols and cutlass.

"You must sail the *Delphine* for us Helena. I will fight if need be, as best I can but first we need a quick way for you to understand my orders." From his pocket he produced a yellow piece of cloth and a blue scarf. He tied the yellow scrap to Helena's left bicep and the blue around her right.

"When I say half yellow, move the tiller to the side of you which has the yellow ribbon. When I say hard yellow, you push the tiller hard that way as quick as you can. The same goes for an order half blue and hard blue, do you understand?"

"Yes Klaus – I won't get confused," Helena assured him. She moved the tiller half blue, half yellow: then hard blue and hard yellow to show him she understood. The boat answered but sluggishly to the helm as she swung it back and forth.

"That's right, you are doing well," said Klaus. He chose to ignore the nagging worry of how they were to evade the approaching ship without a lift in the wind. "I will haul the sheets and control the sails. Our brave *Delphine* has a keel; and her triangular sails and big rudder will mean we can tack or gybe to turn much quicker than they can."

Helena nodded-she was gaining confidence because he was so certain they would prevail. Klaus began to check and load his muskets as he continued, "Whenever they get close we will turn, using the wind to make any distance on them that we can. We can do this for as long as we stay afloat and they don't set our sails alight. Each time we get near I shall shoot one of their crew or more with my muskets. I have three muskets; on each engagement I shall fire all of them. I will reload each time we break off the fight and outmaneuver them, while they seek to re-engage us. Do you understand, Helena?"

"Yes Klaus, you make it sound so simple." She smiled at him.

"Well naval battles are simple so long as you fight to your strengths. Our strength is my fire power, and the speed of our boat; theirs are their archers and the strength of their rowers.

Now, I will tie off the tiller and check all the rigging, you go below and prepare us some food and get the water and wine ready to drink. We will fight on full stomachs at least."

While Helena was below, Klaus tied the tiller to keep a steady course running with all the wind he could find on their beam. The *Delphine* picked up speed pleasingly. As he gazed around, Klaus could see clouds on the horizon and some puffs of wind ruffling the surface of the warm silvered sea. He checked the halyards were tight. Found spare sails below and readied them for use. Made sure all sheets ran freely to control the main and head sail. Satisfied all were in working order and he could bring the yacht about easily with Helena on the helm, he picked up the telescope and studied the ship more closely. He counted the double bank of oars either side and estimated that there must be crew of more than fifty men.

He saw a man standing on the top spar pointing at the *Delphine* and giving a heading. Two more were climbing to join him, both carried bows slung over their shoulders and a quiver of arrows each. Klaus trembled a little as he saw a smoking fire pot being handed up to the lookout. It was clear this ship meant them harm. A trading ship would not pursue a small boat or attack one.

By thunder, they are not Greeks, they are Persians! Said Klaus to himself as he looked closely at the crew. I'm willing to wager they are pirates who have captured this Greek ship and they are a long way from home. We are not much of a prize. Seems they are hunting any shipping they can find. That scum will have no mercy on us if they catch us.

He stood, stretched and took a deep breath. I shall show no mercy towards them, Klaus tightened his mouth in determination.

I will not let them take Helena alive. I shall save my final pistol bullet for a shot to her heart if they do manage to capture us. Klaus was not afraid for himself; he was a naval man, born to fight ships at sea. I shall die swinging my sword until the end.

He sat in the cockpit watching his course and the activities of the pirates as he loaded his muskets. Klaus was a crack shot with long barreled muskets; he had been firing them since he was a young boy. The guns he brought with him on the voyage were a new design with rifled barrels, an accuracy innovation recently invented. A marksman with a rifled musket could now kill a man three hundred yards distant.

The naval armorer had developed a new round which was cylindrical with a pointed end. This round could fly faster and kill a man at over five hundred paces. It was loaded by tearing the end off a paper cartridge filled with a measured amount of gunpowder with the bullet inside. This was then packed into the breech with a long rod. A percussion cap was fitted in front of the hammer, then the hammer was cocked and the rifle was ready for firing.

Klaus knew he could load and fire each of his muskets in twenty seconds. He laid the weapons and ammunition supplies out in the cockpit so they were within easy reach.

Helena brought their meal up from the galley. They ate in silence as the ship closed the distance between them. The wind brought them the sound of the swift beat of the rower's drum, the creak and splash of the oar strokes; and the cries of the men urging each other on.

44

THE PIRATE CREW WERE RUNNING A GOOD SWEAT.

"Row! You proud Persians, row! The prey is right before us!" roared Ainyu. The vibration of the trembling deck beneath his feet felt wonderful. We can sustain this until we are close enough to ram the prey, he thought. When we are within bow range I will lift the oar-stroke to ramming speed. He waved to the archers positioned in the shrouds.

"Be ready to shoot at my command," he shouted. He felt confident that those two and the four spaced along the railing near the bow were all he needed to set the small ship's sails alight. Their fire arrows were tipped with burning rags soaked in tar. With sails ablaze the small boat would be easy prey. Ainyu smiled and looked down at the grappling hooks on the deck. Once we are alongside we will haul her to us and make short work of their crew.

Ainyu had never seen a sailing vessel of this type before. All the sails and mainsail were shaped like triangles. She looked fast and graceful. I would like to take her intact if we can, he thought. After we have shared out the food and water on board I will put a small crew aboard and sail her in company with our ship. He licked his dry lips in anticipation.

"Soon we will be eating and drinking like kings!" he yelled. The rowers cheered and bent to their work with renewed vigor.

Klaus put down his telescope. He could see the enemy clearly without visual assistance and now there was no doubt – they were pirates who intended to capture his vessel. He placed a wide wooden board against Helena's back and wound strong linen sailcloth around and around her body many times giving her back and neck, which faced towards the advancing ship, some protection from arrows. He could find nothing which would serve as a helmet to protect her head.

He buckled on his wide belt over a heavy leather jerkin. His pistols and cutlass hung from the belt within easy reach. Then he wrapped a piece of cloth around his forehead to soak up sweat and keep his hair from his eyes. He looked down at Helena manning the tiller; she looked up and smiled at him.

"Standby Helena! Take a solid grip of your tiller but do nothing until ordered!" he commanded her.

"Aye sir!" she said, eyes shining with excitement. She had never felt so alive or as afraid as she did at this moment of impending conflict with a huge foe.

Klaus took aim at one of the bowman in the shrouds. He estimated the range at four hundred paces and closing. He took aim and fired. There was a scream and a bowman fell from the mast and crashed onto the deck of the enemy ship, his chest spouting blood.

Klaus picked up the second musket, aimed and fired; the other bowman tottered then fell bloodied to the deck below. Bowmen hidden at the bow of the ship fired flaming arrows at the *Delphine* but they fell short sizzling in the sea. Klaus jumped to the sheet ropes and grabbed them in readiness.

"Hard blue!" he ordered. Helena pushed the tiller hard over as fast as she could. Klaus loosened and then fastened off the sheets for the mainsail and foresail and the agile *Delphine* swung about, hardened onto the light breeze and headed quickly away towards the stern of the pirate ship. The bireme towered above them as she passed them. Helena could see the huge oars dipping up and down, each with a wake foaming around it.

Klaus picked up his unused musket, carefully aimed a shot and the big man in the turban controlling the tiller crumpled to the deck.

"Well done Helena, hold your course now. First blood to us! The hunt is on!" Klaus cried.

"Klaus, the guns are so loud! My ears hurt," yelled Helena, holding her ears.

"Aye, but you will get used to it soon enough. We have all day to fight!" Klaus replied, relishing the conflict. Helena saw someone jump to the tiller on the privateer and the big ship slowly rounded to give chase. Klaus watched; intent on counting the seconds until the enemy ship once again laid a course for their stern.

"Now I know how long it takes for them to turn." He smiled grimly; it was clear that these men were unfamiliar with their ship and were under-manned. Another advantage to him; every crew member shot changed the balance of power in his favor.

Helena relaxed and tied the tiller off and watched the ship because the wind had picked up to several knots of steady lift but this was hindering the bireme as they now rowed into the wind, the square sail bellying backwards against the mast. The captain cried out and some crew shipped their oars and ran on deck. There they struggled and swore as they tried to reduce the sail too fast and jammed the ropes in the blocks. A smile crossed Helena's face watching their confusion.

Klaus swiftly reloaded his muskets in readiness for his next action.

"We have a few minutes before they close again. We will tack across their bows this time." He watched the wind and the enemy ship closely as he readied himself to shoot once again.

Slowly, oh so slowly, the bireme came about. The rowers could be heard cursing the small fishing boat in the foulest words the Persian language contained. It was like magic, the way it had so easily out-maneuvered them. Many were white eyed with fear because they saw the effects of the strange device which killed with loud thunder and smoke.

Six of the crew shipped their oars and carried the three slain men and laid them before captain Ainyu. He noticed that two of the corpses had penetration wounds in the front and exit wounds in the back of their bodies. The third body was different, a wound in front and a bulge in the man's back with much bruising. The captain pulled out his dagger and cut the bruised skin open. Among the congealed blood and torn flesh Ainyu found a small flattened piece of metal.

He rotated it between his fingers and thought hard. The enemy's boom stick fired a metal shard like this. It was no bigger than the tip of his thumb yet it did so much damage. That weapon was worth more than his whole cargo, even if it were solid gold! I must take that boat at all costs! He decided. Ainyu pointed a finger at one of the rowers

"Take over the tiller! Follow her!" he ordered. Then he shouted to his crew. "The man who killed your comrades has a weapon which fires a small metal ball. We are many and he is only one man! We will prevail and avenge our brothers!" Ragged cheers erupted from the rowers benches.

"His weapon is not magic. It is not the weapon of a God! The metal will only pierce flesh not our wooden hull. Drummer! Beat for ramming speed!"

The drummer beat faster lifting the tempo. The privateer began to make white water at the bow. The crew grunted in unison and the ship surged towards the little sailboat.

"Archers to the bow - flame the sails!" roared the captain.

Helena heard the drum beat increase and looked behind. She could see the pirate ship was moving faster now. She saw Klaus looking at the water and the sky; he didn't seem interested in the boat bearing down on them.

"Klaus what are you looking for? The pirates are gaining on us!" she cried.

"I am looking for wind. It's coming in puffs and when it does, it darkens the water with small waves. See ahead? On the side of your yellow ribbon," said Klaus, pointing.

"I think so," said Helena staring hard at the water, but not really sure she saw anything different.

"When we reach that patch of wind. I want you to push the tiller to blue as hard as you can! This time we need to cut across their bow and timing is everything. This tack we will get a lift from that breeze and have the wind with us on the beam, if I am right."

Helena looked at her right arm and the blue ribbon, rehearsing the move in her mind. Her throat was dry, she needed water but she could not leave her post. Sweat dripped down her cheeks and she tasted the salt with her tongue. The drum was louder now but she dare not look. She concentrated on keeping the boat straight. Then she felt a puff of wind on her left cheek, the sailboat heeled over a little.

"Hard blue now!" commanded Klaus.

Helena felt the rudder bite into the water as she pushed the tiller over with all her might. Klaus let go the sheets and jumped under the boom where he swiftly pulled the line tight. Now they had the wind on their starboard side and it was freshening. It took a lot more strength to hold the tiller to keep to the course Klaus wanted. Helena could not help herself-she looked left and saw the bireme's sharp prow approaching, the water foaming around the deadly bronze ram. The huge painted eyes staring soullessly straight at her.

Boom! Klaus fired one of his muskets.

"Center the tiller!" he roared, "We will run close!"

Helena centered the tiller and the boat shot forward as the new breeze filled the sails, Klaus let out the sails a little which added more speed. Then they heard the drummer on the bireme quicken the beat. It was right on course to ram them.

Captain Ainyu saw the crewman on the tiller push it hard to starboard; the big crewman hauled the sails around and quickly sheeted them in. Then he realized the little craft intended to cross his bows.

"Ramming speed!" he screamed. The beat changed up to a beat that the rowers had to give everything to keep up with the stroke.

"Turn 15 degrees to port to ram them!" he commanded the tiller man. He could see only the mast of the sailboat ahead as the hull of his ship obscured the small craft from his view.

"Shoot for the sails," he ordered the archers.

Boom! An archer pulling back on his bowstring fell to the deck, his head a morass of blood, splintered bone and brain. Boom! Wood splinters of the railing shattered in front of two more archers forcing them to duck down. The fourth archer jumped up to the railing at the bow and loosed his arrow at the sails.

Boom! His body flipped sideways and he disappeared over the side. His arrow had found the mark and struck the head sail lodging in the heavy stitching of a seam. Flames swept up the linen sail.

"Aiiieghh!" Ainyu yelled triumphantly. Now he would take the little sail boat as his prize. He looked closely at his quarry and was shocked to see the person on the tiller was a woman with shining golden hair.

Klaus did not have time to admire his shooting as a flaming arrow loosed by the archer he had just shot lodged in the head sail and it caught fire. He picked up a canvas bucket of water hanging ready on a belaying pin and threw it at the source of the fire. It almost went out but one bucket was not enough to extinguish the blaze. Klaus ran to the mast, unfastened the halyard rope and dropped the head sail. It flapped down, still burning and smoking. He took off his leather jerkin and beat out the flames. There was a ragged hole in the sail but he hoisted it again and ran back to the cockpit to sheet it tight once more. A sail with a hole is better than no sail, he thought grimly, looking at the bireme which was making an all out effort to run them down. It loomed huge and terrifyingly fast beside them. The *Delphine* had lost speed while he doused the sail and it would be a close thing if they missed colliding.

The privateer turned, trying to match the course of the *Delphine*, working the galley rowers to exhaustion, as they did their best to ram her. By the barest of margins the agile sailboat swept past the sharp prow of the bireme.

"Duck down!" yelled Klaus as the first three of the port bank of oars struck the stern of the *Delphine*. A loud cracking and splintering followed as the oars shattered on the sturdy timbers around Helena's cowering body. Fear froze the scream in Helena's throat where she fell as deadly shards of wood rained down around her. She could hear the cries of the rowers as their broken oars jumped from their hands, smashing and crushing their bodies mercilessly. She still held the tiller by the tiller-rope and prayed for their salvation as flaming arrows splattered in the water around them. The privateer was moving away fast, despite the rowers struggling to turn her towards them once more. As Helena began to get up there was a woosh and something thwacked painfully into her back. Slowly she turned and saw a long red fletched arrow quivering embedded in the fabric below her left shoulder. Blood was on the sleeve of her gown.

"I've been shot Klaus!" she cried out. He stepped up to her; she saw the bright blade of his cutlass swinging past her cheek. Snap! The arrow was gone.

"You are unharmed Helena," said Klaus, "You are lucky, the arrow was lodged in the board on your back. Now tie off the tiller to keep this course."

Klaus began reloading his muskets. The splinters left bloody gashes in her hands and arms, but she could find nothing serious.

After Helena had pulled the wood splinters from her hands and hair and the tiller was fastened off on a course to his satisfaction; Klaus spoke in a measured tone.

"Go below. There is a spare head sail in the smaller bag by the berth. Bring it up on deck."

Helena picked up the heavy bag, grunting with the effort and shoved it out into the cockpit. Klaus had finished reloading and was laying out new ropes.

"Here you are Klaus, will it slow us down much changing the sail?" asked Helena.

"No, we have a little time. I will attach the new sail to the fore-stay with a spare line and hoist it beside the other head sail; then drop the damaged one. Watch out for the enemy, Helena, let me know when they start to close on us again." Klaus grinned and looked towards the horizon behind them.

"The wind is freshening." he gestured aft and Helena saw clouds and choppy waves had developed behind them.

As Klaus began to attach the new head sail, Helena kept the *Delphine* making as much speed as she could. It was easier now; the wind on her cheek was stronger and colder. She looked back at the bireme. They had almost completed their wide slow turn and were lowering their big square sails to make use of the strengthening following wind. The pirates were 200 yards behind, there were many gaps in the oar banks now, yet still they rowed strongly. Helena wondered how long they could do that before the rowers were exhausted. She used her free hand to gather up shattered pieces of oar and throw them overboard.

The *Delphine* heeled more, her bow wave and wake growing as Klaus hauled up and sheeted in the new head sail. He folded the damaged one carefully and stowed it.

"The wind is increasing further, even with the sails up they won't catch us now," Klaus stated with satisfaction, picking up his telescope. He looked at the gathering clouds behind them.

"We are in for a blow soon. It's time we put paid to this battle before we get into a skirmish we cannot outrun with that storm approaching. I'll take the tiller now," said Klaus sitting beside Helena.

Helena went below and brought them much needed water and food. It felt wonderful as their dry throats felt the flow of cooling relief. Klaus eased the tiller slowly changing their course to run before the wind in a freshening breeze. He loosened off the main so it caught the wind squarely as it blow now from behind their stern. The fishing boat caught a small swell and surfed for a few seconds. Klaus relaxed, and grinned at Helena.

"Now we are in a straight race. The Persians will fill their sails; but we are faster in these winds and will pull away. Their oarsmen must be all but exhausted by now." He stood and handed the tiller to Helena.

"Now I plan to leave their captain with a parting gift." He picked up a musket and aimed, supporting the barrel on the boom. There was an ear-splitting crack, fire spat from the muzzle of the musket. The masthead lookout slumped forward clutching his shoulder, then lost his grip and fell forward tumbling through the rigging to land on the unforgiving deck below.

With his next shot the man on the steering oars was thrown backwards and the bireme veered off course. Now Klaus caught sight of his intended target. The man he had been watching intently during the whole battle; the privateer's captain. Klaus watched the pirate take hold of the steering oar and pull with all his might to stop the bireme from swinging broadside to the wind. He was successful until Klaus shot him with the third musket. The captain flung a hand to his stomach before pitching forward. Now without steerage the big ship heeled over dangerously and the crew stopped rowing when they realized their commander was down.

Klaus put his arm around Helena's shoulder and she leaned into him. The Delphine sailed on, Helena took over the steering while Klaus reloaded his weapons but this was not necessary as the pirate crew were in disarray. With no one commanding the rowers the bireme wallowed in the water. As the sky behind them blackened with rain clouds, Helena and Klaus faced a new danger direct from Boreas, God of storms.

45

AS THE STRENGTH OF THE WIND GREW, Helena struggled to keep the *Delphine* steering steadily as larger and larger swells generated by the storm began to run across their path. Klaus dropped the main sail and left a kerchief of head sail, yet that was enough sail aloft for the boat to make maximum speed.

White caps appeared on the waves as the wind whipped up huge storm swells. Rain clouds blotted out the sun. Rolling thunder and jagged bolts of lightning ripped open the skies. Torrents of stinging, wind driven rain began to lash them. Klaus ordered Helena to go below where she prayed to Apollo for salvation. It was a relief as she felt ill. Her stomach so steady in the fair winds of their passage now froze and she was pale as she prayed kneeling on the tiny bunk amidships.

When Helena looked up next from the shelter of the cabin she saw Klaus had tied himself to the stern railing. The tiller was tied with strong rope and bucked against it as the waves rushed under them. Klaus's strong arm rested on the tiller while he held himself steady with the other. His head was bare, his wet hair plastered against his forehead, his wet weather gear streaming water. Her lover was staring into the storm, a wild untamed look in his eyes. Klaus looked down for a moment, feeling her gaze upon him, and their eyes met. He grinned at her, swung his head back and laughed. Helena understood. Klaus was a sea captain and he was in his element.

Klaus excelled at sailing. The sea was his playground, this storm caused their voyage to be exciting for him. Klaus was testing himself and his boat and he adored every moment of the challenge. As a lion rules his kingdom, so Klaus Meinbach ruled the ocean. Helena looked at his broad grin and felt safe. The Gods may have caused her trials and tribulations but they also sent Klaus to deliver her safely home.

All night and into the morning Klaus controlled the small boat as the storm raged. Helena lay wedged into the tiny berth as he relentlessly trimmed the boat and fought the storm for their right to survive. Helena gave him food, cups of water and wine to keep his strength up. As dawn broke she could see huge waves surrounded them. Klaus admitted that he had little idea of where they were, or what heading they were making. Helena thought it did not matter, they were alive and she was grateful.

It was mid morning before the wind abated and Klaus came below, stiff, pale and tired. The waves were still high but not dangerous. Where they would land now, he did not know but for the time being all he needed was sleep.

Helena went on deck and stood watch. Snuggled into a sheepskin jacket she thanked the Gods for their deliverance; but saved the largest praise in her thoughts for the sleeping man below who conquered all before him and captained her heart.

High above the *Delphine*, invisible against the gray storm clouds, a melon-shaped silver object drifted silently. A telescope was readjusted by large long fingers, as an eager eye gazed longingly at the blonde woman standing at the helm on the tiny boat far below.

"Klaus – if it were not for you we would never have met. If ever you leave her, I promise you she will have a true friend in me." A finger tapped on the buttons of a brass fonier.

"Good day," a voice answered, "Have you seen any sign of them?"

"No. It is all clear below. Shall I search more to the South West?"

"Yes, that will assist the search, but do not leave sight of the coastline; you are too valuable to be lost."

"Turning South West now, I will call if I see any sign of them." The call ended and two gray eyes looked long at the small blue sail moving away to the North East below.

"Fare well, fair wind and may your Gods bring you happiness."

THE END OF PART ONE

If you enjoyed this book, a review from yourself would be appreciated on the site where you purchased this book. If you have found any faults in the editing please email us at quintessence.publications@gmail.com

Our Atlantea The Secret Empire blog is at http://longshippublications.blogspot.co.nz/

Twitter @loveleov & @bullburton

Follow our progress as we write book Two of Atlantea Discovered – Escape from Atlantis.

MAPS

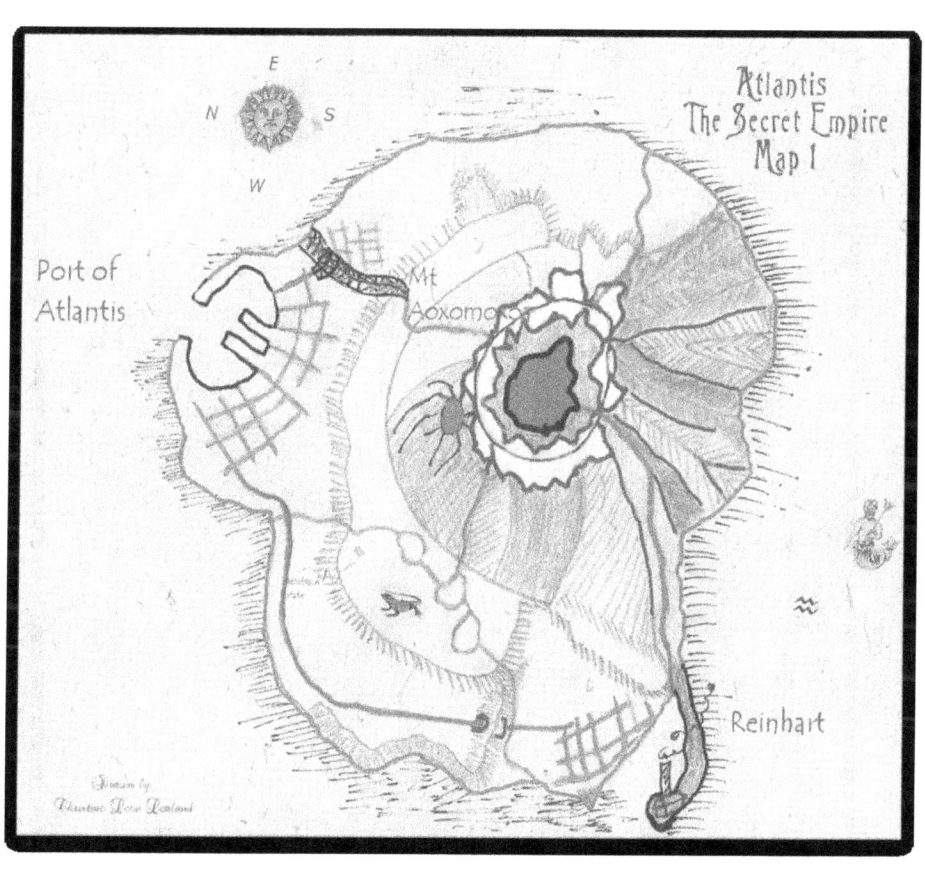

Island of Atlantea showing Ports of Atlantis & Reinhart

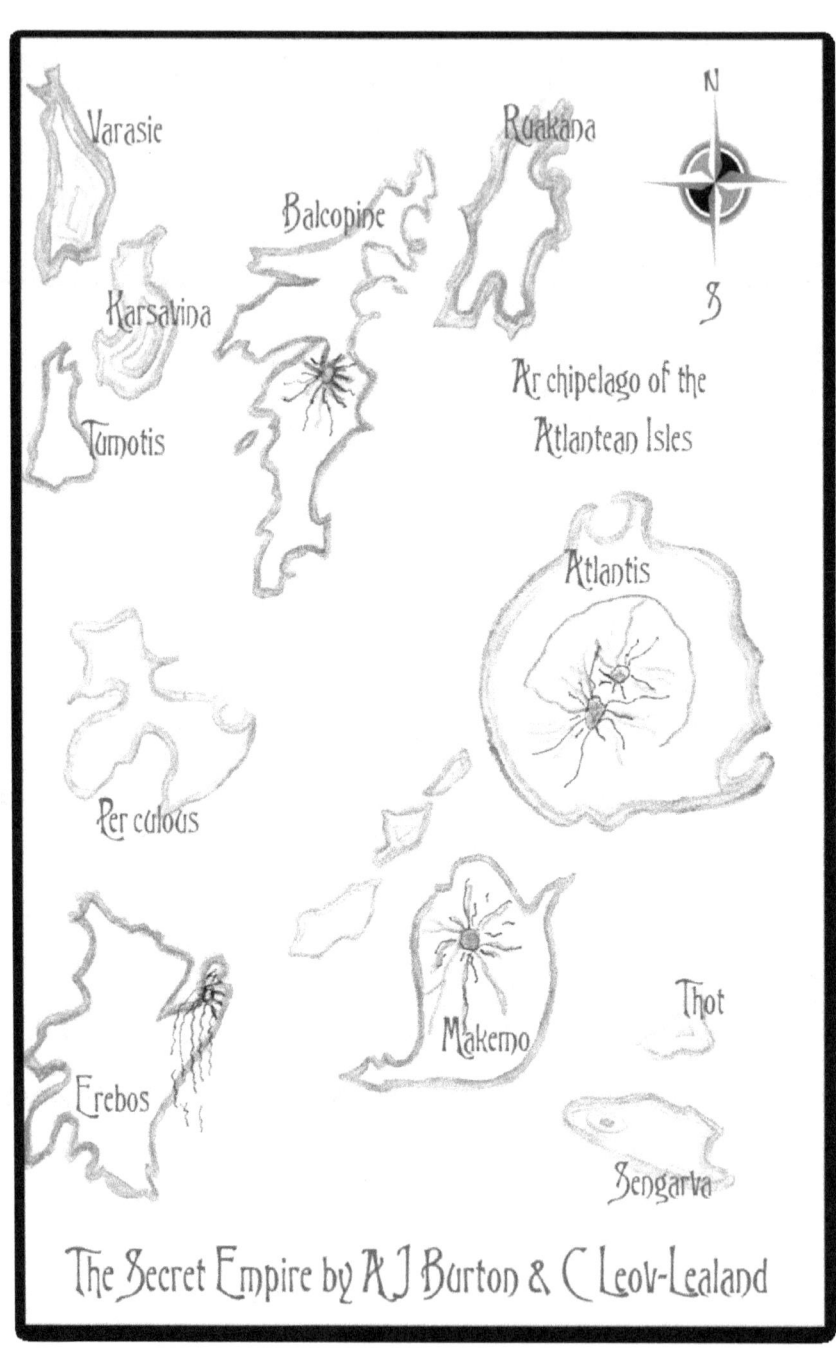

The Archipelago of Atlantea

ESCAPE FROM

ATLANTIS

A Steam Punk Adventure Romance
Book Two of the Atlantea Discovered Series

By A J Burton and Christine Leov Lealand

A sample of the excitement to come...

CHAPTER ONE

Antonius Bortz' occupation was dangerous and potentially fatal, but then so was being a trader, marine or fisherman. The Politico Party had stringent training and testing for their covert assassin guild which provided very special rewards for the few successful graduates. Antonius smiled, his thin lips in an unthinking leer, considering the hard work and stupendous luck which had led him to this place, as he always did before one of his more interesting tasks. He was the best of the past ten years of trainee assassins; his skills honed against many foes. He knew it and his client undoubtedly knew it. The memory of her scorching gaze still chilled him as it had at their interview yesterday. Spiders, he had images of spiders, giant spiders stalking across the city when he thought of the heads of the Politico Party. The powers behind the name of Empire.

He turned up the collar of his heavy woolen coat and pulled the tip of his stiff tri-cornered hat lower over his eyes. The constant regular loud whirring of giant steel wheels winding cables in and paying them out were the only sounds in the terminal as he waited for a sky tram to respond to his call. As expected he was alone in the lobby. The streets of Atlantis were deserted on a wet cold midnight like this except for occasional police patrols. Antonius tapped the toe of his knee length leather boot to a dance tune he had heard on a audi playing in a street bar earlier in the evening. The tone of the cables changed to a more intense sound and he saw a sky tram approaching, rain vibrating off the wet aerial cables as it drew into the platform with a ringing of bells and clanked to a halt. Antonius stepped in and found a seat near the rear door. The tram was empty except for the attendant who barely acknowledged his presence. It was warm and steamy inside, the wooden seat was hard and worn smooth, as usual paint was peeling off some of the interior. The sky trams were in constant use and did not get a lot of time for maintenance. Antonius settled down for the journey to his destination.

A bell clanged on the platform and the tram lurched forward, then settled down and smoothly climbed a gradient of support cables suspended high above the city. Slowly the tram wound between massive steel and concrete supporting towers and made stops at terminal platforms set high up on the sides of apartment and office buildings. At the third stop Antonius touched a button which informed the attendant he wished to disembark. The attendant rapped a lever back and forth and the tram came to a stop. Antonius kept his face turned away from the attendant as he opened the door and stepped out onto the windswept platform. The bells rang and the empty tram moved on to the next terminus.

Bortz paused in the pursuit of his task to lean on the guardrail and enjoy the view. The great glowing heart of the metropolis of Atlantis sprawled out below him in all directions. It was a dazzling sight as sheets of rain moved in formation across the island. The platform was ten stories above the streets below and there were a further ten stories beyond this until the building ended in a large cable terminus and garden. From this vantage point he could see the docks where men worked all hours preparing the trading ships both great and small. Columns of smoke and steam streamed out in the wind from funnels far below. An occasional steam tram clanked by on the many steel tracks below. He looked for police patrols but he was too high up to pick them out with any certainty.

Antonius took a deep breath of the fresh damp sea air. So to work, he thought and turned to the pair of huge steel and wood framed French doors which led into the foyer of the tower apartment. This was a Noble apartment building and the concrete structure was decorated with beautiful red, cream and grey stone slabs. The entire facade of the building had an expensively decorative mottled appearance and on the glass of the doors were etched images of steam engines and the Colossus. There were no guards, tenants used their own keys to come and go from the platform. Antonius withdrew his set of master keys from a pocket with a soft clinking. He took out a pair of thin black leather gloves and forced them over each hand.

Now he slid his view scope out on a slide attached to the brim of his hat and activated a small light which he focused on the door lock. He manipulated several long shiny keys in and out of the lock until he heard the right kind of click. The door opened silently but his stealth was spoiled by the loud sound of his boot heels on the stone flagstone floor. He paused, listening to his footsteps echo down the long corridor. Curse my vanity he thought, I should have worn the soft soled pair but they are so dreadfully unfashionable. It would be a disservice to Minister Dachau if I arrived at his apartment dressed in unsuitable boots.

Walking as quietly as he could past the lift doors the assassin strode up two sets of stairs to the twelfth floor. The interior was warm from the steam boiler heating which circulated through each hallway. From his coat Bortz brought out soft leather shoe covers and slipped them over his boots. Silently he walked down the corridor lined with widely spaced handsome wooden doors counting off the numbers. Outside the windows rain lashed against the glass.

He paused outside number 375 and smiled. My, my, Minister of Genetic Purity, Herr Gabriel Dachau; what a truly exquisite door you have, he thought. He caressed the highly polished panels, feeling the perfect fretwork and seamless joins. The seal of the Atlantean Empire; a steam engine and steamship encircled by blue ocean waves was painted in gold, blue, black and white in the centre of the door. Minister Dachau's name was embossed in proud gold lettering under the seal.

I'm sure your apartment will be elegant and delightful, I am ready to enjoy it, mused Antonius as his supple fingers maneuvered the skeleton keys in the brass lock. There was a faint click - clack. Easing the door handle down slowly he opened the door and glided inside allowing the door to click softly shut behind him. The light from the city below cast eerie shadows inside the room which featured large windows and a door which opened out onto a balcony with an ornately curved brass and steel balustrade. He moved quietly across the room to the balcony door, it was easy to open.

The wind from the harbor swept past him with a damp chill, the lace curtains hanging beside the doorway fluttered into the room. Antonius grasped the metal railing attached to the balcony and shook it. Satisfied it was sturdy enough for his needs the assassin opened his coat and removed a length of thick hemp rope that he had coiled around his waist.

Deftly he made a noose at one end of the rope and tested it to make sure it slid easily. The other end of the rope was secured around the railing and the rest of the rope neatly coiled in readiness on the deck of the balcony. Bortz stretched, preparing his body for the task ahead; stepped back into the doorway and checked the elegant room. All was silent, warm and glinting with wealth. Wealth had a particular welcoming smell, just as poverty had an unpleasant smell. The smell and warmth of this room was a feeling Bortz liked very much and he dawdled a little. Once more he looked out over the glowing city; the streets were deserted, gleaming wet in the rain. The lights were of every colour, red, green, blue, gold and orange. The rain created moving rainbows against them as it fell in squalls.

Time to begin, Antonius reminded himself, checking that his weapon was ready to use. His eyes were completely accustomed to the dim light and he walked softly, swaying like a dancer across the room to the door of the bedroom. He pulled a small metal container from one of the many pockets inside his greatcoat. Tiny drops of oil were placed on the exposed door hinges making sure the door would open without any sound. Replacing the can in his pocket he took hold of the door handle and pressed it downwards. A smirk played across his lips as the door opened without a sound. Antonius was a man happy in his work.

A lamp shed a soft glow, revealing a grey bearded man sleeping on his back, snoring loudly. Softly as a panther stalking prey Antonius moved to the bed and looked down at the sleeping figure. Minister Dachau slept blissfully unaware, his breathing slow and measured.

The assassin drew a wire and handles into his left hand from his sleeve. The other he clenched tightly into a fist. He raised his fist high above the sleeping man, drew a long breath and filled his lungs. Using the force of his out breath Antonius drove his fist down like a hammer into the soft belly of the sleeping man.

"Uuuugh!" gasped the man sitting up bolt upright in the bed. The victim could say nothing else as all the breath was driven from him by the blow. The assassin jumped up onto the bed behind the Minister; the garrote was wrapped rapidly around his helpless neck and twisted until Dachau's eyes bulged and his hands and legs thrashed. Antonius was not a large man but he possessed great strength in his sinewy arms. He stood over his prey holding the garrote mercilessly until it did his awful work and the Minister slumped forward unconscious or dead. Satisfied Antonius replaced the garrote back in his sleeve pocket. He dragged the limp figure of his victim up and over his shoulder and stood slowly grunting with the effort.

"Humph! You are a fat man Minister Dachau," Antonius muttered. He staggered slowly as he carried his victim out to the balcony weighed down by the body which was almost too heavy for him to handle alone. He slumped the minister's body over the railing and placed the rope noose around Dachau's neck. Making sure the knot of the noose was at the back of the neck and just behind the left ear Bortz maneuvered the minister over the railing and let him drop with a sickening twang. The body twitched for a few moments and was still. As Antonius watched the body began to sway in the strong wind blowing past the tower. The windows of the other apartments around him were dark, and blank. No one had seen this dark deed occur.

Antonius took out a crumpled letter addressed to the minister and left it lying open as if much read on the dining table. He returned to the bedroom and neatly made the minister's bed. He locked the front door behind him, removed his gloves and the covers from his boots and ascended to the roof where he caught a sky tram to the central terminus.

Within the hour Antonius entered a fashionable restaurant frequented by the noble men and women of Atlantis. The owner flouted the law about early closing of eating and drinking establishments; he had powerful friends and the officials were well paid to turn a blind eye.

At this late hour the restaurant was busy with richly dressed patrons, clouds of sweet smelling Tobac mingled with perfume filled the opulent room making it difficult for Bortz to locate his employer. Then he noticed her; dressed in a dark red and blue flowing dress, a tight leather corset over it, adorned with gleaming brass gadgets. Her ash-blonde dyed hair coiffed beautifully and her wealth openly stated with bright glints of gold and glowing precious stones of all colours ornamenting her hair, wrists and fingers.

Her booth was discreetly situated near the back of the restaurant. She twirled a silver wine goblet in one gloved hand. Noticing him as he approached she raised her hand a little and subtly signaled that he should discretely approach and speak to her.

"Is your task complete?" asked Ada Schmitt raising her eyebrows.

"Yes noble lady. The minister unfortunately committed suicide this evening after reading a letter. It must have contained bad news."

Ada threw back her head and laughed.

"Well of course, my dear Bortz, we nobles are bound by honor and he simply did what was required of him. I will reward your employers and make sure you receive a handsome bonus." Bortz bowed his thanks.

"Besides, you have provided us with much needed entertainment," she continued, "The papers are full of tedium now that Klaus Meinbach and his slut are no longer news. They need something new and scandalous to write about and I'm sure that Minister Dachau's unfortunate dalliances with a young island woman will be an excellent diversion."

"Thank you Madam, I take it you have plans for captain Meinbach?" Bortz sensed a new opportunity in her tone.

Ada's smile was replaced by a scowl.

"Klaus Meinbach made a fool out of me, and I will have my revenge, Do not doubt that!" she spat. "The new minister of Genetic Purity will make finding that traitor and his uitlander whore his first priority. A proper search must be carried out, worldwide if necessary."

"If madam wishes to retain my services for duties off shore I am sure an arrangement could be made..." Antonius suggested smoothly. "My training was very extensive and I can speak Greek like a native,"

"Thank you Bortz, I shall consider the next actions which will be taken once the new Minister of Genetic Purity is sworn in." Ada paused, "Perhaps you could attend my daughter's wedding next month, to monitor the guests."

"As you wish, Madam. Please send the details to the Chief Politico Office."

"Thank you, that is all." Ada was brusque now. The hour was late, it had been a long tense day and she was still seething over Rainia insisting on marrying some young upstart from a backwoods island fishing enterprise instead of finding a naval captain of wealth and ancient lineage for a husband.

To be continued....

ABOUT THE AUTHORS

CHRISTINE LEOV-LEALAND

Adventure has been a recurrent companion in my life as I grew up on an isolated island, travelled frequently, qualified for my bachelors' degree in History, had a family and finally left everything to pursue my passion to write. I wrote and bound my first book at the age of 8 years, moved to poetry, then wrote a novelette on a portable typewriter at sixteen.

I love cats, sailing, earth houses, old Victorian villas and my garden.

Best-selling author of erotic romances set in New Zealand: 'Quintessence', 'Astride', & 'Avocado' I also wrote a biography of potter and railway magnate Barry Brickell. These books are available as ebooks at all good online retailers.

Fantasy novel 'Doors' is on the desktop along with family history and 'Escape from the Secret Empire'.

A J BURTON

I have lived a life of action as a policeman, horse trainer, plasterer, mechanic to name a few. Writing called to me all my life but I was too busy to listen. Now that I am retired writing has finally come home to roost. Each day I get my comedy and action kicks via my imagination and my laptop.

I enjoy many genres: sci-fi, murder/mystery, adventure, and comedy with a satirical bent.

'Seeking Angel' is my first published novel and The Secret Empire the second; with a comedy paranormal novel in edits.

My main hobby is boating and fishing. If you want to know what it's like to be a boat owner take a cold salt water shower while ripping up $100 notes. Remember many a promising fisherman has been ruined by a good woman.

www.ingramcontent.com/pod-product-compliance
Lightning Source LLC
Chambersburg PA
CBHW060539180626
46817CB00002B/639